Forget Me

Forget Me

A Van Allen Brothers Romance

Kimberley Ash

Forget Me
Copyright © 2019 Kimberley Ash
Tule Publishing First Printing May 2019

The Tule Publishing, Inc.

ALL RIGHTS RESERVED

First Publication by Tule Publishing 2019

Cover design by Llewellen Designs

No part of this book may be used or reproduced in any manner whatsoever without written permission except in the case of brief quotations embodied in critical articles and reviews.

This is a work of fiction. Names, characters, places, and incidents are products of the author's imagination or are used fictitiously. Any resemblance to actual events, locales, organizations, or persons, living or dead, is entirely coincidental.

ISBN: 978-1-950510-58-0

Dedication

To all the ladies everywhere.
You *all* deserve a happily ever after.
Don't let the magazines tell you different.

Acknowledgments

Love and blessings to my agent, Veronica Park, and everyone at Tule, who have nurtured my cinnamon bun Van Allen brothers throughout their lives. Kind of. You know what I mean.

Thanks to my RWA/NJRW/WFWA friends, and everyone who takes the time to send a fistbump of congratulations or a sadface emoji of support. Especially to Carol Van Den Hende, beautiful, sophisticated woman and marketing guru extraordinaire, who has helped me not to fear the part of a writer's life that requires me getting out of my chair and into the public eye. I am so lucky to have you in my life, lady!

This book—the whole series—centers around one man whose alcoholism affected everyone around him. Being an adult child of alcoholics is a thing, and if you're struggling with it, please know that you are not alone (as you may have felt you were your whole life), the feelings you're feeling are valid, and there is help. You can go to www.adultchildren.org and www.nacoa.org to start with. I'm not endorsing either charity, but their website information has been helpful to me.

Chapter One

"LAUREL, STOP!" A deep voice shouted from above her.

Laurel Moore jumped about a foot, dropped one of the catering-size tomato cans in her arms on her toe, yelped, and looked up. The can rolled into the road, where a bus drove exactly where she'd been about to run. Its left rear tire squashed the can like a juicy tick, sending sauce flying everywhere, landing on her white chef's scrubs and oozing into her working clogs.

"Shit!" she shouted, distracted from trying to find the source of the voice. She looked like a crime scene from the waist down. Glancing up, she saw people in the back of the bus, gazing at her as though she were an interesting stop on a tour.

"Hold on!" came the voice again, turning her attention to the building across the street. Laurel had grown up across from this building. She'd thought she knew everything about it, from the real estate office and café on the corner to the uniform set of windows and old-timey fake roofline above. But she'd never really considered who lived there.

She couldn't see more than a shadow beyond the window screen. All she could do was back up from the sidewalk into the alley, so she wouldn't be run over by commuters heading to the train station two blocks over—and who were looking at her with curious expressions, damn them—and wait, her last precious can of tomatoes still pressed to her breast.

The door sandwiched between the realtor's office and the lawyer's opened, and a tall, slim man with dark red hair and a short beard loped out and jaywalked across the street to her. He was wearing a button-down blue check shirt with the sleeves rolled up, dark khakis, and suede boots. As he got closer, she saw tattoos on his exposed forearms and snaking out of the collar of his shirt.

Yep. If the hair and beard didn't brand him, those tattoos sure did. Jonah Gardiner. Town bad boy. The one her mother had always—and uselessly—warned her about. "That Jonah Gardiner," she'd told Laurel in high school. "You stay away from him. He's no good. Getting into everything bad, he is. He'll be in jail or dead from drugs before he's twenty-five, mark my words."

Laurel, being a good girl, *had* stayed away from him in high school. In college, however…

All she could do was stare at him as he joined her in the alley. What was he doing across the street from her father's bar?

"You okay?" he said.

"Yes!" she squeaked. Because she certainly didn't want Jonah Gardiner, of all people, to witness any more of her stupidity than he already had.

Jonah raised an eyebrow. "Sure?" He looked behind her. Laurel belatedly remembered the laden SUV, back hatch and doors open, crooked piles of food filling the inside. Her feet squelched softly in her shoes.

Well, she'd had to start saving somewhere. Her beloved, flawed father had died and left her with all the bar's accounts in arrears and no one but her to fix them. The delivery charges from the local wholesaler had seemed like a good place to start.

She was strong, wasn't she? She regularly hauled and butchered entire sides of beef, didn't she? Her hands could knead enough dough for a whole restaurant, and she'd spent so many hours on her feet as a chef that sitting down was an anomaly. A carload of cans should have been a piece of—well, a can of—cake. Or something.

Yet somehow, the cans hadn't known this. The cardboard had buckled as she pulled one case out of the teetering pile on the passenger seat. Every one of the eight cans had slithered out of her grasp and onto the ground, making popping sounds as they landed, then rolled away.

Laurel had managed to save two of them by clutching them painfully against her chest. Two rolled under the truck—she considered them lost. But she was damned if she was going to lose the rest. Sauce was money, and apparently the patrons of Sullivan's Bar and Grill—Grill? That was a laugh; nothing in that restaurant had been anything other than reheated or fried in years—needed their mozzarella sticks to come with sauce, or there'd be an uprising.

So, she'd run for the cans. Awkwardly, because of the two she still clutched to her chest.

And now Jonah Gardiner had seen her screwing up. *Just great.*

"It's fine!" she said as breezily as she could while dripping. "My brother will be here any minute to help."

Too late, she remembered that Jonah knew Brett. Possibly better than she did. Jonah would know that Brett was more likely to be sleeping off a hangover right now, not showing up on time to help his sister run the bar.

Jonah's eyebrow returned to its proper place. *Don't pity me, don't pity me, don't pity me.*

"Until he gets here, can I help you get these out of the car?" Jonah said.

Laurel really wanted to say no. Reeeeeally wanted to. Accepting his help would mean accepting that this had been a terrible idea—not just the fetching of the food herself, but the notion of relying on Brett. It also warred with her healthy feminism. She *could* carry everything herself. She just had to take it slower.

But she had lunch to prepare, other orders to place, suppliers to placate with promises of installment payments. And she was already sick of the sight of this so-called food.

"Don't you have to… be somewhere?" She nodded at his neat shirt and khakis. Apart from the beard and the tattoos, he didn't look the way she remembered. The wicked grin was gone. He was frowning at her a little. The wiry energy he'd had, the middle finger he'd pointed at the world ten years ago, had gone. With it, he'd been tempting and naughty. Without it, he was gorgeous. And frightening.

She pressed her remaining can harder into her chest. *Not the time, Laurel.*

"I have time," he said and, walking to the back of the car, took a box of frying oil in each hand. Each box weighed over thirty pounds, but he picked them up as if they were helium balloons. He waved one of them at the passenger door of the car, which was blocking the way to the kitchen.

He'd been a part of her father's life, a part that had destroyed Frank. But now he was… normal. And helpful. And, as she slipped past him to close the door, he smelled good. Freshly showered and groomed.

She was glad she'd already unlocked the kitchen door, because she wasn't sure if she could handle keys right now. *Because of this can that your fingers are going into spasms around, you're holding it so tightly.*

She hurried through the door in front of him and dropped the can on the nearest counter, then turned around and shook her fingers out while she prepared to direct him to the pantry.

But for some reason, he'd paused at the threshold. He

was looking at the doorframe as if he was afraid it was about to move, or bite him, or something.

"What?" she said.

He didn't answer, and after another short pause, he stepped over the threshold and into the stainless steel and tile of the kitchen.

For a bar that didn't serve a whole lot of food, the space was large, dominated by the long griddle along the back wall and the four fryers on her left. Sullivan's was perfectly equipped for its patrons—the town's drinkers, who drank, ate what would soak up the alcohol the fastest, and then drank more. Fried food ruled here, as shown by the pounds of expired frozen breaded chicken that Laurel had had to throw out when she'd taken over.

Stainless counters stood between them and the stove, and doors led off to the bar on their right. Jonah looked left, to where an old-fashioned, heavy wooden door led to the pantry and refrigerator.

"Over here?" he said.

"Yes," she answered, following him through the door. "Just—" She slid past him, coming up close in the small space. She didn't dare to look up at his face, and so got a full view of the vine tattoo snaking its way up his neck, and his straining bicep as he held the fry oil. Well, no one ever said he wasn't hot.

Laurel snapped to long enough to open the door, revealing a half-empty pantry and another door beyond. She indicated a spot close to the door for him to put the fry oil. Without the can in her arms she suddenly felt exposed. Now when she dared to meet his eyes, she could see that he was observing her—checking her out. *Let's be honest.* Ha, tough on him. The apron she was wearing hid most of her, only her arms and her neck and the nipping in of her waist with the apron strings visible.

His eyes slid off her again, and Laurel fought not to be insulted. He was only putting the fry oil away, after all. Did she expect him to gaze at her the whole time they brought the stuff inside?

Within five minutes he had the SUV emptied and the cans stacked. It would have taken Brett four times as long.

His job was done. He was supposed to be going… wherever he was going. To work, she assumed. And yet he leaned in the doorway as she slammed the tailgate down, the crack of it echoing in the alley. She reached up to rub her nose with the back of her hand.

"What happened to the regular delivery?" he asked. "Why did you have to go to the wholesaler?" He pointed up to the window he'd shouted to her from this morning. "Doesn't the truck come almost every day?"

The muscles across Laurel's back tensed up. She'd had to make so many decisions in the last few weeks based on spotty information, but she'd seen the delivery charges from the catering warehouse and had freaked out. "It was too expensive," she said.

"Easier on your back, though," Jonah said. "And your clothes."

Then she remembered her dripping apron. A blood-like trail led from the sidewalk to the kitchen, her hands were sticky, and her feet were sliding around in her working clogs. She made a *tchah!* sound of disgust. At her clothes, but also at him. "You wanna maybe not question my decisions before eight thirty in the morning?" she snapped.

"Sorry," he said, backing up a step. Wow, was she that scary? Cool.

But her eyes focused on the car that was now empty because of his help. There was a line of dirt across the middle of his shirt, where the cases had hit him. She sighed. "Look," she began again. "Thank you. You saved my bacon." She waved behind her at the kitchen. "You want a brownie? I just made them."

His eyes widened. "You made brownies and went to the store already today?"

Finally, Laurel felt that she was cutting a slightly more impressive figure—slippery feet notwithstanding. "Chef's life," she said with a shrug.

"Are you serving the brownies later?"

"Uh-huh." Sullivan's had hardly cared about dessert before. Fluorescent, store-bought lemon meringue pie packed with high fructose corn syrup, and tasteless imitation-vanilla ice cream, had been about its limit. Yet another thing Laurel was going to change. "There's plenty. Least I can do," she added grudgingly.

"Thanks," he said, and smiled at her. "I've heard you're an excellent cook."

"Chef," she corrected at once, though his smile was appreciative and made the morning less overwhelming, somehow. He'd known what kind of a cook—chef—she was ten years ago, but he had no idea how much she'd improved. "Come on through."

Again, he seemed to hesitate at the door, and didn't come far into the room. The brownie trays were cooling near the door to the bar, so Laurel brought a pan and a knife over to him. She cut a chunk out and looked around for a plate.

"Whoa," he said, looking at the brownie. "That's huge."

It was also satisfyingly gooey and rich in the middle, just as she wanted it. "I'm sure you'll be able to lift it, those big biceps of yours," she replied.

And then the room got very hot. *I should not have said that.*

"Uh," she said, not daring to meet his eyes. "Let me get you a plate."

"I don't need one. I'll just—" And he lifted the knife that was under the slab of brownie so that he could take it out of the pan without touching the rest, put one hand under the other, and brought the rich, dark food to his lips. And Laurel knew all this because she watched every. Single. Movement.

The metallic, slightly greasy tang in the kitchen was suddenly hidden by the heavy scent of chocolate. This was why

Laurel's fingertips were tingling, right? Not because when she followed the brownie up to Jonah's mouth, she saw that his eyes were darkened and his pale skin betrayed a hint of a blush as well?

His eyes slid off hers to look at the brownie. "Oh, God," he said.

Precisely. "Is it good? There's a little coffee in it."

"Oh. God," he repeated more forcefully, and took another bite, closing his eyes and chewing slowly. Saved from being observed, Laurel noticed that her lips were parted, and the tingling had gotten a lot worse.

A thump from upstairs, of a door closing and then feet on the stairs that led to Laurel's family apartment, snapped them both out of it, judging by the way Jonah's eyes opened and his blush deepened. Laurel shut her mouth.

"Um," he said. "I have to go."

The moment had happened; she knew it had. But the man in front of her had morphed back into Jonah Gardiner, erstwhile bad boy, now in a button-down and khakis he would have laughed at ten years ago. Not a combination Laurel wanted to be touching with a five-foot hoagie.

"I have to get back to work too," she said, as if he'd been stopping her. "Thanks again."

There. That sounded sufficiently dismissive, didn't it? Apparently it worked, because Jonah turned around without another word. Laurel was left to watch the movement of his back muscles under that damn button-down as he pushed open the heavy exterior door.

"Jonah?" *Shit.* There weren't enough stairs on that staircase.

Jonah turned around to face her brother. "Hi, Brett," he said, his voice low.

"What are you doing here this early? What are you doing here at all?"

Jonah paused before he answered. "Your sister needed a little help getting the delivery in."

"Yeah, I know. That's why I'm here." Brett sounded immediately on the defensive. "I was coming. Jesus."

"Okay. It's all yours."

"Wait," Brett said. "You've been in the bar? You told me you'd never go back."

"I haven't—"

He swore he'd never come back? Even when it meant denying Dad a friend?

That was why he'd hesitated at the doorstep. Yet he'd broken his promise, to help her. As far as the kitchen, anyway.

Then why the hell does he still live across the street?

"Dad missed you, for some reason," Brett went on.

Another pause. "Does it help if I say I missed him too?" Jonah said. "But that's what it does, Brett, it messes with your head—"

"Oh, don't get all on your high horse with me, Gardiner."

Jeez. A lot had changed. Brett had always idolized Jonah.

"Brett!" she said, unable to let the insult lie. She stepped closer to Jonah, not even realizing she was doing so. "Jonah was here when you weren't. How did I know when you were planning on showing up?"

"It's all right," Jonah said, putting out a soothing hand to her. To *her!* When she'd been sticking up for him! "Thanks for the brownie," he added, while she fumed. Then he turned back to her brother. "I'll see you, Brett."

And with that, he was gone. She followed him to the door and watched him jaywalk back across the street, presumably to change into another straitlaced, button-down shirt with the sleeves rolled up. Laurel swallowed.

"Not if I see you first," Brett mumbled when he was out of earshot, and pushed past her into the kitchen. He was of medium height, like Laurel, and had her strawberry-blond hair and wider build. His cheeks and eyes looked puffier than usual this morning.

"Hey, Sis," he said, his face going from thunder to sunshine in a moment. "Here I am, ready to work! Are those brownies? Got any coffee to go with them? My head's killing me."

"The coffee's upstairs. No brownie until you help me clean up this mess."

"I just came from upstairs." He held out his hands, clasped together in supplication, and batted his eyes at her. "Would ya do me the biggest favor and get me a cup, Sis? I promise I'll work for it."

She could tell him to get it himself, but if he went up there, she wasn't sure when he'd come back down. So Laurel went up, poured him a mug of coffee, black, no sugar, then brought it down and microwaved it for him. Brett began to complain about the microwaving, but one eyebrow lift from Laurel and he stopped.

When the microwave beeped, Laurel went to the cleaning supply closet. She threw a cloth and cleaning spray at him, narrowly missing his mug and eliciting a curse.

"Cleaning? Don't you want me to set up in the bar?"

Laurel sighed and got her own spray and cloth. "Of course not, Brett. I don't want you anywhere near that bar."

Brett pouted, squinting at her through his headache. "It's my bar, too, you know."

"Yeah, and Mom's. And she never comes downstairs and you're beginning to drink the profits away just like Dad did!"

Laurel hadn't meant to snap, but Brett never did know when to shut up. As if he didn't know that she'd had her dream job in New York City and had had to give it up to come here and take over the bar when their dad had died, because she was the only one who knew how to do it. As if he didn't know that her mother was buried in grief and no help to her at all. As if he didn't know that Laurel couldn't even take over the kitchen properly, because she'd spent the month since Frank's death going through his papers to find out how much they owed, and negotiating with the debtors.

"Look," she said, trying to calm down. "You're welcome to help me with any part of the bar, except standing in front of those bottles. You know I could use your help in the office."

Brett took a sip of coffee, presumably to hide how little that idea appealed to him.

What did he want out of life? Younger than Laurel by seven years, he'd been the surprise baby, the much-loved boy who looked exactly like his father and had learned all his lessons, good and bad, from him.

Maybe from me and Mom, too. Laurel turned her back on him. *Mom never did keep the apartment liquor-free.*

In her teenage, and most self-righteous, years, Laurel had tried this once. She'd seen real panic on Frank's face when she'd dramatically poured a bottle of single-malt down the sink and added the six bottles of wine Gail kept for special dinners. That look had haunted her; it was then she'd really seen the reliance her father had on the stuff. And later that night, after his shift in the bar, she'd lain in bed and heard him lumber slowly and as quietly as he could up the stairs, and cursed herself for her naiveté. What had been the point of throwing out two hundred dollars' worth of liquor, when Frank could take his pick of thousands of dollars' worth right downstairs?

Since high school, Brett had done nothing but take a few courses at the community college and work with a landscaper for minimum wage. As busy as she'd been with her career in the city, Laurel had allowed herself not to worry about him. Now, he was as much a responsibility to her as her mother and the bar.

"Oh, have a brownie," she said. "You need the sugar. Then get to scrubbing."

He grinned and forked up a huge slice with two fingers. Laurel looked away while he stuffed half of it in his mouth. "Thanks, Sis," he said, his mouth full. "You're the best, you know?"

"Yeah, yeah. I know." Laurel pointed at the cleaning supplies and went out to close up the car.

Chapter Two

What indeed? Laurel's voice still rang in Jonah's head, and the taste of the brownie was still on his tongue as he climbed the stairs to his apartment over the real estate agent's office to change his shirt. What had he just done?

Jonah didn't do anything on impulse. He'd learned years ago that road only led to trouble. Nowadays, he carefully weighed all his actions and assessed all their repercussions before he acted. His morning had been a perfect ballet of timing to get him to the office early, so he could study a little before his first client. He'd taken his coffee to the window, idly observed the commuters walking to the station, and noticed the SUV in Sullivan's alley.

And then he'd seen Laurel, and before he could process what the sight of her did to him, he'd thought *she's going to get creamed by that bus*. The next thing he knew, he was in the alley, staring at an entrance to a building he'd sworn he'd never enter again.

It's not the bar, his logical side had told him, though it didn't stop his heartbeat from racing as though he were looking over a cliff. *Just the kitchen. Are you going to flake out now, when her only other option is Brett?*

Relying on this logic, he'd gone inside. And then Laurel had passed close by him to the pantry and, as she always had done to him, sensation had taken over. Jonah had smelled tomatoes, yes, but also chocolate, scents which made the metallic and fried food tang of the kitchen recede.

Even after ten years, she was about as familiar to him as his own reflection. Several inches shorter than him, her strawberry-blonde hair was hidden under a brightly patterned bandanna, so he could see the exhaustion in her pale blue eyes more easily. Her T-shirt and apron revealed her broad shoulders and strong, rounded arms, the apron strings tight around her waist, emphasizing her Rubenesque breasts and stomach.

She'd watched him just as closely. Tall and thin like his father, he'd also inherited Peter's red hair, though Jonah had grown a beard. His tattoos were mostly hidden by his shirt—he did have work to do today, after all—but her eyes had flicked over the designs that escaped from his rolled-up sleeve and onto his wrist. One of the signs he'd had to stop drinking was when he'd woken up one day with two tattoos he didn't remember getting.

The other sign had been when Laurel dumped him.

With this reminder of their current status smashing into his appreciation of her body, he'd broken eye contact and followed her to the pantry, where he stored the fry oil and went back out for more, before Laurel could follow him with that can which was pressing her breasts up into a very distracting cleavage.

Laurel had always brought out the hedonist in him. He'd grown up knowing about her, crossing paths occasionally in school, seeing what everyone else saw—the popular girl, the funny girl. The girl with the dad who loved his job just a little too much. Jonah had stayed away from her, telling himself he didn't subscribe to her brand of happy.

Then he'd met her one summer break, working behind the bar while he propped up one end of it, and something had been different. She had gained a seriousness he didn't remember seeing before, a darkness that attracted him, if her looks hadn't already done that. Jonah had had no qualms about giving her a slow smile and watching her stiffen, but be unable to keep her eyes off him for the rest of the evening.

Falling into bed with her was the easy part. But he'd found himself, for the first time, with a woman who saw past his carefully husbanded bad-boy image. They both had unreliable fathers and, try as he might to avoid it, they understood each other in that respect. Laurel, however, had been trying to fix her father for years. Jonah's answer to his father's faults had been to ignore him.

Still, being understood had felt real good. Had made him feel worth more than the kid whom everyone was waiting to get arrested.

They'd kept their liaison secret that whole summer, the secrecy adding to the spice. Until Laurel wouldn't stand for his drinking any more.

Jonah ripped off his stained shirt and threw it into the hamper in his bathroom, before going to the sink. Running the water until it was ice cold, he splashed some on his face, as if he could shock the memory out of his system. He'd thought he'd known exactly what his problems had been, back then. He still had half of them. He hadn't needed his PhD in psychology to figure that out. He hadn't tried to contact his father, even though he understood him better. His own flaw, his inability to forgive, made his mouth twist with wry sarcasm when he thought of it. Now that he was done being the town's bad boy, Jonah had to be perfect on the outside until everyone forgot. This, his little knot of dislike for Peter who had fathered him and dumped him within three years, was his only vice, and he was sticking to it.

He looked at his dripping face in the mirror, the water stuck in his beard and curling the edges of his hair. *Logic, remember? Now get to work and get back to normal.*

He'd had other relationships after Laurel, healthier than in his earlier years, though all fizzling out within a few months. Jonah couldn't allow himself to let go enough for them, or anyone. Emotion equaled excess, and he wasn't that kind of guy anymore. Reason was his pathway to truth, and he was fully committed to it. Letting his emotions take over had always led him to disaster, so while he wasn't stupid enough to pretend he didn't have emotions, he worked hard not to let them distract him from his purpose. To keep his mother comfortable, and to help as many other people as possible from the metaphorical car crash he had only just avoided.

But today, Laurel had given him that brownie, and the taste of it had blessed and cursed him all at the same time. When he'd watched her watch him eating it, she'd caught her lip between her teeth in a way he'd loved when they were together. Even now, his mouth watered at the sight. Or the taste. He wasn't sure which. Suffice it to say that ten minutes with Laurel Moore had scrambled his careful, logical world into a tangle he would have trouble pulling apart before his first client. With slower movements than he would have liked, he dried off and put on a new shirt before driving to work.

Pulling through the main entrance to the college, however, always steadied him. "Morning, Dr. Gardiner," the security guard said, and the taste of that brownie, and the memories it had brought up, receded. He parked his Wrangler in its usual spot and began the long walk to the student counseling center. The walk, rain or shine, cleared his mind even further and helped him prepare for whomever he might meet that day.

He worked at the college where he'd received his PhD, preferring the world of young adults trying to figure out their way. Psychology gave him the logic he looked for in people—and in himself—and he was comfortable in his role as the anchor in lives that were sailing on choppy waters. If he hadn't yet found that peace in his own life, well, that wasn't as important.

ONCE THE LUNCHTIME cooks had arrived and she'd made sure they were doing what they were supposed to, Laurel climbed the stairs to her family's apartment above the bar, a plate of brownies in her hand.

She'd grown up with the rumble of the bar under her pillow, had slept above it as peacefully as if they lived in the countryside. Until she'd hit thirteen and had realized what her father was and the problems his illness was causing the bar. All their lives had revolved around the fortunes of Sullivan's, their vacations few and far between, and nonexistent for the last few years of Laurel's childhood. The apartment was small but worked for them, since so much of Frank's time had been spent downstairs.

Her mother was sitting at the tiny kitchen table, looking sightlessly out of the grubby window at the houses opposite—Jonah's apartment, Laurel remembered with a jolt. She'd been looking at it on and off for years and had had no idea. When had he moved out of his mother's house?

"Hi, Mom," she began, with as much compassion as she

could put into her tone.

Maybe Laurel should make some time to get the upstairs windows cleaned, too. After the funeral, Laurel had suggested selling Sullivan's for what they could get and moving closer to the city, so she could continue her work and still take care of her mother. Gail had looked so scandalized, and had mentioned Frank's "legacy" so many times, that Laurel had dropped the idea, for now.

"Hello, Lor," her mother said, her voice exhausted, listless.

"I brought you a brownie," Laurel soldiered on.

Chocolate had to make everything better, didn't it? Even grief? Raw, newly scratched-in grief that tore at her throat whenever she let it out? Maybe there was some whipped cream around to throw on top of the brownie, to soften that edge?

"How 'bout I make us some more coffee to go with it?"

"Don't bother," her mother said. "I'm not hungry."

"It's not for hunger," Laurel pointed out, going to the coffee machine. She'd made some when she'd woken at four—woken being a euphemism for the way she'd dragged herself out of bed after yet another fitful sleep—and by the look of it, no one had made any more in the seven hours since. "I saw how little you ate for dinner last night, and I don't see a breakfast bowl anywhere here. So have a brownie. Please?"

Gail turned to her and Laurel watched helplessly as tears

came into her mother's eyes. "I'm sorry, dear," she said, but Laurel was already bending over her, enveloping her in her arms, allowing Gail's tears to seep into her apron and onto her T-shirt.

"It's okay, Mom," she murmured. "It's okay."

Not that Laurel didn't want to cry too. And not just because her father had loved them all, as much as he was able, and would have sawn off his arm if it could have stopped him from wanting something more than any of them. His weakness had caused ripples that would take years to settle, and so far, Laurel was the only person around who could fix them.

She set the coffee machine going, perhaps hitting the button a little too hard, but otherwise not betraying her feelings to her mother. Gail wasn't going to eat that brownie unless Laurel sat down opposite her and watched every bite, so she took the other seat at the table and pushed the plate toward her.

Gail sighed and picked up a piece. She nibbled a corner and put it down again, as if she'd forgotten what it was for.

Jonah knew what it was for.

An emotion entirely unrelated—and inappropriate—to her situation flooded her. Her body seemed to swell and the room got warm. She could swear her breasts pushed out her apron more. The image of Jonah's face when he'd eaten that brownie came into sharp focus in front of her, more real than Gail's drooping figure and certainly a lot more fun to look at. She couldn't stop thinking about his mouth, something she hadn't allowed herself to do in ten years. Had she ever met a man who enjoyed her food the way Jonah Gardiner did? Sneaking around the way they had, she hadn't had many chances to cook for him, but when she had, his appreciation had been an aphrodisiac.

Laurel had been twenty, halfway through her culinary degree, when she'd found a twenty-two-year-old Jonah propping up her dad's bar, drinking alongside him, generally not helping Frank's problems or his own. He'd given her a wicked grin, and for three months she'd fallen into it. Three months of giddy lust and secret sex and the one and only time in her life she'd forgotten her responsibilities. She'd known his reactions to her and her food had been some of the most real parts of him. So much of what Jonah had done back then had been to cover up whatever he was really feeling about life, about the father who'd abandoned him and the mother who never let him forget it. He'd tried to hide those feelings even from Laurel, who, after all, was only supposed to be the girl he thought he was seducing. Laurel had let him believe that, though she'd seduced him right back; anyway she'd enjoyed every minute of it, and Jonah's agenda had matched hers.

Until his drinking had become too much even for her to ignore, and she'd broken her own heart by leaving him to it.

Their few months together had been enough for Laurel to recognize the pain in him and begin to put together a plan to fix it, the way she was sure she was going to fix her father, one day. But the plan had backfired on her. Ironically, it might have been because she was falling in love with Jonah that she'd told him that last day that she was done. The pain of not being with him was never going to be as bad as the pain of watching him destroy himself. And she'd been working with Frank for ten years by then, and he was in the same place he ever was. She couldn't handle two doses of the same painful, helpless love.

Jonah had also been the catalyst for her to cement her dream in her own head and tell her parents she would be moving to the city. Frank's delight had been tangible, though he'd had tears in his red-rimmed eyes when he'd encouraged her to go. "I'm so proud of you, pickle," he'd said.

She'd known that was true, wanted to leave it there. But she couldn't. "Work hard, too, okay, Daddy?" He knew she didn't mean getting the bar to make money.

"Sure thing," he'd promised. A promise he'd broken, like all the others.

Work had been a demanding lover on its own, though she'd had some relationships over the years, usually with other chefs who understood her hours and her ambitions. As far as she could be, she had been content.

Now it didn't matter that her stomach felt as though she'd eaten a pound of raw dough every day, or that she was in Tanner, Albany County, instead of Greenwich Village.

Her mother needed her to be the strong one, and so did the bar.

The coffee finished brewing, so Laurel brought a cup to Gail's unmoving hand and went to shower, then to her childhood bedroom to put on clean chef's whites. When she came out again, Gail was just where she'd left her. Another crack worked its way through Laurel's heart. But she had the lunch service to supervise, and no time to indulge her own unshed tears.

"I have to go down to lunch," she announced from behind her mother. Gail's head barely turned in her direction. Laurel cast about for something constructive Gail could do while she was gone, something that wouldn't require too much nostalgia. "You know what?" she went on. "It'd be great if you could bully Brett into doing these dishes when he reappears."

For Brett, once he'd cleaned up the most obvious stains on the kitchen floor, had grabbed two more brownies and vanished up the stairs as quickly as he'd arrived. Now his bedroom door was closed, and she was unlikely to see him again until he came to the kitchen looking for his lunch at about two o'clock. So, she went downstairs to begin the cooking day.

Reggie, Frank's lunchtime head chef, was checking the fryer temperature. The huge plastic tub of breaded chicken cutlets was on his right-hand side, an even bigger tub of french fries on his left. As she watched, he dumped a pile of fries into the fryer and turned around.

It was eleven o'clock. Lunch service didn't start until eleven thirty. The fries would sit, cooling and congealing, for a half hour before anyone got to eat them. Laurel would have her usual indecision of wasting them by throwing them out, thus drawing more ire to herself from Reg, or letting them go out and confirming the mediocre reputation of the bar. Dollar signs warred with her perfectionism.

Dollar signs won, these days. "Couldn't you wait twenty minutes?" she said. *Okay, good. Passive aggression, let's go with that. Don't do anything about it, just complain.*

"I'm busy," he grumbled, moving to the refrigerator.

As befitted a man who only ate what he fried and who moved a total of twenty steps from the fryer to the refrigerator to the griddle in his workday, Reg's belly went ahead of him, his apron already stained, his bald, bullet-shaped head gleaming pale in the bright lights of the kitchen.

Miguel, whose title was officially "line cook" but who did everything Reg didn't feel like doing, including cleaning, was at one of the counters, unwrapping the bread that had been put away after last night's service and now needed warming up to hide its slight staleness. In contrast to Reg, Miguel was small, dark and quick. He had the bread in the warming oven and was at the pantry, pulling out one of the cans of sauce Jonah had put there earlier, before Reg reached it.

"Move over, Sancho," Reg grunted, using his sizable hip

to make way for himself at the pantry door. Miguel dodged him and his face tightened at the nickname, but he let Reg go first.

One of the things on Laurel's to-do list was to check Miguel's immigration status. The bar took taxes out of his paycheck, but his subservience to Reg suggested he was preternaturally afraid to lose his job.

Laurel had already asked Reg nicely to call Miguel by his name. He'd glowered and grunted and given the bare minimum of agreement, but his little joke was obviously too funny to him to give up. Today, for some reason, something had shifted inside Laurel. She followed Reg into the freezer. This left Miguel outside with empty hands, but it couldn't be helped.

"Why do you call him Sancho?" she said abruptly.

"Huh?" Reg didn't take his eyes from the shelf where he was supposed to be pulling out the battered fish fillets.

"Miguel," Laurel confirmed, filling the doorway. "His name is Miguel. Why do you call him Sancho?"

Reg didn't reply. He put a finger along the shelf, as if he'd forgotten where he kept the fish he'd been cooking for fifteen years.

"Reg," she said, her voice getting cold. She hadn't had time to deal with a lot of things in the last month. Today, apparently, it was time to deal with Reg. One part of him, anyway. "Look at me."

The authority in her voice was enough to make him turn

his head, though his shoulders also hunched up. He looked ready to fight.

"Why do you call him Sancho?" she repeated. "Because if he's Sancho, that makes you Don Quixote, which means you're insane and I shouldn't let you near a hot fryer."

Reg frowned. He probably hadn't thought it through that carefully. His education being what it had been, he might not even know who she was talking about.

"Or do you fancy yourself as Paul Newman?" This, to Laurel, was more likely. "The genial working-class hero with the stupid assistant?"

Reg's eyes narrowed. Bingo. He'd seen the movie *Nobody's Fool*. When she'd seen it on TV it had reminded her of her town, of families trying to make it through a working-class life in a society that no longer provided work for them. The movie had put a good gloss on the story, showing that a community could be a family, that they would all make it through in the end. The main character had even been called Sully, a name people had sometimes called Frank, because of the name of the bar.

But then she'd read the book, and had seen the original had no such gloss to it. The characters were hanging on to their lives with bloodied fingernails, and Sully was in a slow and literally painful decline that his own decisions would accelerate. Just like Frank. She'd been in college then, and her trips back home had reinforced her horror of her father's condition and the town she'd grown up in.

"'Cause you know, the guy in that story ended up with no money, no job and a bum knee," she went on. "So if you're looking for someone to copy, you might want to look somewhere else." She narrowed her eyes. "Show my employees respect, or you can leave."

Reg's shoulders went an inch further up his neck. He mumbled something about "...don't have to take this."

"No, Reg," she reminded him. "*I* don't have to take this. I know neither of us wanted it this way, but I am your boss. Now please don't put that fish in the fryer until someone actually orders it."

She walked out of the pantry to find Miguel where she'd left him, his eyes wide. "Waiting to get to the veggies?" she said.

"Uh-huh."

Veggies at Sullivan's came on top of a burger, in a house or a wedge salad, or cooked almost to a pulp and grudgingly served to crazy patrons who asked for them. Another thing Laurel planned to change.

"Let me ask you something," she said on a whim. "How would you prepare a side of veg for... say... a main of chicken fingers?"

His eyes, she couldn't believe it, got even wider. She wondered when he'd last been asked his opinion of something.

"Apart from fries?" he said.

"Apart from fries."

The words came from him fast, as though he was afraid she'd shut him down. "Something green," he said. "Chicken fingers and fries are yellow—orange."

Laurel winced; the quality of the cheap stuff Frank had ordered was definitely suspect.

"You need something to brighten the plate. Something that can offset the barbecue sauce," he went on. "Coleslaw, but better. Collard greens and bacon tossed in ranch, not too much—homemade. Broccoli slaw—use up the stalks, chop them up small. Or like with the wings—celery and blue-cheese dressing. Cucumber and apple salad."

Wow. Heck, why not say it out loud? "Wow. Those are all good ideas, Miguel."

He beamed. She was going to have to find out his immigration status soon. His accent and careful attitude around Reg suggested he hadn't been born here, but she might be assuming something that wasn't true. Anyway, with ideas like that bursting out of him, she didn't want to lose him. "Can you make the cucumber and apple salad for the lunch crowd? I'll run out and get you the ingredients."

Now Miguel's mouth fell open. "Now?"

"Yes, now." She nodded at the clock which ruled all their lives. "Lunch starts in twenty minutes. Get the rest of the veg prepped while I'm out, okay?"

"O-okay." He nodded.

Plainly, he couldn't wrap his head around the notion of a new menu item finding its way into Sullivan's. Well, he didn't know what was about to hit him.

"Cool." Filled with an energy she couldn't have believed she'd have an hour ago, Laurel grabbed her purse and, still in her chef's whites, dashed out of the kitchen door to run down to the farmer's market that was permanently set up on a corner of farmland just outside town. She could swear the alley still smelled of tomato sauce.

Chapter Three

THE MARKET WAS an example of the rejuvenation the region had undergone while Laurel had been in the city. Already a large town, Tanner had been expanded when commuters to Albany had realized they could get a bargain there and in Boon, its sister town on the other side of the railroad tracks, which had always been a tonier place anyway. The commuters had brought their city ways with them, according to her parents, and also their money. There were now five coffee shops within ten minutes' walk of her old high school. Someone had opened up a wine store, bringing new bottles from the Finger Lakes every week, and the farmer's market had swiftly followed.

And thank God for it. She muscled the Expedition up the main drag and out of town. The supermarket which used to support her neighborhood had closed down years ago, and she didn't have time or inclination to drive out to the Walmart. Driving past the old supermarket, though, she saw a sign pasted in the window that hadn't been there last week. A new... what did it say? Health and Hearth? What was that? Whatever it was, it boded well for the clientele to Sullivan's, if she could just get the place spruced up, and drag Reg away from that fryer.

In an even better mood, she picked up fresh vegetables and apple cider vinegar from the farmer's market.

"What's going up in the old A&P?" she asked the cashier.

"Another food store," the woman said, gloom taking her welcoming smile from her face. "Whole Foods knockoff, 'pparently."

"Oh." Part of Laurel thought that was great. She'd be able to get organic ingredients. She wasn't about to say this out loud, though. "But you guys have the local produce, right? They'll never be able to outdo that."

"Depends what they pay the other farmers," the woman pointed out. "Our margins aren't much."

Laurel could imagine. The oversized shed that they stood in was clean and quaintly decorated, but the heating system was louder than it should have been and the refrigerators also buzzed like the bees whose honey stood next to them. The fall displays were out, pumpkins and spice donuts and a Crock-Pot filled with hot apple cider. "Do you have pumpkin picking? Apple picking? That kind of thing?"

"Sterling Farm up the road does those," the cashier said.

Laurel wanted to ask more about the area, but she didn't have time. She'd ignored that her restaurant was opening for lunch without her on this mad whim to get fresh apples and cucumber, and she had a ten minute drive back again to handle.

"Anyway," Laurel said, "I'll be back. Your produce is beautiful and so is the atmosphere. It's all local farms?"

That brightened the woman up, and, with her smile, Laurel found a little hope. "Almost all. We take Sterling's pumpkins, depending on the weather. But most come from out of state. And they pick too many for one farm to grow anyway."

"Right. Well, I'm Laurel Moore." She stuck out her hand and the cashier checked her own hand, rubbed it on her apron, and shook. "I've taken over Sullivan's. On Bridge Street in Tanner?"

"Uh-huh." The woman's smile faltered. Laurel didn't blame her. Sullivan's reputation obviously preceded her. "Sadie Kurtz. Nice to meet you."

"You too. I'll see you soon," Laurel promised, and turned away with Miguel's ingredients.

Sadie's customers could be my customers, she thought as she drove home. *People who'll pay a little more to get quality food they can really taste. The new folk in town. The ones who'll drive all the way from Boon to buy honey from a beekeeper they could meet.*

Could she make *this* restaurant her dream? Not sell up after she'd figured out the debt, like she'd planned? Allow her mother to stay in the home she'd known for thirty years? Get Brett a job and an apartment somewhere healthier? With flavors like Miguel had suggested, and local produce like the farmer's market wanted to sell her, it might just be possible.

Jonah had grown up in Tanner, like Laurel. His father, everyone knew, lived in Boon with his new wife and their son. He was a professor, they said, and had been a drunk, but now his life seemed to be just fine. She, Jonah, and Jonah's half brother had attended the same high school, but Matthias was three or four years younger. As far as she knew, Jonah had never acknowledged his brother, at least in class. Hell, if the person didn't have several piercings and a hipflask of whiskey in his backpack, Jonah had hardly acknowledged anyone at all.

When she'd hooked up with Jonah that summer, she'd thought his rebellion involved a plan to get out of Tanner, something she could wholeheartedly support. She'd quickly learned it involved just escaping from his circumstances with alcohol as often as possible. "You look like shit," she'd said more than once.

"Thank you."

"Where were you last night?"

He'd squint. "Out?"

"You know what this is?" she'd retort, her fists digging into her sides. "This is pathetic. You're ruining that brain of yours just to piss off a man who did something to you *twenty years ago*. You should be ashamed of yourself."

He'd stopped at some point, she had to remember, if this morning hadn't shown her for sure. He was all kinds of respectable now. If she didn't look at those vines creeping up his neck.

Or offer him a brownie.

Yet he'd stayed. He hadn't left the town he hated to fulfill his dream; he hadn't even moved to Boon. He'd done it right here, across from the bar where he'd started on a path her father had finished.

She'd heard Frank talk of him now and again. "Won't even come in for a bite, anymore. Too good for us now he's found his twelve steps."

"The twelve steps work for some people, Daddy," Laurel remembered saying.

"Not for me, pickle," Frank had said, his eyes twinkling despite being continually bloodshot.

And there he was again. As clear in front of her as the faded awning over the bar, that she tried not to look at as she drove around the corner to park. When the car came to a stop, she allowed herself to slump over the steering wheel for a few moments. "How could you have left us, Daddy?" she asked the ether. "How could you have left *me*?"

The heaviness in her chest tightened; the lump in her throat grew. *No time, no time,* her logical side told her. *Lunch. Now. Remember?*

Laurel walked into a kitchen that was now in full lunchtime mode. Brian, the other line cook, and his son, who washed the dishes, were at their posts. As she put her bag on the counter, one of the servers came in and picked up an order of burger and fries and a footlong hot dog.

"Hi, Jennie," she called.

"Bethany hasn't shown," Jennie replied in lieu of a greeting. "Migraine."

Laurel sighed, already slipping her phone out of her pants pocket to call one of the other waitresses. And for the next two hours there was no time to get philosophical. No time to breathe, almost. She just put out fires—metaphorical ones, thankfully—chivvied unfulfilled staff, and tried to make the food that went out of her kitchen look and taste a little more appetizing.

However, she did find time to shove the bag of groceries in Miguel's hand and point to a chopping board. Five minutes later she circled back around to him. He'd found a mandoline Laurel hadn't known they owned, sliced the apples and cucumber into long, thin strips, and tossed them with chives and some kind of creamy vinaigrette. She grabbed a fork and took a bite. The gentle heat of the chives offset the sweetness of the apples and the apple cider vinegar he'd used in the dressing.

"Mmm," she said. "Yes. Put it out."

That was all she had time to say, but she patted his shoulder as she rushed by. Miguel looked as though he wanted to beam at her but was afraid the others would see him.

Minutes later, he'd put the salad in ramekin dishes and added them to the orders of chicken fingers that Reg slapped onto the counter. A small side dish, almost like coleslaw, apart from the texture and the darkness of the cucumber skin and the chives.

The plates came back empty.

At two thirty the kitchen closed. Laurel spent some time in the front with today's bartender, made sure he had what he needed for the quiet afternoon, then went back into the kitchen.

Reg was already gone. His go-slow protest only lasted as long as he was being paid for it. Brian had taken off his apron and was washing his hands. Miguel was helping Brian's son stack the last of the dishes into the dishwasher.

"Miguel," she said. "Looks like your slaw was a success."

Miguel blushed.

"Yeah," Brian said, his blond hair sticking up every which way as he took off his white cap. "What the hell was that stuff?"

"It's called food, Brian," Laurel said. "Fresh, green food. And there's going to be a lot more of it around here."

"You think what I cook isn't food?" Brian said, his voice rising. His son and Miguel paused in their task and looked at the two of them.

"It isn't *good* food," she corrected, and then held up a hand before he could bust a vein. "Not your fault. I know. It's the food. That's going to change." The rows of wholesome, fresh fruits, vegetables, eggs and meats from the farmer's market swam in front of her eyes.

"Jesus Christ," Brian said, bringing her back to earth. "You and your goddamn fancy degree. Coming up here and shitting all over what your father built. People *like* this food, for Christ's sake. Why do you think the bar's still here?"

She'd seen the accounts. It barely *was* here. "People shouldn't have to put up with cheap breading and zero imagination just because they're used to—"

"They're *tired*!" Brian shouted. "These guys have been out *working* all morning, unlike your fancy pants 'clientele'"—he sneered at the word—"who can get by on some fucking frou-frou salad out of an eggcup." He scowled at Miguel, who looked down.

This wasn't who she'd imagined she was going to have this argument with, but here they were. "You know what, Brian?" Laurel replied. "I don't have time for this conversation right now. Let's have a staff meeting. Tomorrow morning, ten thirty." She glanced at the door through which Reg had skedaddled, thought of the waitresses who had already left. "I'll tell Reg and the others."

She could just fire Brian. But she needed the experience the staff had to get them through the transition period. They knew how the restaurant worked in a way she didn't, and training up someone else would be too much work. Plus, if Brian left, his son probably would, too, and she needed a lunchtime dishwasher. So she gritted her teeth and said, "I need your expertise, Brian. But the bar is in trouble, and we have to make changes. Tomorrow, ten thirty?"

Brian scowled but nodded, then grabbed his son and pushed him out of the back door without saying another word. Laurel let go of another sigh and turned back to Miguel. "Good job, today, Miguel. Thank you. Did you get yourself something to eat?"

He nodded. "I have to go, sorry. Next job."

Frank had already cut the hours they served lunch and dinner, forcing everyone into second and even third jobs. She wondered where Miguel's second job was—or was it his third?—but didn't feel she could ask yet. She had a lot of relationship building to do and about twenty staff to do it with. She said, "Sure. See you tomorrow, then," and let him go.

Locking the kitchen door, she told the bartender to call her if there were any issues, and went upstairs to change. Peeling off her stained whites and cap, she put on her industrial-strength running bra, leggings and T-shirt and hit the road. She didn't see her mother and swallowed her guilt that she didn't go looking for her. If she didn't burn off some of this stressed-out energy she was going to burst.

Since she hadn't had time to find a place to do her beloved Zumba, and running was free anyway, that was what she'd settled on for exercise, walking briskly to Tanner's windswept park and jogging around it for an hour, the punctuation of the train coming by the only interruption to the birdsong and the sound of children playing on the swings.

The movement of her body was always a relief after the prescribed, small-motor-skill motions of the life of a chef. It was a travesty that being on her feet all day didn't count as exercise, but it didn't, and in any case her body told her it needed more any time she skipped on stretching and moving. When Frank had first died, she'd had no time to run, and after a week she'd felt as if her skin was trying to leave her body. Now, no matter how much else she had to do, she gave herself an hour each day to run off the stress.

Not that the pressures of her situation left her alone while she ran. The bills, the staff, the food, the building, her mother, her brother. They all clamored to be solved yesterday. But not having to talk to anyone for an hour was helpful, and she'd come up with more ideas on her run than sitting in her father's tiny office behind the bar.

Today, however, there was a new subject that intruded upon her thoughts. Jonah Gardiner, eating that brownie.

His hands. Cradling it. The way the brownie broke apart in his fingers. He had to lick his hand to catch the crumbs.

Holy crap. She was more breathless than usual. She stopped by a water fountain and took a drink, shaking her head to clear it.

Jonah was a long time ago. What was the point of thinking about him? Not that she'd chosen to; he'd just been getting in her head all day.

Dating, and sex, hadn't been on her agenda for a couple of months, and still weren't. Would it be so bad if she imagined Jonah again, and all the fun they'd had before they'd broken up, to get her through this time? A little pleasure to cut through the depressing thoughts she usually had. That wouldn't be so bad, would it?

Besides, he'd done her a favor this morning, and she'd barely said thank you. Maybe she should thank him properly—bring him a muffin or something.

The jolt of desire that shot through her surprised her so much she bent over at the waist and put her hands on her hips to get her breath back.

That was not why she would bring him a muffin. It would just be to say thank you.

Yeah, right.

Chapter Four

Jonah had no business looking out of his living room window at eight o'clock the next morning. He should be checking his files, doing some reading… something other than leaning against the window frame, glancing every few seconds at the empty alley across the street while he pretended to be people-watching the commuters on their way to the station.

He didn't move, however, and was rewarded at 8:05 when the kitchen door opened and Laurel came out, carrying a tray of something. Unconsciously, he straightened and checked his shirt was tucked in and he hadn't spilled coffee down himself without noticing. So much for their meeting yesterday being a fleeting thing.

Laurel looked up at his apartment windows, and when she narrowed her eyes and kept staring, Jonah's heart skipped. She was looking for him. He knelt on the floor so he could open the lower half of the sash, got close enough to the screen that she could see him, and waved.

Seeing the motion, Laurel smiled, and this time Jonah's

heart thudded harder. She held up the tray. If that had more brownies in it, Jonah was a goner. Then she pointed at his front door and lifted one shoulder in question.

Could she come up? Hell yeah. "Come on up," he called, making several heads turn, the way they had yesterday morning. Thankfully, only Laurel took him up on the offer. She dashed between a bus and a delivery van and across the road. Jonah left his door open, ran down the stairs and had the front door open before she could find his doorbell.

Since when had an apron that covered most of someone's body been so sexy? Or perhaps it was the cinnamon scent she brought with her today, or the tendrils of strawberry-blonde frizz that had escaped her ponytail? Whatever it was, as he had yesterday, Jonah felt as though his brain had seized up. "Hi," he said. *Slick, dude.*

"Hello." She smiled uncertainly and held up a tray containing six muffins. "I wanted to say thank you for yesterday. Lemon poppy or cinnamon crumb?"

Jesus. Just watching her say the word *crumb* was turning him on. What was it with this girl? He'd believed his attraction to her when they were young was the usual sort—her effusive curves, her clear, slightly freckled skin and, let's face it, her interest in him. But he was older now, more logical. If he thought about having a relationship, he figured it would be with someone like him. A psychologist, someone as interested in books as he was, in long intellectual conversations about the human condition. He'd had relationships like that over the last few years. Those relationships had been… acceptable. Adequate. They had provided the service for which they were required.

Nothing about Laurel Moore was merely adequate. She was short-circuiting his logic chip as surely as if she were made of pure light.

"Come on up," he said. *You already said that, genius.* "Um…" He stepped aside so she could pass him. "Second floor." *She knows that, too. Dammit.*

Laurel didn't seem to be as affected, although to be fair, she didn't have to follow her own beautiful butt up the stairs to his apartment. She stood back at the top of the stairs so he could smell the cinnamon scent on her—uh, coming from the muffins—as he went by to let her into his apartment.

Jonah kept his belongings to a minimum, apart from his books—not that he had much choice, with student loans to pay off—and the railroad apartment was tidy, at least. The living room looked over the street, and the kitchen ran along the wall opposite the front door. On their right was a short hallway leading to the bathroom and Jonah's bedroom. He quickly wondered if they were acceptable, as well, before remembering there was no reason on earth for Laurel to go into his bedroom.

Pulling himself together with an effort, he pointed her to a stool at the tiny kitchen island and said, "Can I get you some coffee?"

Her cheek dimpled and she kept her eyes on the tray she

was putting onto the island when she replied, "Sure, thanks."

He couldn't miss a single movement she made. "What's funny about that?"

She waved a hand and sat on the stool. "Nothing! It's just... not what I remember of you."

"Asking if you want coffee?"

"Asking me *politely*. Anyway, you were usually too preoccupied to think of it."

Jonah didn't answer her, but poured her a large white mug of coffee, put it on the counter, then found milk and sugar and a teaspoon and watched her doctor the mug to her satisfaction. He remained standing on the other side of the island.

Laurel took a sip, her lips closing around the edge of the mug. "Oof," she murmured. "That's good."

He could watch her drink his coffee all day, but now she was here, there was something else he had to say. "Laurel," he began.

"Uh-oh," she smiled. "You've gone all serious."

"Serious is kind of my MO these days. It works a lot better for me than reckless."

"Everyone has room for a little reckless, don't they? Have a muffin."

He wanted the muffin, but it would distract him worse than she did. "In a second. I need to tell you that I'm sorry for the way I treated you back when we were dating."

Now he'd rendered her silent. Her mouth fell open. Her

mug clinked on the counter as she almost lost her grip on it.

Taking advantage of her silence, he went on. "There's no excuse for the way I was back then. I was selfish and arrogant, and immature, and I shouldn't have been inflicting myself on anyone, least of all you."

"We were kids, Jonah," she pointed out. "And you had a lot of shit to deal with."

"I was twenty-two. Not a kid. And you had shit to deal with too, but you didn't turn into the town rebel."

Her cheek dimpled again. "Only if you count going out with you in the first place."

That pulled a reluctant smile from him. "I've always felt that you could have used a friend in those days, not an… outlet."

Laurel shifted in her seat. If he didn't know better, he might have said she wriggled. Either way, she fixed him with a lowered-eyelid look and said, "You were quite an outlet, you know."

Now he was grinning. "Right back atcha."

He'd made her smile too, in a way he loved. For a second, he'd taken her out of her problems. As he should have done ten years ago, instead of adding to them.

"It's okay, Jonah," she said, spreading her hands between them. "No hard feelings. Honest. In any case, if I judged you I'd have to judge my dad the same way, and where would that get me? Also, for a long time I felt that I should have stuck around. Helped you more."

"Not at all." He widened his eyes, hoping she'd take this away from his apology, if nothing else. "Laurel, no one was responsible for the way I was but me. Don't ever think you should have done something. In fact, you did something by walking away. It was because of you that I didn't go down Frank's path. You made me see more clearly. Quite a feat in those days."

"Maybe I should thank you, too, then. You made me more determined to stay in the city to work on my career." Something passed across her face, but he couldn't put a name to it before it was gone. "Water under the bridge. Okay? Have a muffin."

If he'd expected his apology and her acceptance of it to assuage his guilt, he'd been wrong, but he couldn't resist her food any longer. He pulled one out of the pan and broke it in two.

It was perfect. Light inside, browned on the outside, the sugar and crumb falling onto the counter—he'd forgotten a plate again—and he put his hand underneath, as he had done yesterday so as not to lose any more of it. He could see her watching him the way he'd watched her when she'd sipped her coffee.

The explosion of cinnamon and sugar on his tongue was intoxicating, a pure decadent pleasure. Perhaps even better than yesterday's brownie. "God," he said, his voice tight—then again, his mouth was full. "So good."

Laurel gave a satisfied little wriggle—yep, this time it was definitely a wriggle—and took one for herself. Unlike him, she took the top off and ate it first.

"Now you've eaten the best part," he teased. "You have to eat the rest without the crumb."

"Seize the day, buddy," she replied. She took a sip of coffee to wash down the crumbs, then said, "Can I ask you a question?"

"Sure."

"If you're so different now, why are you living across the street from a bar? From *the* bar that was so tempting ten years ago? That you've sworn never to go in again?"

"Oh." He pulled the paper off the rest of his muffin. He'd made quite an impressive pile of crumbs on the counter now. "You remember that, huh?"

"I mean, I get the not going into bars thing, kind of, but in that case, why live *here*?"

"Well, first of all, because it was cheap, and small. And I liked the brick walls and space for my books." Laurel raised an eyebrow at him. "Okay, okay. Because it was part of the challenge. Part of not letting that side of me take over again. If I could live across the street from Sullivan's and not feel the pull to go in there, I'd won."

"And have you?"

"Yes. It's no longer an issue." *Until yesterday.*

"Brett was right. Dad missed you."

"Yeah." Dammit, the whole muffin was crumbs on the counter now. He'd been crushing it with his fingertips while he dodged around with his words. "I missed him, too. You know that Sully was like a father to me. More than my own. But..." He chose his words again. "There were parts of him I couldn't follow without destroying myself."

"I understand. That's what they tell you to do, isn't it? Break off with the people you used to drink with?"

"In a way. I didn't do AA. I found a therapist. She pretty much said the same thing. But you should know..." He looked out of the window at the upstairs windows of Sullivan's. "I know Sully was a good man inside. I know you tried to help him as much as you could. And I know he knew that, too." When he looked back at her, her eyes were shining.

He didn't mean to make her cry, but who else would tell her this? Who else had listened to her back then, had this kind of history with her?

"So, losing my relationship with him was painful. Real painful. I don't want you to... to think that Brett was right about that."

Her smile was crooked, but she nodded. Then she pushed the muffin tray toward him. "Try the lemon poppy."

She was letting him off the hook, and he could have kissed her for it. This conversation involved his emotions, and hadn't they just ascertained he was crap at those?

He took the offered muffin, because what else could he do? But the tang of the lemon and the crunch of the poppy seed didn't help him find his way back to his logical life any more than Laurel and her cinnamon scent had.

"I have another question," she said.

Damn. He'd kinda hoped they could move away from this topic. "Shoot."

"Did you drink before you hung out with my dad?"

"Yeah, of course!" He knew what she was thinking—that Frank had been the one to lead him down the destructive path he'd been on, that Brett might still be on, from what Jonah had seen of him yesterday. "Lor, you knew me in high school. Did I ever come in without a hip flask?"

"I don't know. I didn't know you then. I just heard rumors."

"The rumors were true. From junior year, anyway." From when his younger half brother started becoming a star on the football field, he'd realized later. "So Frank didn't lead me on, if that's what you're thinking. I was all too ready to follow him. Until someone with a lot more common sense slapped me upside the head." He smiled at her, making sure he caught her eye.

She gave another watery smile and bit into her muffin. They sat in silence for a moment.

"How are you doing?" he said at last. "With the bar and everything?"

"Good," she said, finishing the top of her muffin, not looking at him.

"You've had so little time to process it all. And now you have to run a restaurant you didn't know anything about."

She bristled. "I *do* know how to run a restaurant."

"I didn't mean—"

"I know." She subsided, pulled the wrapper off the bottom half of her muffin and looked at it. "I don't know how to run *this* restaurant. At least, I don't want to run it the way it's been run." She began folding the wrapper into a tiny parcel. "Dad left a lot of debts."

"I'm sorry."

Her mouth twisted, her shoulder going up in another half shrug. "Everyone's been very understanding, but if I don't turn things around in the next six months... At least, that's how long I'm giving myself to either get it back up to scratch, or sell it at a loss. And break my mother's heart."

Jonah wanted to reach across the counter and take her hand. But he'd given up that privilege years ago. "If I can help," he said, an empty request. How could he help her?

She shook herself. "Well, let's not get all mopey with this much sweetness in front of us."

He couldn't agree with her more. The sun was coming through the living room windows now, highlighting the red in her hair and making her skin glow. And the scent of cinnamon and sugar that surrounded her was better than a shot of tequila.

"Tell me what you've been doing," she went on. "You're a psychologist?"

"Uh-huh."

"You went back to school for all that time? You? You hated college."

"I didn't really. I just half-assed it to embarrass my dad." Yet it was because of his father that his student loans weren't as bad as some people's. "Once I sobered up and paid attention, I found what I wanted to do. Had to work my butt off to convince the school my grades were an anomaly, not really what I could do. In the end, I found I liked helping college kids, especially ones who are about to lose their way. And the college where I got my PhD offered me a job."

She sat back on her stool, appraising him. "I would never have pegged you for an intellectual, back then. But it suits you."

"Thanks. And it's not how I would have wanted it for you, but being in charge suits you."

She laughed. "Yeah, I really made a good impression yesterday, nearly getting creamed by that bus and then looking like a crime scene, thanks to that can of sauce."

He smiled with her, but said, "Still. Whatever you decide to do with the bar, it'll come out great. I know it."

She blushed lightly. "You haven't finished your muffin."

"I can't give it the attention it deserves when you're sitting in front of me."

Had he just said that out loud? Apparently so, given her deeper blush and the satisfied wiggle of her shoulders. *Not part of the plan, genius.* But what was he going to do? Take it back?

"You're very kind," she said, putting her hand to the flyaways in her hair. "I've been up since four and baking since then. I'm probably covered in flour."

He shook his head. "Perfect."

Her eyes met his and she narrowed hers a little, trying to figure him out. Now it was his turn to get hot under the collar, if it wasn't obvious he'd been that way since she'd come across the street to him. There she went again, scrambling his brains. "Anyway," he said, perhaps louder than he needed. "I should get to work."

"Yes, of course," Laurel said, slipping off the stool. She began to walk the few steps to his door, leaving the tray on the counter.

"You forgot your muffins," he said behind her.

"No." She turned around. "I made them for you."

And ten years of study and about a billion words read, and Jonah Gardiner couldn't utter one sound as she walked out of his door and down the stairs. He also couldn't take his eyes off her butt, with its slight swing when she walked.

She was so strong, doing this all by herself. Leaving behind everything she'd built in New York with no complaints, and looking for no sympathy past the telltale sheen of tears he'd seen in her eyes this morning.

Jonah thought of Brett, squaring off against him yesterday morning. The kid had been ready for a fight just because he was hungover. Frank had brought Brett into the bar as soon as he could get away with it, making games out of concocting drinks and generally showing Brett that a life without booze wasn't a life for a Moore.

Without him, it wasn't surprising that Brett was floundering. And Laurel would be suffering on his behalf. Jonah could see she was already buried under the combined problems of her father's business and her family's grief, and Brett wouldn't be any kind of support to her any time soon.

Who would fill that gap? As he turned into the back street that led to the parking lot behind his apartment, the flashing lights from Sullivan's neon beer signs caught his eye.

Not you, you dried up old stick, he reminded himself. There was a reason he didn't get involved anymore, and it wasn't about to get plowed over by the mere taste of the best cinnamon crumb muffin in the history of muffins.

Chapter Five

LAUREL'S MORNING MEETING had her out of Frank's office and back in the kitchen by ten thirty. There, lined up against the counter like tin cans she was about to shoot down, were Frank's hand-chosen employees—her employees, now.

Reg was in the back, his arms spread, holding onto the griddle as though she planned on taking it from him. Brian and his son were together on one side of the room. Miguel—whose paperwork was just fine; it was Brian's son whose age had been fudged on his papers five years ago, so he'd begun work at the bar at thirteen—had taken the other side, though it wasn't hard to know that they didn't get along. Jennie, Bethany, and the other lunchtime servers were in a bunch in the middle, a few sipping from mugs of coffee they'd already picked up in the bar. Jennie, a woman in her fifties who dressed in the same way she had in her twenties, was blinking slowly. She'd worked a double shift last night and probably didn't appreciate being asked to come in a half-hour early today. Pascale and Maureen, the lunchtime bartenders, stood nearest the door.

The first time Laurel had held a meeting like this, days after Frank's death and before the bar reopened, she'd looked at this group and been terrified. She was responsible for their income—at least some of it. Even with the cuts Frank had made in their hours, she might still have to let some of them go.

She'd told them as much that day, but added she wasn't going to do anything for at least a month, that she wanted them to go about their business as usual so she could learn the ropes. Some of them had taken offense at the idea that they were on probation. Some had used the intervening weeks to suck up to her, the kitchen crew being the notable exception to this. But generally they *had* continued to do what they always did, and while there were some efficiencies Laurel could make, she'd learned that the biggest money-loser they'd had—Frank's habit of drinking several bottles of scotch a week—had gone.

Laurel took a deep breath. "Thanks for coming," she said. "Have a muffin." She nodded to the counter against which they all leaned. None of them had touched the tray she'd left there, and none of them touched it now. They were looking at her too hard.

"I'm not letting anyone go," she added. Maybe that should have been the first thing she said, as evidenced by the distinct change in atmosphere and the lowering of several sets of shoulders. "*Now* have a muffin?"

Most of them laughed and turned to the trays. Reg wasn't buying it, though, and neither was Brian. His son looked longingly at the muffins but stayed with his father.

When they'd turned back to her, Laurel went on. "Thank you for your patience with me. Sullivan's was about my dad, but it was also about all of you. The fact that you stuck it out has a lot to do with why we're doing all right."

She noticed a pained look on Bethany's face. Maybe her migraine hadn't quite gone away. "Now," Laurel went on, "I *do* want to make some changes to the food." This was what had kept her up half the night—the promise in the shelves of Sadie's farmer's market and the surrounding farms and fields. That visit had opened up a new vision in a world Laurel had thought permanently narrowed. A gastropub in the middle of Upstate New York that people would travel miles to visit.

Reg scowled. Everyone else looked apprehensive. "This is my job, don't forget," she reassured them. "What I've been working toward all my life. Tanner is changing and if we change with it, we can all stay employed for the next twenty years."

They shifted on their feet. Clearly, she wasn't going to sell them in one conversation. She held up her hands. "I just want to introduce a few specials, and a few extras, like Miguel's slaw yesterday."

That put the attention squarely on her line cook, who blushed and stared at his shoes. "Did anyone mention it when you served it?" Laurel asked the waitresses.

They flicked their eyes at each other uncomfortably. "Did you ask them?" she pressed. But the answer was on their faces. They'd all been stuck in their familiar ruts for too long to break out of them just because something new appeared on the plates. Laurel succeeded in not rolling her eyes at them. "Today, ask. Okay?"

"Okay," they mumbled.

"They liked the brownies, last night," Jennie said unexpectedly. With everything else in her head today, Laurel had forgotten she'd offered them.

"Yeah?" she said.

"Yeah. 'Much better than usual,' Mitch Hill said."

"What was so different about them?" Brian asked. He sounded belligerent, but couldn't have as much invested in the desserts when the servers put those together themselves, from the meager offerings the restaurant gave out.

"I made them."

This was not a selling point to Brian, who still hadn't gone for a muffin.

"There might be a few left, if you guys would like a taste."

"Don't you need them for lunch?"

Laurel was already halfway to the refrigerator. "Just a taste. The servers got to taste all the meals in my old restaurant. That way, you knew what you were offering the customers."

This was a new way of doing things, but no one was

complaining when she took out a few brownies and cut them into bite-sized pieces for everyone to try. Even Brian's son got one while Brian was making up his mind. The noises of appreciation made her smile in relief. In this one tiny battle, at least, she was winning.

"I'll be making some more changes, like this," she finished, "but with your input, and we all get to taste them before they go out. Okay? Okay, thanks."

The waitresses filed out, and Laurel expected Brian, Reg and the rest of the lunch crew to begin their tasks as usual. When Reg and Brian exchanged looks and stayed at their places in front of the cold griddle, however, Laurel squared off opposite them.

"That was it, guys," she said.

"Well, we're not done," Reg said.

Laurel sighed. She pushed a stray hair out of her eyes with one wrist. Normally she did what she could not to piss Reg off, because she needed him, but now that she had a direction to take the restaurant, his attitude was pissing her off more and more. "You really do brighten my day, you know that, Reg?"

Reg wasn't to be deterred. "I told you yesterday. The restaurant doesn't need changes. The customers like what we cook just fine."

"But we need *more* customers, Reg. A half-full bar won't keep anyone employed."

"So you're going to push out our regulars by upping the

prices for this new stuff?"

"I hope not. But you have to realize that—"

"God." Now Brian took over the lecture, his sneering face coming closer. Behind him, his son cringed in the act of putting on his apron. "You have no fucking idea, do you? You're going to run this bar right into the ground with your stupid fancy ingredients and your freaking frou-frou food."

"And how do you plan on paying for this?" Reg came in close behind. "You tell us we're in all this debt and then you want to throw out perfectly good food!" He waved a hand at the freezer, where the damnable cheaply breaded chicken still sat, waiting for its hot fat bath.

"You let me worry about that," she said, shaking now. She *was* terrified of the gamble, but she knew how to budget, and with the staff at their current pay, she thought she could manage it.

"I'll worry about it if I please, Miss High-and-Mighty," Brian said, pointing a finger at her. "It's my job you're killing off."

The finger-pointing really set off Laurel's raw emotions. "I'm trying to *save* your job," she snapped. "We can keep doing it your way, and be closed within six months, or we can try something new, and—"

"Close in three," Brian finished, his voice bright with glee. Then he turned his back on her and spoke to Reg. "You know what, Reg? I don't think I feel like sticking around to watch it all fail."

As if they'd planned this all along, Reg got a terrible, gloating grin on his face. "I think you might be right about that, buddy. I'm sick of this bitch dissing everyone who's ever walked in here, running, begging after the yuppies who won't give her the time of day."

"There aren't even any yuppies anymore, you moron!" she shouted, losing her cool completely. "You ever heard of the recession? That's what this bar is still in, and unless you get with the program, it'll sink and you'll be out of a job anyway!"

"Better choose to go now, then," Brian said loftily, and began to untie the navy-and-white striped apron he'd only just put on.

Some sense got through to Laurel. "Wait. Are you two serious? We open in an hour!"

"You hear that, Reg?" Brian said. "She opens in an hour."

"Aw," Reg said. He hadn't even put his apron on yet, so he was able to just begin to walk to the door. "Shame, that, innit, Bry?"

"Shame," Brian nodded, following him.

The room swam in front of her eyes. For a second, Laurel was afraid she was going to faint, but she was just getting angrier. "Get the fuck out of my kitchen," she said, her tone icy but furious. "Don't come back. Don't ask for a reference, and good luck with your future careers at McDonald's."

"Good luck with your *bistro*," Brian sneered. "Come on,

Brian."

His son, who had stood, almost glued to the sides of the kitchen, while they'd argued, stared at him with his mouth open. "What?"

"Let's go," Brian said impatiently. "Haven't you been listening? Come on."

Brian's son's mouth opened and closed a few times. "But she doesn't have anyone for lunch service."

"The fuck do I care?" Brian replied. "Get over here."

His son went bright red, gaped a couple more times, and then said, "No, Dad. That wouldn't be fair."

Holy shit. Laurel had not expected that. *I am really going to have to start calling him by his name.*

"What?" Brian's face began to go red too, and his voice got tighter. "No. You just quit. Why don't you listen when people are talking?"

"I'll work today," Brian Jr. said, his tone as even as his father's was angry. "Then I'll come home."

"Not to my house, you won't," Brian snapped.

"You're going to throw him out because he said no to you one time?" Laurel burst out.

"You keep out of this." Brian didn't even look at her.

"Dad. I'll be home after this shift. That's it. I just don't think it's fair to leave her with no one to make lunch."

Laurel noticed that Reg's face was red, too, as he stood a little behind Brian in the door. A beeping behind them hailed the arrival of the bar truck, snapping them all out of it. "Fine," Brian snarled. "But if you aren't home by two thirty, don't bother coming home at all."

Brian Jr. lowered his head. Laurel wanted to hug him, but she didn't know if her legs would carry her over to him, and she wasn't about to fall flat on her face in front of the two turncoats at the door. "How about you get out of the way of my delivery," she said, her voice cold again. The men disappeared. "And it's a *gastropub*!" she couldn't help but shout after them.

The kitchen suddenly echoed with silence. Laurel looked at Miguel and Brian Jr., who looked back at her, their eyes wide. She had to act, and act now. "Miguel, you're promoted," she said abruptly. "You've worked the grill before?"

"No," he confessed. "They wouldn't let me near it."

Laurel cursed. "I'll teach you today. It's nothing but timing, and anyway, it'll be less important once we start the new menu. Junior?" She couldn't stand to hear the name "Brian" one more time. "You want to be sous chef?"

"Whuh?" Now he did look as dopey as his father always said he was. "I can't, I—"

"You can, if you want to. I'll pay you more and you can move out of your father's house. You can bunk on our couch if you have to. For now, you're promoted. You can decide later if you want to make it permanent."

Feeling better for having made some decisions, Laurel went over to Junior and put her hand on his shoulder. "You're a good kid, Junior," she said, shaking him a little, "and you've got a home here, and a school, if you want it."

To her surprise, his eyes filled with tears. "Thanks," he said, his voice choked.

Poor kid. "Don't mention it." She shook his shoulder again, making his whole body move. "Seriously. Don't mention it. Get to work."

He laughed wetly and reached for the paper towels to blow his nose. Laurel started handing out orders left and right, trusting Pascale and Maureen to handle the drink delivery, as they did every day, after all.

The boys could only learn so much in one day, but they did their best, and with Laurel darting about filling the gaps in their knowledge, the lunch service was completed with almost no one the wiser. The servers all came in and observed Laurel and Miguel working the grill, and a distinct lack of Reges and Brians—or rather, one Brian—but didn't say anything until the bar had died down. Then they all said they didn't know how she'd put up with the two men for so long.

Neither did she. In her chef's whites, her muscle memory kicking in as she took orders and set the food on the griddle, Laurel finally felt that she'd come home. She should have fired Reg right off the bat. She couldn't do a whole lot about today's menu, but she was more careful with the fry oil, making sure whatever had to be fried was properly drained before it went on a plate, and having Junior cut up fresh coleslaw to put alongside.

She still needed more help. Junior couldn't do all the prep himself, and the dishes piled up on every available surface. Luckily—or unluckily, depending how she looked at it—it was a quiet lunch, and they didn't run out of plates until she could take Junior off chopping and send him back to his old job.

With some qualms, but not knowing how else to help, Laurel sent him home at two fifteen and she and Miguel finished the dishes. "You're welcome back tomorrow, Junior," she reminded him. "But I understand if you don't come."

"Thanks, chef," he said, his voice thick, and he left. She and Miguel looked at each other.

"Now what?" he said.

"Hell if I know," she answered.

Chapter Six

DESPITE HER "NEW" position as head chef at her own restaurant, Laurel was still up early the next morning for another trip to the wholesaler. She hadn't seen Brett for a day so she'd left a note on his bedroom door, but didn't hold out a lot of hope that he'd show up the next morning, even if she had made two-bite apple pies.

She could maybe ask her other delivery man. When she drove past Jonah's windows at seven thirty, Laurel couldn't help but look up, but she didn't see any movement. *It's not his job. And what's the point, when you two would be doomed from the start? A bar owner and an ex-alcoholic?* It was about the worst idea she'd ever heard.

This time she was smarter about what she ordered and how she loaded the SUV, so she was more than half unloaded when a shadow fell across the tailgate at half past eight.

"Hello." She smiled, squinting up at Jonah in the morning sun that reflected off his apartment's windows and down into her alley.

"Hi," he said. "Can I help?"

"You don't have to. See? I'm tomato-free today."

"I'd still like to."

Was there a rumble in his voice when he said that? Or was it just Laurel's humming body, indulging in a spot of wishful thinking? He looked all kinds of edible today, in black jeans that emphasized how long his legs were, and a green shirt with a subtle check that contrasted perfectly with his red hair and beard. When he squinted back at her, he resembled some kind of hipster cowboy.

"Okay," she said, hoping he wouldn't notice her breathlessness.

As before, Jonah more than halved the time it took to unload the truck. And, as before, he hesitated for a moment the first time he approached the kitchen door. Not as long as before, but she noticed.

When they were done, she pulled the apple pies out of the warming drawer she'd kept them in, in case he showed up. His eyes widened as he followed the tray to the counter. "Laurel," he said. "You can't keep doing this to me."

"Doing what?" she teased, getting two plates and a canister of homemade whipped cream out of the refrigerator.

He didn't answer at first. What exactly *was* she doing to him? Was it just her food? He'd been happy with her before whether or not she fed him, but that had been a different Jonah. Who cooked for him now? As far as she could remember, cooking wasn't his mother's strong suit.

"Giving me this..." he said, his voice trailing off. "I haven't had food this good in... years."

"That's very sad," she declared. "Very, very sad." She popped a tartlet out of the pan onto his plate and added a perfect swirl of whipped cream on top.

"It's not sad," he said, his hand already reaching for the plate. "It's... necessary."

She didn't understand what he meant, but he'd already picked up the tart and she wanted to watch him eat it, not make him talk more.

The cream got on his nose, which was funny, but the noise he made when he bit into the pie anyway was so sexy that Laurel had to clutch the counter behind her.

"Jeez," he said, closing his eyes, his mouth full. "I don't know how you do it," he added thickly.

"Butter, sugar, eggs, flour." She let go of the counter long enough to take a bite of her own mini pie. Completely as she wanted it—crumbly pastry giving way to firm-but-not-undercooked apple chunks in a light syrup that didn't soak the pastry. She nodded. The perfect dessert for fall. "It's science," she added to Jonah.

He shook his head, pointing at the pie in his hand and rolling his eyes. "Nuh-uh. This is art."

"I'm glad you like it," she said, preening inside. She'd had Michelin-starred chefs praise her food with more eloquence than this, but it was Jonah's reaction that mattered to her the most right now.

He finished the pie and licked his fingers. Laurel swallowed.

"Thank you," he said. "I'm sorry I didn't bring coffee over."

His coffee was good, too, but right now Laurel was fixating on his hands, the long fingers of which were a little sticky. What would he do if she reached over, picked up his hand, and sucked on his fingers herself?

Oh, God. She was really losing it.

"Laurel?"

"Jonah?" she echoed, stalling.

Her problem was she didn't have the kind of chest that sat quietly when she was breathing fast. He could probably see her desire all over her body. She was probably blushing, too, if the heat in her cheeks was anything to go by.

His blue eyes got darker while she watched. Yeah. He could see.

The cavernous kitchen suddenly seemed very close, yet the counter between them stretched for miles. She could hitch herself up onto it and reach him that way…

"You want another?" she asked, her voice strangled.

"Laurel," he said again, his voice lower. "Stop tempting me."

"A little temptation never hurt anyone." She couldn't believe she was saying this. A little temptation could hurt plenty.

"You are more than a little temptation to me," he said.

You. Meaning her. Not her food. Her. He'd said it again.

Laurel's own attempt to resist temptation blew away like a handful of flour. "Then kiss me, you idiot," she said.

Jonah put out one long arm, hooked a finger into the top of her apron and pulled her across the counter toward him. They met in the middle, his mouth covering hers gently at first, but quickly going deeper when Laurel put her hands on his shoulders and pulled him in.

God, he was better than she'd ever remembered. His lips were fine and warm, his beard softer than she remembered. He tasted of apples and sugar, and a hint of the coffee he must have drunk earlier. He moved over her lips as if getting to know her, but now that she'd said the words, Laurel needed more, and she opened her mouth and hitched one hip on to the counter at the same time, just as she'd imagined it.

Jonah groaned and leaned into her, his hand moving to the back of her hair, his fingers finding their way under her braid to massage her head while he kissed her with long, slow strokes of his tongue.

Now it was Laurel's turn to moan; his fingers felt so good. When was the last time a man had had his hands in her hair? So much of her job was spent making sure her feminine assets were hidden away. Jonah's hands seemed to say, *I see you. I know who you are in there.*

Laurel swung her knees up onto the counter so she could slide closer to him on one hip. So she could place a hand flat on his shirt and feel the muscles, the heavier build he had since the last time they'd been this close. It suited him, the extra weight. He was rangy and strong, and those words alone made her skin tingle.

He was almost holding her up, one hand in her hair, the other sliding around to her back so she could feel his arm against her breast. She used the hand that wasn't touching him to press that forearm closer to her. She wanted him all kinds of closer to her.

But suddenly he was gone. He broke the kiss, backed away from the counter. Left her almost on her side, her hair mussed, her lips cool in the kitchen air. He put a hand out, as though she were advancing on him, and said, "Don't."

She couldn't handle the change in mood. What had gone wrong? "What's don't?" she said stupidly, sitting up on the counter and swinging her legs down so she faced him.

"Don't... start this," he said, running a hand through his hair, not looking at her. "This is a bad idea."

At least his voice was as shaky as she felt. "Who said it had to be a bad idea?"

"It always was," he insisted. If he would just look at her. "I was bad for you then and I'd be just as bad for you now. You have to forget me. Forget 'us.'"

"Why? What's so terrible about you now?"

"I can't give you what you want—what you deserve"—and when she began to talk, he went on—"and I don't want to."

That made her close her mouth with an audible click.

Then he did look at her, a brief glance that deepened his frown. "Look," he said. She remembered he spent his life explaining emotions to people. How was he going to explain this to her? "The last time we were together, I was… immature. Overemotional. I was mad at the world and I didn't care who I hurt while I railed at it. You got mixed up in that, and it hurt you."

"I already said I—"

"I don't mean that," he said. "I'm saying that now I'm better. I don't let my feelings dictate the terms anymore. I'm grateful for what I have. What I've achieved, despite doing all I could to derail things back then." He sighed and began to stroke his hand down his beard, as if it helped him collect his thoughts. "I can't open it all up again, don't you see? I don't do well with emotions. They take over. I'm better—and I'm better for my clients—when I make my decisions based on logic. You…" And finally he did look at her. "You are everything that would send me back there."

Laurel's mouth fell open. Her bewilderment changed to anger in a heartbeat. "So because I make you *feel* something, you're rejecting me?"

"God, no, don't use that word." He flinched away from it.

"Okay, genius, you're the one with all the 'booklarning,'" she went on sarcastically. "You give me the word for what you're doing, when you were just offered on a platter something you and I both wanted."

His cheeks reddened, but he said, "Don't you see? I *don't* want it. I don't want to stir all that up again. My life is good now and I intend to keep it that way. I'm sorry, but—"

"I *hate* those words!" she exclaimed. "'I'm sorry, but—' means you're not sorry at all. You're just going to go back to your safe little world and not even acknowledge that *ten years* have gone by and maybe if you don't start working on your social life a little, you'll end up alone, looking around and wondering where all your relationships went."

He winced again, but said, "That's my point. I don't have any relationships now, unless you count the joy of listening to my mother complain. I still can't go back to my father and tell him it's water under the bridge, as you so kindly said to me. I can't do it. You see? I would never let one of my clients get away with that, and here I am, doing it."

That tempered Laurel's anger a little. "Still? But what about Matt?"

He shook his head. "Same thing. Different reasons. He's a freaking war hero now and whenever he comes home, I still won't be able to welcome him with open arms, because of something that happened thirty years ago that he couldn't even help."

He stopped, his mouth tightening. "Sorry. TMI. I'm just trying to say… Thank you. God, thank you for even these few minutes we've had together these last few days, but no thank you to any more."

"Wait just a minute—!" she called, but it was to his back as he let himself out into the alley, leaving her pained and disheveled on her clean stainless-steel countertop.

Chapter Seven

"Mom!" Jonah called that Friday night, as he let himself into the house he'd grown up in. The little bungalow on the Tanner side of the tracks stood a couple of miles from the center of town. A bay window and a tiny front porch were all that could be seen from the street, but his mother had planted whatever perennial flowers she could get for cheap when their season was over, so the front yard was a profusion of black-eyed Susans, hollyhocks, coneflowers, peonies and astilbes at different times of the year. The display helped to hide the cracking wood in the porch railing and the paint job the house needed.

Inside, not much had changed since Jonah had moved out. The walls were a pale yellow and all the soft furniture a pale blue. The kitchen cabinets were the same oak color they'd been when they'd moved in just after Jonah had turned three. The carpet was the same, though Pam kept it as clean as she could. Sometimes it seemed that cleaning was Pam's only joy. That, and the consignment store she'd worked in for as long as he could remember.

"Take your shoes off, for the love of God!" was her greeting that day.

Since Jonah knew her, he already had one boot off and in its designated mat by the front door before she spoke. He obediently slipped off the other one and bent down to kiss her hello.

She didn't look much like him, though they shared blue eyes and a tendency to be too thin. Her hair was long and straight, with more than a few strands of gray invading its black color. Much of what pissed Pam off about Jonah was how much of his father he'd inherited. She'd been a model before she met Peter, and had dreamed of a baby with her hair and Peter's eyes. Instead, she'd gotten russet-haired, pale-skinned Jonah.

"Must you keep that beard?" she complained.

He rubbed it. "I like it."

Pam tutted, but drew him into her small dining room, where they sat down to her spaghetti and meatballs. The meatballs were more like little round burgers dunked in pasta sauce, but he appreciated that she'd cooked for him. Pam felt that having cooking skills would bring her down to the level of the other moms, than whom, she'd told Jonah almost every day growing up, she was much smarter and prettier.

Of course, now he knew someone who could cook a hell of a lot better…

"Jonah!"

"Uh-huh?"

"You're dripping on the table! No, don't use your napkin. Here." And she hopped up and brought over a kitchen towel. She provided fabric napkins but got twitchy if he ever used them.

"Your father called," she said, when she'd cleaned up the dot of sauce.

Jonah stopped chewing for a moment. The mention of Peter stopped him in his tracks every time.

"Yeah?" he said, feigning disinterest.

"His other son's coming back."

That was news to Jonah. He looked up from his plate. Funny that his mother would mention Matt the same day that he'd had to explain his feelings for him to Laurel. "On leave?"

"No." Pam was triumphant that Jonah was finally looking at her. "He quit the army. Coming home for good, your father said."

"Why? I thought he loved the army."

"He should do. It was the only place that would take him, wasn't it? With his learning disability and all."

Usually—and for too long, he remembered with a guilty pang—he let his mother go off like this about the boy who'd usurped her son's place in Peter's home and his life. She could spend hours calling Peter names and bewailing what he'd done to her "career," but her anger at Matt's mother and therefore at Matt himself often left her speechless.

But today Jonah remembered what he'd told Laurel, and

how she'd called him on his bullshit. He'd known it was bullshit; he just hadn't been able to move past it. "Mom. He's not… mentally handicapped. He has—had—ADHD."

"How do you know that?" she snapped.

"First of all, because you told me the second you found out about twenty years ago. Secondly, because it was all over the school that he only got through his exams 'cause that Raya did his homework for him."

Pam snorted. "Yeah, well. That Raya obviously got sick of bailing him out. That was why he went into the military, I heard."

Jonah swirled some spaghetti onto his fork. "Still," he said. "Joining the military wasn't exactly a soft option."

"Where did all this *sympathy* come from?" Pam pointed a piece of bread at him. "It's not like you to defend your brother."

A week ago he would have kicked himself in the nuts before defending Matt. And he still found it hard to talk to the guy, the few occasions he'd seen him in their life. Matt had done everything right, even with his challenges. An army medic, for crying out loud. The town about wet itself every time he came back. Whereas when Jonah had made good, everyone had kept on looking at him sideways. Just waiting for him to screw up again. He still kept his distance from most people in town.

Not from one, though… He didn't seem to be able to stay away from Laurel and her family.

"Sullivan's is open again," he said, apropos of nothing.

"What?" His mother took a second to follow the change in topic. "Oh, the bar? Yeah, well." She took a sip of her wine. Jonah was having water. "That Frank Moore was cut from the same cloth as your father. Same lack of backbone, same immature—"

"I don't think so, Ma," Jonah interrupted. "He loved his family. He was just sick. And he ran a bar, for God's sake."

"He could have sold it. Done something else."

"What else is there to do in this town? It's only in the last ten years that things have begun to look up. You know that from the business at the consignment store. Sullivan's was a good living, back then." He took a deep breath. "And I know that he sucks as far as we're concerned, but you have to admit that it looks like Dad figured it out right the second time around. He and Mariah have been together for decades."

Pam sat back in her chair as if he'd shot her. "Are you... defending... your father... to *me*?"

"No, Mom, I just—"

"Because I'll tell you something, mister." He was sure she was about to tell him something she'd told him a hundred times before. "That man doesn't know the meaning of love. Mariah's convenient to him, that's all. He figured out a young, pretty little Hispanic girl looked good for his reputation at the university—which, may I remind you, was in the toilet because of his drinking—and so he sobered up and she was naïve enough to take him back. You know how much time he spent with that boy once he knew he had a problem?"

No, Jonah didn't know. And neither did Pam, except through hearsay from her equally prejudiced friends. This was another reason Jonah kept emotions out of his decision-making. Pam overreacted to everything. She loved to hear about any digression of Peter's duty to his other family, so she could find new reasons for her complaints.

But then she said, "She barely spoke English anyway, it's not surprising—"

That did it. Jonah couldn't listen anymore. "Mom!" he said, more sharply than he'd spoken to her since his teen rebel years. "Mariah spoke perfect English then and now. And besides, ADHD is nothing to do with what language you speak."

"There's no need to raise your voice," she said, ignoring his words with a wave of her hand. "Suffice it to say your *sympathy* for your father won't go rewarded, so don't even try it."

Jonah put down his fork. He'd never bothered challenging her before; figured if she needed to vent, he was available, and then she'd be satisfied and wouldn't go off about Peter in the store or somewhere more embarrassing. But something had changed in him. He thought of what Laurel had told him about her father. She'd forgiven Frank every time he'd betrayed her trust. Jonah had told himself at the time that she was a sucker for punishment, but deep down he'd been awed at her ability to see the good in Frank and work to bring that out.

Then again, he wasn't going to change Pam's prejudices over one meal. "Let's drop it, okay? Maybe you can spare a thought for Frank's kids. They just lost their dad, and now Laurel has to manage a bar Frank almost ran into the ground. Brett's going off the rails—like I almost did—and they could use a little… sympathy."

"You lost your dad years ago," Pam pointed out, but her face did soften. "That Laurel was always a good girl."

She sure was.

"Poor Gail."

Jonah was surprised that Pam could spare a thought for anyone else's pain. "I didn't know you knew Mrs. Moore."

"Oh, yeah. She used to come in the consignment store a lot."

Half the town had shopped in his mom's store while he was growing up. He'd used their reliance on second-hand clothes as another excuse to hate his life. Laurel had never said a word.

"We're pretty good friends. Or were."

"Have you seen her since the funeral?"

Pam finished her wine and looked uncharacteristically sheepish. "I can't," she said. "Not after all the things I said about Frank when he was alive."

"I get that, but she could maybe use—"

Pam stood up, making him stop talking. "Now," she said, "can you get my air conditioners out of the windows?"

Thus dismissed, he stood up and took his plate to the sink. Then he got on with the main reason he'd come. Maneuvering the heavy air conditioners out of the house's old windows used enough of his brain that he didn't have time to think of anything else until his mother was putting a tub of vanilla ice cream and a bowl out on the kitchen table and reaching for the fudge sauce.

"Why did Dad tell *you* that Matt's coming home?" he asked.

"He wanted me to pass on the message to you."

"What?" Jonah almost dropped the bottle.

Pam shrugged. "He said he knows you don't answer the phone to him."

This was true, not that Peter had called him more than a handful of times in his life. "He could leave a message."

"I don't know why he called me, Jonah," Pam replied tartly. "He just did, all right? The point is, Matthias is coming home and for some reason Peter wanted you to know that."

There was a lot to chew on there. Her marriage to Peter had been short—they'd married when she was pregnant with Jonah, a fact she reminded him of frequently, which of course made him feel *not at all* guilty that he'd been the reason she'd gotten into such a disastrous marriage—so she'd only received alimony for a few years, and it had been a long time since she'd been eligible for child support. "When is Matt coming home?" he finally asked. The sauce bottle made its usual fart noises as he poured out the fudge.

"Next month? I think that's what he said. And can you please stop making that bottle make those disgusting noises?"

"You bought the stuff, Mom."

What would Jonah do about it when Matt did come home? Was he going to man up and stop blaming the guy for things that were out of his control? But it was a short trip from that to rebuilding a relationship with their father, and... no. Jonah wasn't there. Peter didn't deserve a relationship with him; that was the bottom line. Jonah was glad Peter had been a better father to Matt than he had to Jonah—and from what he'd seen of Matt in high school, the kid had seemed happy—but Jonah wasn't going to get that for himself this far down the line.

Well, he had a month to figure out about Matt. He could kick the emotional can down the road for that long.

They finished their ice cream in silence, apart from the hum of the refrigerator and the background of the radio which Pam kept on at all times.

Then suddenly Pam said, "He sounded tired."

"Matt?"

"Your father!" she snapped. "Of course not Matt." But then she subsided. "It's been a long time since we spoke. He sounded... different. Tired. He didn't ask me to ask you to call him. Just asked me to tell you." She scraped her spoon around her bowl, not looking at Jonah. "I think he's given up on you."

Jonah thought about that. This was what he wanted, wasn't it? To cut his father and the painful emotions he brought up out of his life? *Yes. That is what you wanted.* He nodded to himself, put his bowl in the dishwasher, and bent down to kiss his mom's still unlined cheek. Pam showed him out with a list of jobs she wanted him to do next time he came around and a dose of guilt that he didn't come over more often.

The truth was that Jonah didn't want to come over more often than he had to. He'd learned a lot about toxic relationships in his studies, and Pam was his. But he was her only son, her only child, and at least she wasn't Peter.

The nighttime air was refreshing and Jonah appreciated the long walk back to his apartment to clear his head from the last important words she had said. *Dad's given up on you. Job done. Now you can move on.* He tried to fill his head with the needs of his clients for the next day.

Only that wasn't what happened. Because in the forced absence of any emotion for Matt or his father, the image of Laurel, spread over the counter this morning, her face turned up to his, her lips swollen from his kisses, his hand buried in her hair, overwhelmed his senses and wouldn't let go. And yes, he felt like a heel for putting a stop to it. What was it that guy in *Love Actually* had said? "It's a self-preservation thing." In the same way, cutting Laurel out was a self-preservation thing. That was what it was. So why were the guilt and the frustration making his skin itch?

You're just going to have to apologize. Not change your decision. Just apologize.

The idea wasn't going to solve either the guilt or the frustration, but it was the best he had right now.

With this unhelpful decision made, he walked down Bridge Street, past the other bars and restaurants that were open with Friday night revelers spilling out into the streets despite the chilly air. Closer to his apartment, though, all was quiet. Sullivan's wasn't the kind of bar that offered outdoor seating or a young crowd who didn't mind the cold.

But then he saw a couple struggling outside the bar, and heard someone say, "Let go, Sis, or I'll make you let go."

Chapter Eight

LAUREL'S DAY HADN'T gotten any better after Jonah had rejected her kisses. She had to work in the kitchen instead of calling suppliers. The lunch service was busy today, and she, Junior and Miguel could barely keep up. Junior told her his dad had thrown him out when he'd told him he was going to continue to work at Sullivan's, and he'd spent the night on a friend's couch. The waitresses began coming in with complaints about the delay, which made Laurel furious and embarrassed at the same time. She couldn't get her afternoon run in, and that made her even more jumpy, not only because she was afraid her schedule would never allow it again.

That night the second bartender didn't show. When she texted him, he texted back to tell her he'd found a new job and wouldn't be coming in. So Laurel had to do that, too. She had to go upstairs, change out of her whites, and put something on that looked bartender-y. Which meant something low-cut. She had money to make, after all.

She chose a loose sleeveless V-neck blouse in a royal blue,

black leggings, and flat boots. Adding long earrings and shaking out her hair, she remembered makeup, which she hadn't bothered with since her father's funeral. When she checked her reflection in the mirror she couldn't help but think, *now why couldn't Jonah have seen me like this? That would have stopped that stupid puritanical speech he gave this morning.*

But he'd kissed her anyway. In a schlumpy old T-shirt and apron and with flour in her hair, he'd still given her the hottest kiss she'd enjoyed in years.

And then he'd taken it all back, the bastard.

She strung a gold chain around her neck and went to the stairs. She could hear a sitcom playing on the television in the living room, so she put her head in. "Hey, Mom. I'll be in the bar if you need me."

"Okay," Gail said with little enthusiasm.

"Why don't you come down and have some dinner? A little conversation? Everyone would love to see you."

"Oh, I don't think so. You can just bring me up something when you're done."

"Mom, I won't be done until past midnight." And she had to get down there now. "Just think about it. Okay? I gotta go."

"Okay, dear." But Gail's voice was as wispy as ever, and Laurel knew she wouldn't see her. She hadn't told her about Brian and Reg's betrayal. She'd have to talk about the changes she wanted to make to the bar, and that would bring her mother down even further.

Downstairs she slipped behind the bar and smiled at her first customer. Walker, the other bartender, a tall African American with a buzz cut and a dour expression, muttered something like "about time," but seemed to remember he was talking to his boss and didn't speak up.

From here, even as she poured drinks and looked up cocktails—not that there were many orders of those; this wasn't that kind of bar—she could keep an eye on the servers and on the food that went past.

She was surprised that many of the customers took time to welcome her back, to offer their condolences on her father's death, even to prop up the bar for a few minutes while they reminisced. Laurel preferred not to think about Frank stuck behind this bar, surrounded by his kryptonite, but his clients—and friends, she tried to remind herself, though had any of them actually helped him when he needed them?—had no such qualms. Thankfully, on a Friday night, the bar was busy and she could spare little time for their memories.

The emergency squad took up one of the large tables in the corner; the firefighters, another. Their friendly rivalry had been a part of the bar for years, but Laurel's business mind couldn't help but notice that they didn't buy much. Other groups of clients came and went—older couples, retired blue-collar workers, students who lived at home and probably worked at other bars when they weren't at this one.

Salt of the earth, the lot of them, but not one with a whole lot of money, she thought gloomily as she poured another domestic beer. And no families.

Then there was the décor. No one in her circle of colleagues in New York would have been able to stand the pseudo-colonial armchairs and barrel tables for a second. The walls hadn't seen a coat of paint in twenty years, and the pictures Frank and his predecessor had put up, of Irish celebrities and landscapes, all needed reframing, if not ditching altogether.

Laurel rubbed a spill off the counter with undue frustration. She didn't want anyone to feel excluded, but damn, could the business carry on this way? She could pay her immediate bills, but how was she going to cover the debts Frank had run up? And there was an entire demographic out there that this bar was ignoring! Who had money! Who shopped at the farmer's markets and the new Wegman's out on Route 32. If she could attract those people to come to Sullivan's, that could only be good for her employees and for their neighborhood, right?

Between her constant movement and her inner thoughts, it took Laurel a while to realize that Brett was on a stool at the other end of the bar. If she didn't know better, she'd have said he'd sat there so she wouldn't notice him right away. So Walker would serve him.

She stopped Walker on his next trip in her direction. "How long has my brother been there?"

Walker peered around at him. Brett saw them, gave her a sarcastic smile and raised his beer bottle at her. Imported, Laurel noticed sourly. "Uh… 'bout half an hour?" Walker said.

"And how much has he had?"

Walker's eyes skidded away from hers. For a big guy, he could sure look sheepish when he wanted.

"You didn't count," she answered for him. "Because he's never paid for a drink before."

She wanted to kick herself right there behind the bar. They'd been open for a month, and she'd paid more attention to the kitchen than the bar area. Brett wasn't drinking like his father had, but he was obviously comfortable turning Walker into his personal butler.

Walker seemed relieved that she'd figured it out. Of course. What else would Frank do? Charge his own son to drink at his bar? More than likely he'd given him a tasting tour of the inventory years ago, made a game of it, made it normal that Brett spent more time there than with his more sober friends.

This was the first time she'd seen Brett today; that was certain. A day that she was having trouble believing had started with the scent of apples, and that fresh, woodcut smell that Jonah seemed to carry with him. The plaid shirt he'd been wearing. And a kiss that had made her lose her mind.

And then bullshit about logic, and emotion being a bad

thing. As if the world could go around on anything else. Look at her right now. She could count at least seven emotions coursing through her body as she looked at Brett and thought about Jonah. But this evening Brett won out over her frustrating memory of Jonah.

If she threw Brett out, he'd just go somewhere else, and she wouldn't be able to keep an eye on him. Taking Brett cold turkey was not a job she needed to add to her responsibilities right now, if she could even get him to do such a thing. Instead, she went for a shitty compromise. "One beer every half hour," she told Walker. "That's it."

Walker shrugged. To make her point, Laurel went over to his end of the bar.

"Hey, Sis," Brett said, using his bottle to point at her. "You look smoking."

She ignored this. "One beer every half hour. I've told Walker."

Brett rolled his eyes. "Yes, Mama."

"And no hard liquor," she said, for good measure. "Unless you pay for it."

"Jesus." She knew he didn't have any money.

As the evening wore on, Laurel recognized the other patrons who relied on the bar for more than friendly banter and a bite to eat. They drifted toward Brett's side of the room and were still there when the kitchen closed at ten thirty. Laurel took the risk of leaving them to Walker and slipped into the back to check that everything was being cleaned and tidied as it should.

"We need another busboy," Karen, one of the waitresses, said as soon as she saw her. "Sam's not keeping up."

"And we need another server for the nights the EMTs and firefighters are here," said another waitress. "One server can't keep up with all their drink orders coming at once. Another bartender, too, would be good."

The dollar signs flashed in front of Laurel's exhausted eyes. She grabbed a hairband from a dish she kept on a high shelf and piled her hair into a messy bun, keeping it off her sweaty neck.

"One of the microwaves blew," Sonny, the evening head chef, added helpfully, while she still had her hands in her hair.

We microwave too much food anyway. Her mouth twisted. "Anything else?" she asked, trying not to make her exhaustion obvious. They shook their heads. "All right. If any of you have any contacts that could get us a bartender by tomorrow night, let me know. I'll give them my firstborn."

While they continued their cleanup, she went back out to the bar. Funny how twelve hours in front of a stove weren't as tiring as five hours serving drinks.

Pushing through the swinging door, she saw Brett quickly hide something on the other side of the bar. His timing was terrible, or maybe he'd wanted her to see. She strode over to him and around to her side of the bar. Sure enough, an old-fashioned glass, a thin line of amber liquid still swaying in it, was on the lower counter.

All of a sudden, Laurel had had enough. "That's it," she said, to Brett at first, then, louder, to the whole room. "That's it! We're closing!"

"Huh?" Walker said.

"*What?*" Brett spluttered.

"Yep, that's it." She looked around at the four or five serious drinkers still in the place. "Sorry. We're closing. Due to illness," she improvised. It was kind of true. She *was* sick of it.

The rest of them began creaking their way out of their chairs and off their stools, putting on fall jackets and baseball caps and shuffling out of the door. Usually Laurel had more sympathy for them, knew they were lost, as lost as Frank had been. That was why they had come here. But not tonight.

"Go upstairs and put on some coffee," she barked to her brother. "Get some fluids in you before bed. I have another warehouse run to do tomorrow and I need your help again."

Brett was still stunned by her decision. "You can't *close early*!" he said, his face going red—redder. "This is a bar! We're open 'til midnight!"

"We're closing *right now*, and it's *my* bar, and what I say goes. Get upstairs." She stalked to the other end of the bar and began to gather glasses.

"*Your* bar!" Brett shouted, getting off his stool. "What are you talking about? It's *our* bar. Mom's and yours and mine. I don't remember Dad leaving it just to you!"

Laurel spun round. "He left *everything* just to me!" she yelled.

The words echoed in the bar, which was now empty except for her, Brett, and Walker. Walker was backed against the drink shelves, looking as though he was trying to get his six-foot-three frame to blend into them.

Her statement had been too much of the truth, and if she'd believed it would elicit sympathy in Brett, she would be disappointed. "Yeah, that's right," he said, changing his argument as only he could. "Everything got given to you, the perfect one. Pretty impossible to live up to, the perfect Laurel Moore, you know."

"*Don't* use me as an excuse!" Laurel's chest was heaving now; she was afraid she was going to break down crying in front of Walker. She'd never had this kind of fight with her father; he'd loved her too much. But Brett was young, and hurt, and had no one else to blame for his troubles. She tried to get her words under control. "Look, Brett. I know exactly what you're going through—"

He snorted. "Yeah, right."

"I *do*. Don't you think I did all the research when I was trying to help Dad? It's a cycle. It goes in most families in our situation. Oh, for God's sake, Walker, go home," she added with bite. He'd been the one to give Brett that shot, and she would have to deal with him tomorrow, but right now he looked like a puppy she'd kicked after it peed on the floor.

He didn't need telling twice, but picked up his jacket from where he'd stashed it behind the bar and headed for the front door.

"I'm going too," Brett announced, walking after him.

"No," she demanded, though she knew the word meant nothing to him. "You're going back upstairs. We have got to deal with this. You wanna end up like Dad?"

Even saying it made an icy shiver work its way up her spine. Her worst nightmare had been Frank's illness and death. If she lost Brett too…

"Look." She tried one more time to be reasonable. Brett had looked up to her, once. "Please let me help you. Let's both go up and we'll talk about what you want out of life, and how I can help you get it."

But she'd said the wrong thing. "Oh, yeah," Brett spat, "because *perfect* Laurel can fix anything. Right? Well, you didn't fix Dad and you're sure the hell not getting your claws into me!"

And before she could recover from the gaping stab wound his words had opened in her heart, or get out from behind the bar, he was slipping through the front door.

Laurel followed him as fast as she could, but he was several steps down the street before she caught up. She grabbed his arm. He wasn't wearing a jacket, and the night was cold. Laurel's bare arms began pebbling with goose bumps at once. "Where are you going?"

"Anywhere you ain't," he said nastily.

"Don't go to another bar," she begged. "Please, don't." She held on tighter. He was built like her, with a broad chest and belly and strong arms. He easily wrenched out of her grip, pushing her away hard enough to making her stagger, but Laurel grabbed him again.

"Let go, Sis, or I'll make you let go," Brett said, and his voice was as cold as the wind swirling around them.

"What did you just say?" came another voice out of the shadows.

Thank the Lord, it was Jonah. Laurel's first, instinctive thought was that she had never been so happy to see him in her life. Her muscles seemed to loosen just at the sound of his voice.

But her second instinct was that she didn't want him to see Brett like this. She didn't want him to react to what Brett had said, because she was sure Brett hadn't meant it and in the morning, if he remembered, would be giving her tearful apologies.

So as Jonah came into the glow cast by the bar's signage, she stepped in front of her brother and stared up at Jonah. "Nothing. He didn't say anything. What are you doing here so late?"

If she hadn't stepped between them, Laurel was sure Jonah would have grabbed Brett by the scruff of his neck and slammed him against the bar's windows. His hands were clenched at his sides and it had been many years since she'd seen such raw anger in his eyes.

But her actions seemed to do the trick. Jonah looked from her to her brother, the anger fading to a frown, his lips a thin line. "I was having dinner with my mom. I'd decided to walk home tonight."

You got your wish. Jonah got to see you dressed up. Only she was so damn cold, and so unnerved by Brett, that she'd wrapped her arms around herself and tucked her chin as far down as she could while still looking at him. "Oh, that's nice," she said, for something to say.

He gave a quick, sarcastic smile, but didn't correct her. "Going somewhere, Brett?" he said.

"Yeah," Brett said, who'd been frozen before but now seemed to feel Jonah's presence was a protection from Laurel, rather than the other way around. "I was just heading away. Bye, Sis."

"Brett, wait—" But he was already at the corner, and short of hanging onto him, there was nothing she could do.

Now, before she was remotely ready for it, or armed with a pithy comeback or some kind of warrior-maiden's shield to hold him off with, Jonah was in front of her again. Closer, even, than he'd been that morning, before she'd dragged herself across the counter and made a fool of herself. And she could still feel that raw emotion coming from him, even muted, even though she could hear him consciously slowing his breath.

"He's that bad, huh?" Jonah said, looking in the direction Brett had gone.

She didn't want to talk about Brett to Jonah. He'd made it clear he didn't want to be in their lives. Yet he'd been here, ready to defend her against her brother. Another tangle of emotions Laurel didn't want to sort out right now. So she kept her arms folded across her middle and glared up at him in silence.

Jonah had the grace to look embarrassed. "Uh, yeah. About this morning... Hey, you look cold." And he swung off his jacket and began to put it around her shoulders, but seemed to change his mind at the last minute and held it out to her instead.

Laurel scowled at him. Damn, she needed that jacket. But her self-righteousness was keeping her warm. Maybe. "About this morning?" she prompted, trying to stop her teeth chattering.

WHEN JONAH HAD come around the corner and seen Brett push her hard enough to set her back a step, a rage had gone through him he hadn't allowed himself in years. He could swear his fist was pulled back ready to let fly at her brother, and he was only stopped by Laurel standing between the two of them. Defending her family, who wouldn't thank her for it. Like always.

But with Brett gone, six seconds of looking at Laurel and Jonah felt like he'd been set a paper he hadn't studied for.

This was a terrible time to bring up his screwup that morning.

Still, he'd started now. "I... I just wanted to... You just took me by surprise, that's all. I didn't... say very clearly what I meant to say."

Laurel raised an eyebrow. Did she know how intimidating she looked when she did that?

He had *not* expected to see her so soon, but he'd been thinking about her all day, whenever he wasn't focused on his clients and all through the usual fun and games that constituted an evening with his mother. This morning had been a disaster, and not only because he'd done something he'd only recently sworn he wouldn't. He'd known he'd hurt her feelings—what had he expected, given what he'd said—and he wanted to take it back. But she scared him, and not just because of that raised eyebrow. This stunk, because he was a grown man, several inches taller than her, and he hadn't been scared of anything in years.

Untrue. Why haven't you gone to see Dad?

See? He was a hopeless case. What part of what he'd said to her could he take back?

"It's not you, Lor," he said at last, almost in desperation. "I mean... dammit, it *is* you, because you're irresistible. Will you just put on the jacket?"

She gave a massive, involuntary shiver. He wasn't sure if the cold or what he'd said had caused it. She smelled of the bar tonight, of alcohol with overtones of fried food and burger meat. He could also smell her perfume, a heavy, musky scent he realized had been there all along, only he'd been too obsessed with her cooking to notice.

She put the jacket on, swinging it over her shoulders and slipping her arms through the sleeves. Even that simple act began to turn him on. He hoped there was enough warmth in the lightly padded jacket to help her.

"You're still telling me you regret kissing me," she pointed out.

"Yes," he admitted, "but *no*. I'm just saying I'm not in a position to do it again."

"'Not in a position.' Jesus, Jonah. Way to make me sound like I was applying for a job."

"I'm sorry," he said, and then he shut up. Words and Laurel just didn't mix in his world. He saw the empty bar through the windows. "No one in the bar tonight?"

"I closed early," she said.

"Shit. I'm sorry," he said again. "Is it the staff's wages? Did Frank leave you that badly—"

"No!" He'd made her mad again. "I just… decided to close. In fact, I haven't told the kitchen staff yet, so if you'll *excuse me*."

She said this last in a fake-formal accent, which Jonah figured he deserved. "Sure, Laurel. You'll let me know if I can help you, though. Will you? With the bar or anything?"

"Oh, yeah, Jonah." She laughed, half-turning away. "You'll be the *first* one I call." But then she turned back.

"No, wait. You *can* help me." Now her blue eyes, glittering slightly in the streetlights, were fixed on his. "You said anything, right?"

"Of course. Anything."

"Then help Brett."

Shit. "Oh, hey, Lor."

"Nuh-uh." She pointed a finger at him. "You said anything."

"Yeah, but he—"

"You're the great therapist. You had a shittier dad than him. You pulled yourself back from the brink. *You* help him."

She poked his chest with each repetition of *you*.

Jonah felt them like a brand under his shirt. "He won't listen to me."

"He doesn't listen to me more. You have to try, Jonah." And to his horror, tears welled in her eyes and tracked down her cheeks, shining in the yellow streetlights. "You have to help him."

There was only one thing to say, and for once, it was the right answer. "Sure, sweetheart. I'll do whatever I can."

She nodded decisively. "That's more like it." The firmness returned to her expression, and she angrily wiped away the tears. "Sorry. I've just had enough men not doing what they're told recently."

Jonah smiled, though he hoped she wouldn't see in the dark. "If they're anything like me, they're shaking in their boots while they do it."

"Not you," she said. "At least, I didn't mean you this time."

She began to walk back to the front door of the bar. Jonah followed her. "Then who?"

He got to the door first and opened it for her. She hesitated at the entrance, then began to take off his jacket. "Don't worry about it. Thanks for the jacket."

"Who?" he persisted, not liking that her face had fallen back into lines of worry.

The two of them stood in the doorway, Jonah blocking the door so it couldn't close. He didn't want to leave and he couldn't get into the bar because Laurel was in front of him. He could see goose bumps already rising on her bare arms from the safety light over the door.

"You don't have to come in," she said, holding out his jacket.

"I know I don't," he said. "It's okay, Lor. I'm not going to leap over the bar and grab a fifth of scotch. Let me close this door."

Now he could see her blush and she moved out of the way. The door swung closed behind him. The waitresses were still tidying up and paused in their work to stare at the two of them.

"I thought it was really important to you," Laurel said, low enough that no one else could hear.

"It was. It's not such a big deal now. Brett didn't know that."

"Oh." Her shoulders relaxed an inch.

"I mean, I don't plan on hanging out here," he clarified, keeping his voice low, too. Once the waitresses had figured out they weren't going to hear anything, they kept on with their jobs. "But I said I'd help if I can, and something else is bothering you. As if Brett isn't enough to deal with. So what is it? One of your creditors?"

"No, nothing like that. I just lost two kitchen staff yesterday. They quit." She waved at the women now making themselves look very busy. "We lost a few at the beginning, mostly waitresses, but they all gave notice. Now I'm down a bartender and two cooks in the space of two days."

"I'm sorry."

"Don't be. They were assholes. The cooks anyway. I'll find someone else. It's just… it'll take a few days, and in the meantime my sous chefs are undertrained and overwhelmed."

God, the list of her troubles just kept on growing. Jonah wanted to pull her into his arms, to promise her that they could fix it together, but the waitresses had begun to look at them again, so he could only look down at her and think of something useful to say.

"I have to close up the cash register," she said.

Well, that was something. "Sure. I'll come by tomorrow to talk to Brett?"

"Thanks." She gave him a smile he wished he could make bigger, and turned away.

Chapter Nine

Now Jonah had to add something else to the life he'd determined wouldn't involve getting involved.

He lay awake that night, telling himself not to, until he heard Brett stumble back down the street and into the side door that led to the family's apartment above the bar. Brett was the same age as he'd been when he'd used alcohol to drown out the world, and Jonah understood him completely. That didn't mean that Brett wanted to be understood.

Then there was Laurel's other problem, of staffing. Jonah couldn't get that out of his mind either, and by the next morning, he had an idea.

It was Saturday and Jonah didn't have to work, though he sometimes went in anyway to man the crisis hotline. But now he had a crisis unfolding right in front of him. And since these days he always did what he said he was going to, he made two travel mugs of coffee and carried them over to the bar at eight o'clock in the morning.

Laurel wasn't in the kitchen. Her car was in the alley, so he figured she was home, but if he was going to look for her he would have to go up the private stairs to her apartment, to which he hadn't been invited.

He sat on one of the stools placed out of the way and sipped his coffee, and sure enough, in a few minutes she stepped through the swinging doors herself.

Even with everything else on his mind, he couldn't stop himself from reacting to the sight of her. She wasn't in her apron yet, so her curves were on full display. Her cleavage tempted him from the scoop neck of a light blue blouse whose short sleeves fluttered against her shoulders, and which fell loosely so that her stomach hardly pushed it out. Her jeans outlined her thighs, and that was all Jonah could see past the counter, but honestly he didn't care, because his mouth was already dry and he'd almost forgotten why he was here.

"What are you doing here?" she said.

He looked hard at her face, framed as it was by another bandanna like the first day he'd helped her. That was better. He could concentrate when he saw the accusation in her eyes. Laurel needed his support, not his raging libido. "Hoping to figure out a way to help Brett."

Laurel looked at him as though his brain was misfiring. "At eight in the morning? He didn't get home till four, you know." Yeah, Jonah knew. His own tired, scratchy eyes testified to that. "You won't see him until at least eleven."

"I know. I came to ask you to let me know when he's up. He might be feeling… delicate enough to sit still and listen for a minute, if we're lucky."

"So why did you bring him coffee already?"

Jonah sighed. He deserved this treatment, but she made it hard. At least she was staying on the other side of the room. That helped. The room smelled like bread, and he could bet that if he nuzzled her neck, she would too. "This one's for you. I got the impression you don't have time to make it in the mornings."

Laurel's beautiful broad shoulders slumped. "I do," she said, coming closer. "Just at about five a.m. when I wake up. Then it's upstairs and I don't have time to go get another cup." She picked it up and some of her tension left her as she took a sip.

"Oh, God," she said in relief. But then she glared at him over the top of the cup. "This doesn't mean you're forgiven."

"That's okay. I actually had an idea for your cook issue."

"I don't need help for that. I told you. I'll find someone."

"Yeah, but—sorry to mention it—but with your current financial situation, it might take a while, and it sounds like you need someone right now."

"Well, not today. I have different staff on the weekends."

"Good." He'd been hoping for this, because he didn't want to make a call to his colleague on the weekend. "So what if we got some of the restaurant management or culinary arts students from my college to intern here? Would you be up to doing a little training?"

Laurel's eyes widened. "Kids?"

"Kids who are hungry to learn. You can set up a program with the school and have more students to help out than you'll know what to do with. I have colleagues over there and I'm sure they'd love to have a new restaurant to put on their list. And you can have staff as soon as… Tuesday, if I can get hold of the guy on Monday."

She caught her lip between her teeth in the way that he loved. "It sounds too good to be true."

Scrupulously honest, he said, "It might be. But I thought it was worth a shot."

Laurel was gazing at him now. "It's totally worth a shot. Sure, I'll teach them. Are these your students? The ones you help?"

"Sometimes."

"Oh." She went a little pink. "Of course you can't tell me."

"No." He smiled reassuringly. "But I think they can help you. And you'll certainly help them. So I'll call him?"

"Yes, please." Laurel looked around the kitchen, perhaps imagining it with a new staff. "Yes, please, Jonah."

He grinned. "Great." He got up from his stool and pulled another one around for her. "Now tell me about Brett."

AT ELEVEN THIRTY, Gail tiptoed down the stairs and waved to get Laurel's attention. "He's up," she said, and scurried back up.

Laurel wiped her hands on a towel, washed up her knives which she'd been using to cut the hanger steak she'd found at the farmer's market after Jonah had left, and got out her cell phone.

"*Brett's up,*" she texted.

"*On my way,*" Jonah replied.

"*Cool. Uh… be polite to my mom, k?*"

"*What else would I be?*"

Maybe she should have given him more of a heads-up. With all the drama around the two of them and Brett, she'd forgotten to mention that Gail considered Jonah the devil's spawn. Still, she hadn't told Gail why she wanted her to let her know when Brett woke.

So when Jonah arrived at the kitchen door, she went with him—telling herself to ignore how yummy he looked in a navy sweater and jeans, and not to tug his sweater higher in a losing battle to cover his tattoos—up to her apartment.

The stairs seemed even narrower with Jonah's big frame walking up them, and Laurel found herself more breathless than necessary by the time they reached the top. Jonah stopped at the front door. The landing outside it was tiny. Laurel had to brush past him to open the door for him. She hoped she didn't have some giant smear of sauce on her chef's whites that she was now transferring to him. Also, pressing up against him was hella fun.

But she had to focus, never mind that maybe his breathing had sped up too. She went through the door first. Brett was sitting at the kitchen table, his head in one hand, a cup of coffee and several pieces of toast in front of him. Gail, thankfully, wasn't there.

"Hey," Laurel said softly.

Brett cringed, not looking at her, but when Jonah followed her into the room Brett caught sight of him and his red eyes stared.

"Hi, Brett," Jonah said.

"Why are you here?" Brett somehow gave off apprehension and defiance at the same time. His hand clenched on his mug, but the other hand didn't give up its job of supporting his tousled blond head.

"I came for a cup of coffee," Jonah said. He was talking as though to a skittish horse—slow and gentle, but matter-of-fact. "And I thought maybe we could talk."

Brett covered his eyes with his hand. "I don't feel much like talking."

"Okay," Jonah said easily. "I'll just sit for a while, if that's okay."

Brett shrugged. Laurel took this as a positive sign and pulled out one of the other kitchen chairs for Jonah. Then she went to the coffee machine and made him a cup.

"I have to get back downstairs," she said to the room in general.

"Don't go yet," Brett said, his voice thick. He didn't look at either of them as he said, "I'm sorry, Lor. I'm really sorry." His hands covered his eyes and she heard him take in a choking sob.

In half a second she had her arms around him, crouching beside his chair. "I know, bug," she said.

"I don't know why I did it," he said, his voice higher from crying.

"It's a disease, bug," she said. "That's what it does."

"It didn't do it to Dad," Brett said in despair. "I'm so much worse... so much worse than him."

"Not if you acknowledge it now," Jonah said, his voice low, but cutting through the emotion in the room with his sensible tone. "If you make a committed effort, now, knowing what the alternative could be."

Brett wiped his eyes with his hands and focused on Jonah. "Is that what you did?"

Jonah's eyes met Laurel's for the briefest of moments. "As far as I remember," he said, "I only hurt people with my thoughtlessness, my selfishness. Not my fists."

"No. Never," Laurel said, before she could think. But Brett didn't seem to notice the slipup. Jonah sent her a grateful half smile.

"Let's talk for a while," Jonah said to Brett. "I'm not offering you a panacea, just a door you can walk through."

"Are you going to make me pray or something?"

Jonah laughed; Laurel was happy to hear it. "Definitely

not. Unless that's what works for you. It does for some people."

"It didn't for our dad," Brett said. Laurel nodded, remembering.

Before any of them could say anything else, Gail's voice came from the living room. "Is that you, Laurel?"

"Yeah, Mom!" she called back. "I'm just leaving."

"Did you tell Brett whatever it was—" The voice had gotten closer and suddenly Gail was in the kitchen doorway. Jonah was right in front of her.

"What are you doing here?" she demanded, her tone nothing like the wispy despondency Laurel had been hearing from her for weeks.

"I invited him," Laurel began.

Jonah had stood as soon as Gail came into the room. "Hello, Mrs. Moore," he said. "I'm really sorry about Frank."

Behind him, Laurel winced. "Don't you talk to me about my husband!" Gail hissed. "What did you ever care about him? When was the last time you talked to him? Ten years ago! Ten *years*!"

Jonah was about a foot taller than Laurel's mother, but it was Gail who seemed to fill the room now. "I'm sorry about that, Mrs. Moore," he tried to say, but she cut him off again.

"Oh, you're *sorry*, are you? Sorry your guilt has been eating at you all this time, more likely. He was your *friend*— when no one else in this town was, may I remind you, the way you ran around causing trouble—"

"*Mom*," Laurel interrupted.

"Well, he did, and don't give me that look, miss, you knew exactly what he was like back then, and told me so, if I remember rightly."

Laurel's face burned. She was still behind Jonah. His head turned a little to the right, as though he wanted to look at her but didn't want to make it obvious to her mother that he did.

She could do nothing but admit it. "Yes, I know, but as you say, that was ten years ago. He's changed. We all have, I hope."

Gail hadn't. Her first, last and always job had been to keep Frank going. No wonder that now he was gone she was lashing out. It was healthy, in fact.

In front of Laurel, Jonah's hand stretched out behind him, making a soothing motion. "You're right, Mrs. Moore," he said to Gail. "I regret not going to see Frank again. But he was only ever in the bar, and back then I couldn't—"

"He was up here sometimes too, you know!" Gail retorted.

Jonah bowed his head in acknowledgment. "True. As I say, I regret not making more of an effort to see him. It's no comfort to you now, but you were the most important thing in his life—all of you."

"That's not true," Laurel said, "There was one thing more important than his family, and he died worshipping it."

Gail's eyes filled with tears. "I can't believe you're saying these things about your father."

"I can understand that he wasn't a saint, and still love him."

"Frank *was* my friend," Jonah said. "He tried to be a father to me, back then. It was just that his environment... and his illness... didn't make that healthy for anyone around him."

Through her tears, Gail glared at him. "All right, you've said what you came to say. You can go now."

Jonah hesitated, so Laurel had time to say, "*I* invited him, Mom. I... I thought he could help Brett."

"Brett doesn't need help from Jonah Gardiner!"

"He's *Doctor* Gardiner now—"

"I don't really use—"

But Laurel shushed him. "Don't you see, Mom? He's right here. He *knows* this stuff. He helps kids at the college. Exactly Brett's age."

"Do I get a say in this?" Brett said vaguely from his seat.

Laurel really wanted to say, "No." But that wouldn't be helpful in getting him on board. "Of course you do," she said instead. "And there isn't a 'this,' yet, unless you want it. But, Brett..." She sank into the chair Jonah had vacated and took Brett's hand across the table. Making sure he was looking at her, she said, "You are very important to me, bug. Very. I need you around, you hear? More than ever now."

Tears were making their way into her voice again. She swallowed and fell silent.

"So let him go to rehab!" Gail said. "Why do we have to use this boy?"

Nothing boy about Jonah. She swore she could feel the heat coming off him behind her. At least the image kept her tears from spilling. She smiled at Brett, who smiled back a little at Gail's term.

"We can't afford rehab, for one thing," Laurel pointed out.

"We can't afford a fancy psychiatrist either!" Gail yelped.

"I'm not a psychiatrist, Mrs. Moore. I'm a psychologist," Jonah said. "And I wouldn't charge you. If not for your sake, for Frank's." Brett was observing him with his red-rimmed eyes. Assessing him. "For the kid I was, who could have used a me."

"You had—" Laurel began, and then stopped. He'd had *her*, but her mother and brother didn't know that, and it was better if she kept it that way. "Your mother," she finished lamely.

"Oh, you figured out what you owe your mother?" Gail put in, her voice still raised. *Jeez.* Laurel's mouth twisted. *At this rate we'll be through the anger stage of grief by twelve thirty.* "What you put that woman through I can't even begin to tell you!"

"I know it," Jonah said, though he frowned. Laurel wondered what was behind his darkened eyes. "I take better care of her now."

"Do you? I wouldn't know, since she hasn't bothered coming to see me in a month!"

"I'll talk to her," Jonah promised. "I know she'd love to come if she… if she knows you'd like to see her."

Gail scowled at him but didn't say any more.

"Can I make you another cup of coffee?" Laurel asked her. Perhaps this would distract Gail for long enough to—

"No, I don't want *coffee*," Gail replied scornfully. "I want Jonah Gardiner out of my house!"

"Well I don't," Brett said, and since he said it to the table and they were all standing above him, they almost missed it.

Gail folded herself into a chair near him and tried to put her arm around him. "You don't have to listen to him, honey. You'll be fine. Your sister just thinks we should all be done grieving by now."

"Oh!" Laurel almost buckled under the injustice of that statement. "That is *so unfair*, Mom! Just because I've been trying to get you to eat doesn't mean I don't understand you!"

Gail fussed over Brett another second. Laurel and Jonah exchanged glances. At least he looked as though he knew how much Gail's words had hurt. He put out a hand and squeezed hers, once, before her mother could see.

"Lay off her, Ma," Brett said, surprising them all. "She's got the bar to run as well as us two to deal with. If it weren't for her getting him to stop at least for a few weeks at a time,

Dad would have died years ago and we'd have nothing."

This time Laurel couldn't stop the tears. She kicked back her chair, knocking it over, and ran blindly out of the door she'd come in through.

Stuck at the top of the stairs, unable to go down to the bar's kitchen or back into her own, Laurel hid her face in her hands and tried to stop her sobs from making too much noise. But they seemed like great, gulping blows that spilled out of her in a way that scared her.

The door opened again and there was suddenly someone with her in that tiny, dark space. Someone who just put his arms around her and let her hide her sobs in his chest instead, who rubbed her back and said, "It's okay," into her ear, and whose warm breath on her neck comforted her until the sobs lessened.

"Sorry," she said, her face still buried in Jonah's chest. "He took me by surprise. It brought everything back... the futility of it all. I couldn't fix Dad. I can't fix anyone."

He didn't relax his hold one bit, so she cried more in his arms.

Finally he said, "You fixed me."

She shook her head. "That's not how it works and you know it." At least getting a little mad at his words helped the tears stop. "All those years of books and I could have told you that with a Google search. You stopped because you wanted to. Like you just told Brett."

He nodded, but said, "You reminded me of the stakes.

You pushed me toward the door. Frank had another twenty years of habits on me. Besides, it wasn't your job to fix him. Parents don't work like that."

She slumped against him, turning her face this time, feeling the wet of her tears on his shirt against her cheek. "It was my life's work."

"I know." He rubbed her back again. "And he loved you for it."

She gave a shaky sigh. "I'm sorry about my mom."

"Don't apologize. You know that she was his enabler, right? It was *her* life's work to give him what he wanted. She doesn't know what to do now that he's gone."

"Mom used to sneak Dad booze when I wasn't around to stop her. She might do the same for Brett. It's all she knows."

"Well, you won't be the only one policing the situation. If everyone's rooting for him—including himself—Brett won't go down the same path." Jonah's chest shook with a laugh she didn't hear. "I think your mom helped by throwing me out. His head hurts just enough to keep me there to spite her."

Laurel hadn't thought of this. "I won't be the only one policing him?"

"No." He squeezed her a little harder. "I told you I'd help you, and I will."

"By hugging me? By being at my side when he questions me? Or by holding me at arm's length and blaming it on some stupid sense of logic?"

JONAH LOOKED DOWN at her. The tears on her cheeks were drying, her emotions turning faster than he could follow.

"How did this turn into you being mad at me?"

"I'm mad at you anyway, after yesterday."

With her face this close, and the space so secluded, and the aroma of coffee surrounding them, Jonah could feel himself getting drunk again. "I apologized for that."

"Not properly. You talk a lot."

Now her mouth was very close to his. Her breasts and stomach were pressed all along his slim, hard body, her thighs against his. There was no way he could stop himself from kissing her now. Jonah pulled her closer and brushed his lips against hers.

If he was aware that her mother and brother were on the other side of that door, Laurel seemed not to care. She melted into him. His kiss became many small kisses, on her lips and down her jaw to the scented spot behind her ear. A small stone in her earring pressed against his cheek. He opened his eyes to look at it. Pale blue. Aquamarine. He'd looked that up once, when she'd told him her birthday. But they hadn't been together by the time her birthday had come around. And there were still many reasons to keep them apart. He just had trouble remembering them right now.

He backed up, causing her to sigh in annoyance. "Go on down and deal with lunch. I'll talk to Brett for a little bit and see if he agrees to something regular. Something at my apartment, maybe. To get away from... from the memories."

"From my mom, you mean." She shoved him a scooch. "Coward."

He smiled down at her. "She'll want to hear, and that's not what this is about." He leaned forward and kissed her temple, then smoothed the spot he'd kissed with his thumb. "Go crack some skulls. We'll be fine up here. Brett got a good hard lesson yesterday, though God knows I wish you hadn't taken the brunt of it."

Back on the subject of her brother, the sexual tension in the hallway began to dissipate. Laurel dropped her arms from his back. If only they could have stayed there all morning.

But then she said, "He only pushed me because I—"

"Nuh-uh," Jonah interrupted. He lifted her chin to make sure she was looking at his eyes. "Don't start apologizing for him. Any show of strength against you, or anyone, is too much. You hear me?"

Her lips pressed together, her emotions changing again. "Jonah, please help him. Please. Whatever it takes. If I lose him as well..."

"Okay, sweetheart." He folded her one last time into his arms. Each time he did this, each time she showed him how easy it was to express her feelings, Jonah felt himself falling into her a little bit more.

Chapter Ten

THE FIRST TWO students arrived at Sullivan's on the following Tuesday, as Jonah had promised. Laurel had promised a bump in pay to Jennie if she took over the bar with Walker on Monday afternoon, and drove up to Jonah's school to meet with the head of the hospitality department.

Jonah met her at the entrance to a squat, one-story building with small windows and several stainless-steel vents coming out of the walls. After her long day in the restaurant, Jonah was the epitome of a tall drink of water, loping out of the doors and putting a hand on her arm.

His grin was huge. "They're so excited to meet you."

Laurel was pretty happy to see him, if anyone cared to ask, but she just unzipped her coat and let him lead her into the building and to a battered door, behind which a small white man with glasses sat behind a desk full of papers.

"Andrew Largo," he said, shaking hands.

"Laurel Moore."

"Please, have a seat. Jonah tells me you have an opening for some of our students needing field work?"

"Yes," Laurel said, hoping she didn't sound as desperate as she felt. "Yes. I think we could make some room."

And that was all it took. She filled out some forms, promised to send over her insurance certificate, and accepted a tour of the teaching facilities. Andrew surprised her by introducing her to some of the students and asking her to tell them in her own words what kind of a place Sullivan's was. About a dozen words she couldn't say flew through her mind, but she thought afterward she'd sold the place well enough. The students had kept smiling, anyway, and the next day, three of them were at the kitchen door at nine o'clock.

Laurel had read up on the curriculum, so she knew what they knew and had found gaps she could fill. Also, she had fries that needed chopping. When Miguel and Junior arrived at ten thirty, they gaped at the industry going on in "their" kitchen. The next day, three more kids came, and the day after that. She'd been assigned fifteen kids, three per day on the weekdays. Just what she'd prayed to the gods of hospitality for. She even had time for her afternoon runs again.

Best of all, every single damn one of those kids called her "chef" and treated her, Miguel, and Junior with respect and admiration. She swore the three of them grew two inches under it all. And Miguel was renting a room to Junior, so she didn't have to worry about that anymore, either.

Laurel hadn't realized, until they were gone, how lowering the presence of Reg and Brian had been to her spirits.

Getting rid of them was like opening up the front and the back of the bar all at once, blowing fresh air through and welcoming her new way of doing business, one that included both regulars and the newcomers.

Even Brett was behaving himself, thanks, Laurel assumed, to Jonah. All of this was thanks to Jonah, but she hadn't seen him for a few days. She was almost too busy to notice. Almost.

Fired up with her ideas of getting the newer residents of Tanner into Sullivan's, Laurel took one morning at the beginning of October and drove over to the farmer's market.

She saw Sadie at once, wrapping a basket of mums for the customer in front of her. The woman in line already carried two paper bags with appetizingly fresh leaves sticking out of the top. Behind her stood another mother with a preschooler who clutched a small painted pumpkin to her, even using her chin to hold the pumpkin in place. Both women were dressed in what Laurel could tell were expensive coats and boots and had hair that was artfully highlighted. And if that kid wasn't wearing a Brooks Brothers coat, Laurel was a monkey's aunt.

She skimmed the refrigerated shelves while the women finished their purchases, admiring the fresh kale and organic lettuces, bright red cranberries and orange butternut squash. Her senses went into overdrive, imagining the delicious meals she could create for her customers—for women like the two who had just left—with these ingredients.

Sadie came out from behind her counter and joined Laurel at the refrigerator. "Sullivan's, right?" she said.

"That's right," Laurel acknowledged. "But I'm changing the menu," she hastened to remind the woman. "And this place is perfect."

Sadie gave her a long look. "Sure you don't want to wait until that new store opens up where the A&P was?"

Secretly, Laurel had to admit that it was likely she *would* have to shop in the bigger supermarket at some point. But she said, "Hang Health and Hearth. Bunch of corporate types pretending to care anyway." And Sadie beamed at her, and Laurel crossed her fingers behind her back and swore to use Kurtz's as often as possible.

"I want to change our whole vibe," she went on. "I know right now Sullivan's has a menu that barely deserves the word, but by this time next year, I want it to be Central New York State's coolest gastropub."

Sadie raised her eyebrows. "Gastropub, huh? You might get some resistance from the local folks."

"Not when they taste my food." Laurel couldn't help the pride which crept into her voice. "Your food, too," she reminded Sadie.

"I like the concept," Sadie said slowly. "So what's sparking your interest today?"

"Butternut squash soup, obviously," Laurel began, picking up a squash. "With local cream and carrots. Real cranberry sauce on a turkey sandwich, with stuffing."

"Did you see these truffle mixes?" Sadie pointed out, obviously getting into the swing of things.

"Oh, my God. Can I open one?" At Sadie's nod, Laurel unscrewed the top of a short glass jar of spices and carefully, but luxuriously, inhaled. "Pure heaven," she declared. "Don't tell me that's local too."

"Truffle farm over in Oneida County."

"I'm putting them in the burgers," Laurel promised. "Tonight."

"Hold on, hold on," Sadie laughed, flapping her hands. "That jar's twenty-five dollars a pop."

Laurel slapped the lid on quick and shoved it back onto the shelf, making Sadie laugh again. However, Sadie's warning had reminded her she couldn't just jump into this wonderful new idea. If she was going to make it pay, she was going to have to be careful where she spent her meager budget. "Okay," she said.

But as she turned away, her fingers stole out and picked up the jar again. "Just one jar," she said. "Just to try it." Even if the only person who she fed it to was herself.

And Jonah.

Dammit. Could she have one thought about food without imagining Jonah putting it into his mouth?

"You don't have to be embarrassed," Sadie said, looking at her hot cheeks with concern. "It is a pretty irresistible taste. You know how popular umami is right now."

"Yes. Right. Umami."

Sadie turned to lead her to the counter and Laurel took the opportunity to fan her face and try and slow her heaving breast. She added more cucumbers and apples to her order, along with the squash, carrots, and leeks for the soup. Those, at least, were cheap additions to the menu she didn't have to feel guilty about.

"Ooh," Sadie said at the cash register. "One more thing you might be interested in. They're a little off the beaten track food-wise, but I thought you'd…"

Laurel looked at what Sadie was showing her and said, before Sadie could even finish, "Yes. Yes, I'm definitely interested in those."

JONAH HADN'T SEEN Laurel for over a week. To be precise, he hadn't been in the same room with her for over a week. He had, as he sipped his coffee and looked out of his living room windows each morning, seen that Brett had gotten up and was helping her bring in the cases from the wholesaler. He'd seen the college students milling about in the alley and all over the bar's entrance, cleaning the windows and hosing down the faded awning. He'd seen Laurel there with them, showing them the order Brett was moving in from her truck. Jonah privately still thought she was economizing in the wrong place by not having the food delivered, but it wasn't his place to say, and it was giving Brett something to do other than sleep in in the mornings.

Once Jonah saw them out there, he would move away from the window and busy himself somewhere else in the apartment. He didn't need to add Peeping Tom to her mother's list of his transgressions.

Brett had come to see him twice, in the evenings when Jonah assumed the pull of the bar was at its height. Brett still didn't completely trust Jonah—or perhaps his qualifications—and two sessions weren't about to cure a man who had been in the habit of drinking for six years. But it was a start. Jonah liked Brett's chances.

"MOM!" HE YELLED as usual, walking into her house that Saturday morning. Today he was in his work clothes—old heavy canvas pants and a couple of layers of tees and Henleys against the chill fall air.

Pam was at the front door immediately, as if she'd been waiting behind it for him. "Don't come in!" she yelped, looking at his work boots. He'd made sure they were clear of mud from the last time he'd worked in her yard, but she obviously wasn't taking any chances. "The tools are in the shed. You can cut back the ornamental grasses and finish deadheading the roses and anything else you see that's dead and messy."

"Okay," was all Jonah could get in. Pam put on a pair of

gloves and zipped up a thinly padded, long black coat that fit her slim frame perfectly. "I have to get to the store. The holiday rush is starting already, can you believe it?"

Yes, he could, since she said the same thing every year. But he shook his head obediently.

Today, however, he needed to tell her something, an idea that had begun in Laurel's kitchen and grown with his conversations with Brett. "Just a second, Mom," he said, following her to the car.

"What, Jonah?" She opened the door, not looking at him. "I have to get going."

He held the door, keeping her from moving. "I wondered if you'd thought any more about visiting with Mrs. Moore."

"What?" Pam looked surprised, then her eyes darted left and right. "Are you still on this?"

"Yes."

His stillness finally stopped her fidgeting. "Why?" she asked, searching his face.

"She needs someone. She's buried in her grief, Mom, and has no one but Laurel to share it with. Laurel's buckling under the strain, and Brett's no good. He's got his own issues to deal with."

Pam brushed at the top of the open driver's side door with her gloved hand, breaking her eye contact. "I told you, Joe. I don't think I'm the right person—"

Her selfishness made Jonah disbelieve she was the right

person, too, but the way Gail had talked about her had changed his mind. Maybe Gail would bring Pam out of her own head for once. "You're her friend, aren't you? You know everything about her life with Frank. I know you're not about to tell her all the reasons you hated Frank, when you know that she needs someone to talk to about him."

A flake of rust fell off the edge of the doorframe. They both watched it float to the ground. "Now look what you made me do," Pam said, but there was no heat behind her words. "I'll think about it, okay?"

"Okay, Mom." He reached in for a hug and kissed the top of her head. "Don't think too long, though. Laurel needs your support, too."

"Yeah." She wiped off his kiss, making sure her hair was still as sleek as ever. Then she got in the car and looked up at him, an appraising look coming over her face. "Speaking of Laurel," she said, "I heard you were in Sullivan's the other night."

Of course she had. Tanner would never get big enough for the rumor mill to fail. "After it closed. I was talking to Laurel."

"Jonah, you promised…"

"Mom." Explaining it to her was a whole lot more annoying than explaining it to Laurel. "I can enter a bar without wanting to drink there. It's been ten years."

Pam didn't make a move to close her door. "Once an alcoholic…" she said.

That truth was part of the reason he'd stayed away from his dad, but coming from his mother, he saw the flaws in it. A lot of people could be needlessly judged with a rule like that. "I'm not going to start drinking again, Mom. I swear."

She searched his eyes again. Perhaps she saw what she wanted to see, because she said, "Awful lot of Laurel talk going on around here."

Awful lot of Laurel thoughts going on, too. But what could he say? He went with, "Bye, Mom," and closed the car door.

Chapter Eleven

WHEN HE GOT home, he found a text from Laurel. "*Are you still home?*"

He needed a shower. He was covered in dirt after Pam's fall cleanup. "*Yes,*" he replied. "*In about three minutes.*"

"*Stay there,*" came the brief text.

Jonah stayed there. Okay, he ran into the shower and scrubbed himself as clean as he could in two minutes and thirty seconds.

His doorbell rang thirty seconds later, and Laurel, smelling of grilled meat and herbs, swept past him and up the stairs. Jonah, in a fresh pair of jeans and an old college tee that fit him snugly, took a deep breath, told his mouth to stop watering, and followed her up.

"Here," she said, before he could even say hello. "Try this." She was holding a small, white plate, on which she had arranged four or five lamb chops, all drizzled with a dark green sauce.

Jonah caught a scent of mint as he obeyed, taking the bony part of a chop in his bare hand and biting into it.

It was perfect, of course. God, he'd thought her baking turned him on. Her grilling beat it hollow. The lamb was pink in the middle, charred just right on the outside, and the brightness of the mint sauce offset the heavy taste of the meat... well, perfectly.

So much for his mouth not watering. He'd finished the first chop and she was passing him another before his brain could come up for air. Their fingers brushed as she handed it over, and it took everything Jonah had not to grab her hand and lick the juices from her fingers.

What was it Laurel and her cooking did to him? He didn't get like this around anyone else's food, and he'd had quite adequate meals throughout the last ten years. Food was usually fuel for him. Only Laurel made it something much earthier, much more exciting, much more dangerous to his equilibrium.

"I don't have to tell you how good these are," he said when he could get his breath back. He'd eaten all but one of the chops.

Laurel giggled and took the last one. "I know. I just like watching you eat them." While Jonah blushed, she took a ladylike bite. Jonah wanted to hold onto something. "Mmm," she said. "I served them at dinner yesterday. The lambs are a little older than usual. They're called hoggets. The flavor's richer, did you notice? The farmer's not even thirty miles from here. Beats the crap out of frozen burger patties, huh?"

"Uh-huh," he said, watching her finish the chop.

"Sold out before the night was half-gone," Laurel went on happily. "People have forgotten what mint sauce is supposed to taste like, with that fake green jelly stuff all over the place." She went over to his kitchen area and dumped the bones in the garbage can. Then she put the plate in the sink—thank God he was a tidy person these days; the dishes were done—and turned on the water. "That farmer's market outside town is a complete revelation. She knows everything about what's available here." She began to wash the plate.

"I can do that," he said belatedly, coming up to her, but not getting too close.

"No need. It's done," she said, turning back to him with the wet plate in her hand. "I tell you, I really think I can make a go of this place as a gastropub. With all the new couples moving here to commute to Albany, and the families, I think there's a real market for decent food."

"Yes," Jonah agreed, but his tone was uncertain. There was a flaw in her argument.

Laurel didn't hear his hesitancy. "I can find organic produce and meat—God, the meat. I need never look at a frozen chicken nugget again."

He'd found the flaw. "Yeah, but, Laurel—"

"I'm banning that disgusting high-fructose corn syrup, yellow number six lemon meringue pie as of tonight." She'd found his tea towel and was drying the plate. "And as soon as I can smooth out my schedule, I'll be making something a lot better. Or buying it. I bet there's a bakery that I could partner with."

"Laurel."

"So." She put the dry plate on the counter and suddenly she was very close to him again, and Jonah's eyes began to glaze over. "Since I'm so successful now, *and* I brought you lunch, *and* you somehow got Brett to help me with the deliveries five days in a row, *and* you're looking pretty appetizing yourself in that tight T-shirt showing off your hot tattoos, then I *think* that I might have to kiss you again."

What he'd been about to say fled from him on a hiss of air. He couldn't keep his mind on sensible subjects for three seconds with her around. "We've talked about this," he begged, his voice coming out strangled.

"*You* talked about it. I told you at the time, if I remember correctly, that your reasoning was bullshit." She cocked her head.

She was close enough he would only have to reach his hands out a foot to touch her.

"For a man who says he lives his life by logic, your argument stinks."

Her abandon, her surety that what she was doing was what she wanted to do, made him feel drunk. The closer her lips got to his, the drunker he became. "I… Lor, don't do this to me."

Her breasts were touching him now. She had him trapped against his tiny kitchen island. She tipped her head up. "If you really don't want me to kiss you, then tell me no."

"Not fair…"

"Just say no." She stopped a hair's breadth from his mouth. "Say no, Jonah."

He'd said no once. He couldn't make himself do it again. Jonah covered her inviting mouth with his. His arms wrapped around her and Laurel pressed into him so he felt her soft curves all along his front. Her hands slipped behind him and began untucking his shirt from his pants in the back.

Jesus, if she touched his bare skin she wouldn't make it out of the apartment. But Jonah was helpless before her, letting her control the kiss and everything else about this, just as she controlled his every thought and feeling whenever she was in the room. Her tongue played with his, and then she broke off and kissed the skin above his beard to his ear, to kiss his jawline and his neck and the flying pulse in his throat, while his shirt released itself from his jeans and she flattened her hand against his broiling skin.

Jonah groaned and told himself to let go of her, but he was kidding himself. Nothing about Laurel made him want to let go. He could bury his face in her chest and stay there till he stopped breathing; the rest of the world could go hang. Schedules, responsibilities, logic… they all fell away while Jonah reacquainted himself with Laurel's cleavage and his hands flexed convulsively, scooping her butt closer and closer until she was standing between his legs.

He began to control the kisses now, finding a way down her jaw and the V-neck of her shirt, pushing the fabric aside with his mouth until he'd revealed the taut, creamy skin of the top of her breast. Laurel shuddered and removed her hands so she could press his head to her.

ONLY NOW THAT Laurel was standing in Jonah's kitchen, looking down at his head at her breast, appreciating his height and warm blue eyes and strength and smell and... well, everything about him, did she acknowledge to herself how much she'd missed him this last week. How much she needed—no, wanted—him in her life.

Laurel recognized the tension that had kept her shoulder muscles bunched and painful all week, and the level of control she'd had to maintain so that she could get through all the obstacles to her goal. With Jonah, she could let them all go, or at least, share them with someone who would listen, and understand.

She pulled his head back up so she could kiss him again, trying to show her gratitude. Hardly letting go of his lips for a second, she murmured, "The students are doing great."

"Good."

"I thought you'd come supervise."

"They're not really my students."

"Not for them," she breathed. "For me. I missed you."

"I missed you too," he whispered back against her lips. "Though I have no right to."

His words didn't stop him from pressing her body against his, her softness taking on his firm muscles. The extra pressure in his groin made her push harder. Her legs parted of their own accord; Jonah's hand went from her back to her bottom and gathered her closer still, so she moaned into his mouth.

She could dimly hear the sounds of the street below through the open window, and a cool breeze played over her heated skin. But otherwise there was only the circle of Jonah's arms and the fire in his kisses, and the next thing Laurel knew, she was sitting on the counter next to her platter so he could kiss her neck and what parts of her chest he could reach from her V-neck. His hand pulled her braid over her shoulder and out of its tie, and he raised his head long enough to loosen the strands so her hair cascaded over her shoulders and onto her breasts.

Jonah licked at the line of her cleavage and then kissed back up her chest to her neck. "I don't know how you do this to me," he said against her ear. "I told you to forget about me. About us."

It sounded like a promise, some kind of reverse spell that, once spoken, the opposite came true. "I can't," she confessed. "I can't."

"Me either. God, Laurel." His hands were under her T-shirt now, tugging it over her stomach and breasts. But he didn't take his lips away from her neck. "You've ripped all my rules to shreds."

"They were stupid rules anyway," she pointed out in a whisper, trying to wriggle out of her shirt while he was still pressed against her.

He laughed and backed up long enough to take off her shirt, revealing a lacy purple bra. "Shit," he breathed. "Did you know this was going to happen today?"

"Possibly." She reached behind her and unsnapped the bra. "But I wear these every day. Just for me."

"God, Laurel," he said again, as the flimsy fabric fell to the floor and her breasts were released in all their glory. He took the weight of one in his hand and it jiggled as his hand shook. "You're the most beautiful, most…" But he ran out of words, or perhaps he'd finally remembered what else he could do with his mouth, because it closed over her nipple and Laurel cried out and her back arched involuntarily.

The sounds of his sucking, searching tongue and lips made her wiggle her hips in frustration. The platter got pushed further along the counter as she began to take over more of the surface, and Jonah followed her with his hands and mouth. He kissed the space under her breasts where they usually rested on her stomach, and he breathed in her scent as though it were the purest oxygen. His hands kneaded and massaged her stomach, and then popped the button on her jeans and slipped inside.

Laurel cried out again and pushed at his shoulders. "You have way too many clothes on," she complained, and popped his jeans button herself, freeing him and taking her own breath away. His clothes joined her bra and shirt on the floor, and Laurel made him stand still so she could run her eyes and hands over every inch of him. His breathing was taut and fast, and he growled at the time she took, which made her feel so powerful she had to take advantage by going even slower. The firm muscles on his chest, the corded strength in his neck and arms, his heavy thighs and flat belly and the lighter skin on his hip, the rose and thorn tattoos on his chest and shoulders, that snaked up his neck; she explored them all before taking him in her hand.

He let out a surprised yelp but Laurel stroked and massaged him in turn, kissing his mouth all the while, until he was swearing at her and twisting away, and his hands went to her pants again. She laughed and let go long enough to push her pants over her hips.

"Wait," he ordered, now that he was less in her power, and she let him slide the material slowly over her hips and thighs. He knelt down as the jeans went lower and his mouth followed the fabric. Laurel was pinned against the counter, his mouth at her core, her toes curling. She was crying and swearing and laughing, swatting at his head but then holding it closer to her.

When she was sure she was going to die from the ache he was conjuring inside her, he pulled back. "Lor," he said, looking up at her.

"That's me," she panted.

"I'm giving you this chance," he said, his voice shaking. "This chance to leave now."

She gaped. She could barely stand, her pants were still stuck at her ankles, her body was screaming at her to get him inside her *right now*, and he thought she was going to leave?

"For my sake," he said, and now he was begging. "For your sake."

"For God's sake," she interrupted sharply, "go find a condom or I'll kill you."

He laughed and slid his hand up her calf and knee to rest on her thigh, which he then kissed. "I thought I had more self-control."

"Are you still talking?" she interrupted, shimmying her hips in front of his face. "Who needs self-control at a time like this?"

"Laurel, I—" But he laughed at himself and stood, holding out his hand so she could take it and he could lead her to his bedroom. Laurel stepped out of her pants and followed him.

The room was dark, with heavy wooden blinds almost completely closed at the window. It was quieter here, facing the back of the building, and the room and its bed felt like a secret chamber where no one would find them. Jonah followed her onto the bed and kissed her more, then went into the bathroom. Laurel turned her head to take in his scent on the pillows and navy sheets, and to look around the room. One wall had a line of closets along it; the rest were filled with books. *The man's too intellectual for his own good.* She wriggled deeper into his bedding.

Jonah was back in two seconds and gazed at her lying in his bed. "You look like…" he began, "like a Rubens and a Botticelli all rolled into one." He moved closer; Laurel propped herself up on her elbows, encouraging him with the movement of her breasts. Unfortunately, the action seemed to transfix him, standing at the edge of his bed. This made him fun to look at, and all, but Laurel got on her hands and knees and crawled toward him.

Jonah made a sound as though he were being strangled. "Anyone ever tell you you talk too much?" she said, kneeling in front of him. "Give that here." In seconds, she had the condom on him and had pulled him on top of her.

Now he was where she wanted him. His weight was delicious and Laurel was almost delirious with wanting him. His steel-strong arms lifted him from her so he could move down to her breasts and kiss them more thoroughly, while his knees gently nudged her thighs apart and he finally—Jesus, *finally*—settled between them.

The heat of him and her need had covered her body in a fine sheen of perspiration. She angled her hips, lifting her knees, and Jonah slid inside her.

Her teasing banter fled. *This* was what she'd wanted, what she'd missed, what she'd craved for ten years. This was what had been lost, that had made her life less. This feeling of her and Jonah, connected so closely their hearts beat in rhythm. She remembered, now, how much she'd loved him and how much more she did today. Tears formed at the corners of her eyes.

Jonah, who had remained still for a moment, saw them. "Lor," he whispered, half-pulling out.

She shook her head hard and put her hand on his butt to pull him in close. "Don't you dare," she muttered.

"I'm hurting you."

"You are not," she swore and to prove it, moved her hips so he couldn't help but follow her rhythm. "Kiss me, you idiot," she said, and the echo of the first time they'd kissed, as if she'd set them both on the path that could only lead them to this, most blissful of places, swelled her love for him and put more fire in her so he was utterly in her power.

To prove it, she flipped and sat on top of him, lifting her hips and driving down so he yelled and his hips rose to meet her. His hands had room to hold her breasts now, slick as they were with perspiration, and, with his fingers flicking her nipples, Laurel lost all of her own control and burst into shards, the feel of him against her breasts and her hips and filling everything inside her she hadn't known needed him sending her out of her body, melting her bones, and making her collapse on top of him.

He hid his face in her hair and lifted her again, one more time, and shouted his own release against her, the heat of his breath a brand she felt hours afterward.

Laurel wanted to stay there forever. What could the real world possibly offer her that was better than this exact spot, with her man's arms around her and her legs wrapped around his, their hips still glued together?

But after a minute or two, Jonah gently slid her to the side and went into the bathroom. He came back with a box of tissues and a glass of water.

Laurel blinked slowly at him. She hadn't moved from where he'd deposited her, wasn't sure if her muscles would ever support her again. "You are the most annoyingly practical man I've ever met," she muttered into his pillow.

He put the box and the glass down on his bedside table, which only held an old-fashioned travel alarm clock and a lamp. "And you are the most passionate, emotional, stubborn, fiery, loving woman *I've* ever met." He held out the box of tissues.

Laurel got one arm out from under her and grabbed a couple. "And don't you forget it."

"I can never forget you," he said, and lay down next to her, gathering her into his arms, the sheets tangling around them, the sound of a downtown Sunday barely pricking their bliss.

Chapter Twelve

MUCH, MUCH LATER, when the sun had almost set and Jonah was telling himself to let Laurel get back to work, though she hadn't mentioned it, she said, "I really should get back to work."

Now real life came crashing in. Because he was going to have to kill the moment. "Lor, would you hold off on changing everything about the bar until we've talked about it some more?"

"What's wrong with changing it?"

"Only that if you go super-upscale with your ingredients and your recipes, and you start charging more for the food, and changing the atmosphere, and all the other good ideas you have, you're going to run out the people who use Sullivan's now."

Yep, that did it. She sat up in bed. Her face, though flushed from his beard, closed off from him. "What are you talking about? Sullivan's hardly has any customers. Why do I want to keep anything the way it is just to serve a few old men who don't care about my food?"

"Because they need Sullivan's. This town is getting gentrified, fast. As you pointed out," he agreed, when she opened her mouth, "the guys who've been here for decades are feeling pushed out. Their house prices are going up, which is good until their taxes go up with them. And their kids can't buy their first home here. There's only one decent supermarket left in town. The hardware store is fighting to stay open now that the new Home Depot opened on 32." He risked a pause, wondering if he was making his point. "Sullivan's is one of the old places they could always rely on."

"They never spend any damn *money* there!" she burst out.

"If we can work out the debt situation and you could increase the number of people coming through the door, would you be that keen to get rid of them?"

"I'm *trying* to get more people through the door. Haven't you been listening?" She tutted at him and folded her arms across her beautiful chest. "Way to ruin the mood, Jonah." She pouted.

Jonah got off the bed and stood before her. He wanted to take her hand, but her arms were folded too tightly. "I'm sorry. You know I'm behind you in every decision you have to make. But I just want you to think about this one a little more. You'll be pushing the regular folks out if you change everything. All I'm asking is that you take it in stages, and don't kill off everything that made Sullivan's so welcoming to those guys."

"That's another thing," she said, apparently ignoring his point. "It's always guys. Why don't the women come in? Maybe 5 percent of my customers are women. What's up with that?"

"Okay, okay. We can figure that out, too. But do you know what I'm saying? Listen." He thought of an example. "The emergency squad and the firefighters. They come in every Friday—"

"Spend hardly anything—" she put in.

"They see you as their clubhouse. You understand? Sullivan's is a second home to them. They don't have a place to get together, all of them at once, with them all having second jobs. Yeah, they can't spend much money, but they could put the word out all over if you made them feel like you valued them."

Laurel's face got redder. "I *do* value them! They're saving lives, for Chrissake!"

"Then tell them that."

She opened and closed her mouth a couple of times. "You're saying I'm a shitty hostess."

"You're an amazing hostess. You're just looking for the wrong party."

Laurel stared at him for a few seconds. Then she said, "You suck at kissing, you know that?"

Not what he'd expected her to say. "Oh?"

"Not the kissing part, but the shooting your mouth off afterward part. Why can't you just shut up and kiss me and all the rest, like a regular guy?"

Jonah laughed. "'Cause I don't know what's good for me. Never have, or I wouldn't have kissed you in the first place."

She rolled her eyes. "Yeah, well. I'm off before you find some other way to ruin my day."

"Not ruin, I hope—"

"Yes, Jonah Gardiner. Ruin. I hope you're happy." But her tone was a shade more pouty than genuinely hurt. She went into the kitchen and began to gather up her clothes. Jonah watched her with a regret so sharp it hurt his chest.

"Will you think about it?" he persisted.

"Maybe." She put her underwear on. Jonah enjoyed the view so much he reached for her. Laurel slapped his hand away, but laughed and gave him another kiss before pushing him off her one more time. "Will you get that stick out of your butt and be nice to me next time?"

It was Jonah's turn to shiver. "Honey, if I was as nice to you as I want to be, neither of us would get any work done all week."

Laurel's eyes widened, then narrowed. "Now I really freaking hate you."

She got dressed, picked up her clean plate and held it in front of her chest like a shield.

"I'm sorry," he said again, hopelessly, because he was sorry for the timing but not for his words. "Can I make it up to you?" His hand snaked out to run a finger down her curvy hip.

She pulled the plate closer to her, but Jonah saw the shiver in her limbs. "What are you doing about one a.m.?" she said.

"Whatever you want me to do," he promised.

"Good. I'll be back then." And she punished him with another blood-boiling kiss and left him to spend the next few hours remembering the last few.

LAUREL SPENT HALF that evening in a fog of delicious memory and sensation that made her hopeless at her job, and the other half clear minded and incensed at Jonah's completely unjust, unfair and missing-the-point argument against her introducing new dishes.

She still hadn't found a new bartender, so that night she again had to change and paste a smile on her face while she served behind the bar. Each person who came in front of her reminded her of the argument with Jonah. But she was beginning to remember drink orders. And she started listening.

The servers told her which groups were sitting at which tables, and usually had a little gossip for each one. These guys were laid off from the electronics factory and had to take lesser-paying jobs in a new technology plant. Those guys near the broken jukebox were given early retirement and had lost a bunch of it in the stock market during the recession. The two men drinking a pitcher of Coors in the corner were partners in one of the garages in town, wondering if they should quit now or wait for one of their rivals to fold so their business would pick up. This woman's husband was on disability, and they relied on her hair-dressing business to pay the bills. If she could get her own space, she could make more money, but she hadn't been able to save enough to move.

Tonight, instead of racing around putting out fires, Laurel let her heart rate and her breathing slow. She served her customers, but she listened, too, and asked discreet questions. Instead of looking behind the bar or at the décor for what needed attention, she focused on the people.

Also, had she mentioned how much she hated Jonah Gardiner about now? Nothing worse than a man turning out to be right.

Despite everything on her mind, she didn't forget to take her mother some dinner. But when Gail came into the kitchen light in the apartment, she said, "Goodness, Lor, you have a heck of a rash." Gail pointed at Laurel's neck and down to the skin exposed by her tank top. "Is that prickly heat or something? Did you get into some poison ivy?"

Laurel looked down. *Fuck.* Jonah's beard had left broad red swathes across her pale skin. She covered the area with one hand, though it didn't do much. "Oh, no. Just hot, I guess. Better take a cold shower."

"Okay." Gail didn't look convinced. In fact, she looked like she was putting two and two together and Laurel began to blush. But she kept up the pretense. "I have some cortisone cream in the bathroom I can bring you."

"I'll find it," Laurel said quickly. It wasn't cream she needed to soothe her heated skin, but time.

WHEN THE BAR was closed up and dark, Laurel slipped out of the kitchen door, locked it behind her and ran lightly across the street. Jonah was waiting for her.

"No talking," she said.

Jonah made the universal symbol for locking up his mouth and throwing away the key.

"No, don't lock up your mouth," she said. "I have another use for it."

Jonah unzipped his lips quick. "Whatever you say, sweetheart."

"Now if you could just take that as a given…"

EVERY NIGHT FOR the next week or two was the same. During the day, they went about their own business. Once or twice, Jonah popped into the kitchen at Sullivan's to see how the students were doing. When he was there, he and

Laurel didn't touch or speak much to each other, and were never alone. He met Miguel and Junior and liked that they demonstrated their respect for their boss to the trainees.

But every night, after the bar was closed, Laurel crept up the stairs to his apartment—he'd given her a key—stripped off her clothes, and slipped into bed beside him. Sometimes, that was all that happened. Jonah would gather her into his arms, bury his face in her hair, and fall right back to sleep. That wasn't what usually happened, though, and Jonah, if he allowed himself to think of it, had never been happier in his life.

At five a.m., Laurel would kiss Jonah goodbye and go back across the street to begin her baking. Jonah would bring her a mug of coffee some time before he went to work, and she would take a break, hitch a hip onto a stool and talk with him across the stainless-steel counter. Jonah mostly listened to her ideas and her stories about the students. He gave what advice he could about the finances, Laurel even showing him her spreadsheets at one point. Jonah appreciated the trust she placed in him, though he learned just as much from her about how a restaurant was run. He'd taken business classes in school, before he'd decided to work at the counseling center, but a restaurant was a whole other ballgame, and he respected her even more for how she was handling the numbers side and creating the most delicious meals at the same time.

He didn't see her in the evenings. His presence in the bar

would cause a lot of talk that neither of them needed. Gail had calmed down about his helping Brett, who came to see him every few days, and Pam didn't have to know anything about it.

But one morning, when the kitchen was quiet and the two of them were sipping their coffees and eating cinnamon Danishes fresh out of the oven, Laurel said, "What are you doing for dinner tonight?"

"I'm staying at the college tonight. Going to a lecture."

"Oh."

"Why?"

"I was going to suggest you come eat here."

Jonah looked hard at her. "Seriously?"

"Of course, seriously." She used her fingertip to pick up some flakes from her plate. Jonah got distracted from their conversation. "Then come tomorrow night."

"Okay." He put his elbows on the counter and leaned toward her. "To have dinner *with* you? Or just to eat dinner in the bar?"

Now she met his eyes. "Does it matter?"

It hadn't, for a while. Now it did. "We're not kids any more. I'm not the bad boy and you're not the… well, you're still the good girl. But we don't have to be a guilty secret anymore."

"I know that." She concentrated harder on picking up the last crumbs of her Danish. "I wish you wouldn't say 'good girl' like that's a bad thing."

"It's not." Hang this across-the-counter crap. He didn't care who came in anymore. He went around to her side and took her hand, putting one finger after another in his mouth and taking the last of her Danish for himself. He was rewarded by a soft moan and she pressed herself closer to him. "It's a great thing," he said, buzzing her cheek with his beard. "Don't ever change."

Laurel squirmed and turned her face so he was kissing her instead of roughing up her cheek. They kissed for a while, Jonah taking in her scent of cinnamon and yeast and flour.

"God, I could eat you up," he murmured.

Laurel shivered, but a noise upstairs made them both break apart. Jonah backed up three steps before he remembered himself and laughed. "Old habits die hard, huh?" he said.

"I guess. We'll work on it," she said, smoothing down her hair and patting her apron, setting off small puffs of flour.

Jonah looked down at himself and saw that, once again, he was going to have to change before work. His black jeans were dusted with white, and the cuffs of his navy shirt, which he hadn't rolled up today because he had a staff meeting, had also been hit.

Laurel laughed at him. "Busted."

"You think your mom would notice if I went up there right now?"

Laurel's smile froze. "Very funny. Just… give me a little while to warm her up. What are you going to say to your mom?"

"Hell if I know. She'll probably tell me you're too good for me. Which you are."

"Shut up." Laurel took their plates to the sink. "What's this lecture you're going to tonight?"

"It'll be an interesting one. The speaker used to work in the Manhattan DA's office, and somehow also has a doctorate in criminal psychology. He's seen it all."

Laurel whistled. "I bet. Well, if you get back from that before we close, come in for dinner."

"Okay." She still hadn't answered his question, but eating together might set off a nuclear explosion in the lines of town gossip, so perhaps they could wait another day or two for that bit of excitement.

Chapter Thirteen

THE TALK JONAH attended that night was in one of the smaller lecture theaters in the psychology department. The theater seated maybe one hundred and fifty people, but it was more than half full when he arrived fifteen minutes early. He recognized the students acting as ushers and nodded to them as he went through the double doors into the auditorium. The room was functional rather than pretty, with wooden chairs softened only slightly by thin cushions, and a blond-wood podium at the front. A man was fiddling with a microphone while another plugged in a laptop.

Jonah had been to dozens of these talks in the past, but he enjoyed any opportunity to increase his learning. He was grateful for the position he held in the counseling center because he had access to these kinds of lectures for as long as he wanted them. He found a seat on an aisle where he could stretch out his legs and nodded to students and faculty who greeted him as they came by him.

The lights dimmed in the house and the head of the psychology department stood up. To his left, an African-

American man with short hair and a broad build sat on another uncomfortable chair.

"Good evening, everyone," the head said, and the room hushed. "We have a very special speaker in tonight for our Psychology in Action series of lectures. Professor Lucas Richardson received his JD from NYU and his PhD in criminal psychology from Columbia University. He has been on the faculty of Mercia College for the last year, after a distinguished career with the Manhattan DA's office. I'm very pleased to welcome him to our program tonight and to hear his work on the topic of 'Empathy and Criminality: Who Deserves It? Who Can Give It?' Please join me in welcoming Professor Richardson."

Jonah applauded along with everyone else as the man changed places with the head and stood at the podium, a shy smile on his face. He clicked the first slide on his presentation and began to speak—and no one else breathed for an hour.

His talk was fascinating. Jonah could bet 80 percent of the people in that room had spent their careers teaching students or sitting in comfortable armchairs, solving problems at arm's length. But this man had had the immediate consequences of criminality right in front of him for fifteen years. Jonah could still see how his eyes tightened a little when he gave examples of his work—although those parts were the ones everyone hung onto the most.

But as the talk went on, so subtly that at first he didn't

notice it, Jonah found himself leaning forward in his seat, staring at the man at the podium, examining his face as though…

He didn't know him. He knew he didn't. Everything about their lives was different, except that they both had degrees in psychology. But there was something about this man that kept sending shots of recognition through Jonah; that raised the hairs on the back of his arms.

He's talking about serial rapists. Jonah surreptitiously rubbed his arms. *Of course your hairs are on end.* But that wasn't it.

Jonah stayed quiet during the Q and A session and the lively discussion the professor's thesis introduced. In the end, the head of the department had to tell them all their time was up. Professor Richardson looked at the clock at the back of the room, his eyes wide in surprise, and laughed, rubbing his hand over his short hair. "Time flies when you're having fun," he said, making everyone else laugh. His voice was low, almost hypnotic. Jonah could imagine he'd been a great champion for the victims he'd represented. "I'll be here for a little while if you have any more questions," the professor said, and received a round of applause that echoed around the small theater.

Jonah hung back while the audience either left or crowded around the professor. It was ten minutes before Jonah added himself to the back of the line.

He listened to the conversation in front of him, observing the professor's face while hoping he wasn't making it obvious he was staring. He had dimples when he smiled. Jonah did too, though his beard hid them.

And so, at last, he came to stand in front of the man. He was a few inches shorter than Jonah, but broader. Jonah stuck out his hand. "That was a great talk. Thank you for coming."

"My pleasure." But he didn't look as though it was his pleasure. He was staring at Jonah as hard as Jonah was staring at him. "Lucas Richardson," he said unnecessarily, shaking Jonah's hand.

"Jonah Gardiner."

"I thought so."

That was an unexpected thing to say. Jonah hadn't made a big splash in the academic world as Lucas had. But what was more bizarre was that Jonah became aware of someone else standing next to him, someone he recognized at once, as soon as he moved his focus.

His father.

"Jonah," Peter said.

"What are you doing here?" His father was a history professor, and he certainly didn't teach at the same school as Jonah. It was the first time Jonah had seen Peter in years. His father's extra wrinkles and stooped shoulders surprised him.

But not as much as when Peter said, "Lucas. Jonah. This is your brother."

JONAH ALMOST GLANCED around for Matt. "What?" he said.

"I thought I recognized you," Lucas said. "Though the beard threw me off. The picture you showed me was pretty old." This was aimed at Peter.

"It's still the only one I have," Peter said.

Jonah couldn't take it in. None of the words they were saying made any sense. He couldn't have a brother. He had a brother already. This man looked nothing like him. He, Jonah, looked exactly like Peter. Even Matt, who'd inherited his mother's looks, was clearly Peter's son. This man was different in every way.

Except for the dimples.

Jonah kept looking between the two of them. Peter, tall, stooped, white-haired, his clothes hanging crooked on him as always; and Lucas, shorter, more solid, dressed in a well-fitted suit, no tie. Oh, and the small fact that he was black. Jonah's brain couldn't compute.

"You never contacted him, then," Peter was saying to Lucas.

"Why? I have all the family I need."

"He's your family, too. Like it or not."

Jonah was still struck dumb, trying to catch up.

"I didn't say I didn't like it," Lucas said. "I just… didn't want to…"

But he didn't finish the sentence because he noticed

something over Jonah's shoulder. Glad for a distraction, Jonah turned to find the head of the department hovering politely out of earshot. When the man saw he had Lucas's attention, he apologized for the interruption. Lucas soothed him and sent him away with the diplomacy of a politician. He seemed completely at ease with the idea of a brother. Meanwhile Jonah had forgotten how to process words.

"Look," Lucas said once the head of the department had been dispatched, "we should probably go somewhere and talk."

"Yes," Peter agreed at once. "Let's go."

"No," Jonah said.

Lucas looked stricken. Jonah pointed at Peter. His finger, he hated to see, was shaking. "Not you."

"Listen, Jonah," Peter began. "I understand that this is a shock, and believe me, I—"

"Believe you? Believe anything you say?" Jonah drew himself up to his full height which, to his surprise, was now taller than his father's. "You wanna talk your way out of this one?" He glanced at Lucas. "Why does something tell me you were as much of a shit to *his* mother as you were to mine?"

"More so," Lucas and Peter said at the same time.

Jonah's mouth fell open.

Peter bowed his head. "More so, to my eternal regret."

Jonah still couldn't take it in. He didn't know what question to ask first, but his main instinct now, as it usually was,

was to get away from his father. Long before this, Peter had stirred up emotions Jonah didn't want to examine, which was why he'd cut off his overtures over the last few years. Jonah's life was ordered, comfortable. It didn't involve his irrational, alcoholic father and it sure the fuck didn't include a secret brother.

"Did you cheat on Mom with her, too?" he spat.

"I wish it were as simple as that," Peter said, and Jonah reeled. After all these years, Peter still had no idea how his actions had affected Jonah and his mother. He would never have said that if he did.

"Let's get out of here and get a drink," Lucas said.

"No!" Jonah said immediately. "I mean, no. Not a drink. Let's get a coffee. Come back to my office. Not you," he said again to Peter. "You can get lost."

"Jonah." Peter's voice was pleading, as it had been the few times Jonah had listened to his voice mail messages. But Jonah was not in a forgiving mood. Not this decade. Especially when he didn't even know what he was supposed to forgive this time.

"Do you know about Matt?" he said to Lucas.

"Yes. Though I haven't met him either."

"Does he know about you?"

"No."

At least Matt didn't have this over him. "Why does *he* know, and we don't?" he said to Peter, pointing to Lucas.

"I'll tell you, if you'll let me," Peter said. His pale blue eyes—Jonah's eyes—were watery.

Jonah wanted to know, but he didn't want to know from Peter. Before he could speak, however, Peter said, "Can I come see you tomorrow? After work?"

Jonah stared at him for a moment, then nodded. He had to get to the bottom of this somehow, and it might take two voices for him to understand it all.

Peter's gaze slid to Lucas. "Your presentation was flawless," he said.

"Thank you for coming," Lucas said, in a strangely toneless voice. "You don't have to."

"Yes, I do." Peter held out his hand and Lucas shook it. Jonah was pleased that he didn't even try that shit with him. He just said, "I'll see you tomorrow," and left them with the long, loping stride that Jonah had inherited.

Alone with him, Lucas suddenly seemed nervous. "Let me just call my wife," he said, pulling out his cell phone. Jonah nodded and they walked out of the theater, passing the janitor with his wheeled bucket, mop and broom. Jonah heard Lucas's low murmur and moved farther down the hall, staring at the notices on the wall without seeing them.

Lucas joined him after a moment and Jonah led the way to his office. It wasn't a long walk. Not long enough for Jonah to corral his thoughts before he was in the room, turning on a couple of lamps against the darkness outside the windows, and facing his brother—it still didn't make sense—across his sitting area.

"You're married?" he began. It wasn't the question he wanted the answer to, but it was a start.

"Yes." Lucas's somber face broke into a smile. "I still have trouble believing it, but I am. You?"

Jonah shook his head, abandoning the attempt at small talk. "Why didn't he—"

"For the reason you assume," Lucas answered. "He was ashamed. That was what he told me, anyway."

"How long have you known about me—us?"

"About a year." Lucas leaned back in Jonah's armchair, the one his clients usually sat in.

Belatedly, Jonah remembered the coffee. "I need a coffee for this," he said. "How about you?"

"All right."

They left the room again to find the machine in the faculty lounge, then resumed their positions, Jonah the incumbent, Lucas the newcomer. In this way, Jonah could listen more closely, use his skill to understand, to hear the nuances. He waved at Lucas to begin.

"My mother met my father—our father—in law school," Lucas said. "In New York."

Jonah shook his head. "He's a history professor."

"Yeah. History of law. Only, when his alcoholism began to affect his work, he had to leave New York and get a job wherever they'd take him."

Jonah laughed a little at hearing his old college being described in such a way. It had taken Jonah with his abysmal high school grades because his father was there, so for that he supposed he should be grateful.

"They dated, but he was…"

"A drunk." Jonah wasn't pussyfooting around it.

"Yes, and one night he…"

It took Jonah a moment to realize where Lucas was going. "He… attacked her?"

Ridiculous that he couldn't say the word, when Lucas had been talking about sexual assault all night. But even for Peter, this was a new low that Jonah didn't want to believe. When Lucas nodded, Jonah shot out of his chair. "Holy shit!" he yelled, walking over to his desk and back again.

"That's about what I thought when I found out," Lucas said.

"That fucking fuck!" Jonah hadn't sworn this much in years. But his brain was burning. "Did he tell you?"

"Yes. But he didn't remember he did. I didn't see him, or know who he was, until I was thirteen." Lucas's eyes became unfocussed, lost in a memory Jonah wasn't brave enough to ask about. "I only saw him twice after that, until last year. The second time, I didn't even speak to him. The third time was just before I got married. That was when he told me about you."

Jonah was still standing, ready to pace his office again. He was still stuck on what Peter had done to Lucas's mother. It was indeed worse than what Pam had gone through. How was Jonah supposed to feel about that? Grateful? The man was still his father. The monster was still in his veins.

"I used to think I was like him," Lucas said. "A monster running through my veins."

Jonah looked up in surprise. "That's what I was just thinking."

Lucas gave him a smile with no humor in it. "I lived with that for years. But my mother raised me, and she was amazing, and eventually… it was brought home to me that I was a product of my environment, not my birth." He traced the rim of his mug of coffee with his thumb. "It brought a lot of peace. Room to move on. To listen to him."

Jonah's beef with his father seemed laughable next to this. "When was this? I mean… how old are you?"

"I turned forty this year."

Eight years older than Jonah. Long before Peter had met, and married, Pam. Mariah hadn't even been an adult yet. "What has he told you about us? Me and my mother, I mean."

"That he lost you."

Jonah snorted. "That's one way to put it. I live right over the damn tracks, but sure."

That wasn't what Lucas meant, and they both knew it. Lucas didn't call him on it, however. "That you suffered because he left your mother for your brother's. That he ignored you for years. That you started down the path he'd been on—"

"Not that kind of path!" Jonah exclaimed.

"No. The drinking. But you pulled yourself out of it,

which was more than he could do. He said only Mariah saved him. You did it yourself."

"That's not—" But he didn't finish. He wasn't about to admit to Laurel's part in his life to this total stranger. "I had help," he said instead, leaning against his desk.

"He says he's proud of you now, prouder than you'll let him say."

"I don't need his pride. I assume you don't either."

Lucas smiled again. "We've both studied the same books. We want to kill our fathers and yet we want their approval."

"I'm not a Freudian."

"Neither am I, but we are human. Everyone likes a pat on the back now and again. And Peter's pretty smart. His acknowledgment of your success would feel good."

Jonah indicated Lucas with his mug. "So you *have* sought his approval?"

"Probably, at some level, even when I wanted to rip my connection to him out of me."

That was how Jonah had felt when he was younger. The impossibility of it had fueled his rage all through high school and most of college. He didn't feel it now purely because he didn't allow himself to go down that road.

"Anyway," Lucas went on, "I'm not here to plead his case." He laughed ruefully and pulled a hand down his face. "Didn't think I was going to be here at all. Not tonight, anyway."

"Why *didn't* you contact us when you found out?"

Lucas seemed to choose his words before he spoke again. "You have to understand... I never believed I'd have a family at all. My mother was everything to me, and she was dying of Alzheimer's. Until I met my wife, I'd reconciled myself to being alone. What Piper's given me... I couldn't begin to ask for more. Like I said to Peter, I had all the family I need."

Thinking of his wife put a light into Lucas's face that was almost too private to look at. "Do you have children?" Jonah asked.

"Yes. A girl. And another on the way." Now Lucas did grin, which made Jonah smile along with him.

"Then I guess I'm an uncle. Cool."

"Hey, yeah. Cool."

They stayed in silence for a moment, contemplating the idea. Both had been deprived of the families they should have had, and both had made a successful life for themselves despite it—perhaps, as Jonah had found out when he'd gone into therapy, because of it. Now Lucas had moved on, found love, was happy. He could open himself up to gaining an uncle for his children, to building a life with an extended family.

"Have you forgiven him?" Jonah said.

The smile left Lucas's face. "No. I'm not perfect. Some days I think of what my mom went through and I want to send his tired ass straight to jail. He's said he deserves it, and he does. But she's passed away now—"

"I'm sorry."

"And he does seem to have turned around his life. A

good marriage, with another wife and a family—oh, I mean…"

Jonah winced. "A family, and a spare."

Lucas scrutinized his face. "Is he like you? Matthias?"

Forced to describe the man who'd taken so much of Jonah's resentment over the years, Jonah found himself embarrassed. "He's a much, much better person than me. Literally a war hero. Also really *nice*. I don't like him very much."

Lucas laughed. "Given your history, I don't blame you, I guess."

Up against what Lucas had been through, though? To continue his grudge against Matt this long? It was pure laziness, and Jonah had to face it. God, he hated emotions.

"Will you see Peter tomorrow?"

Jonah noticed that Lucas wasn't calling him "Dad" yet. "I don't know. But I guess I can't put it off too long. If only to kick his ass."

"Did you inherit his temper?"

That was a strange question. "I was a moody son of a bitch in my teens, if that's what you mean. I milked the rejected bad boy thing for all it was worth."

"You never treated women like he did, though." Lucas's voice went up at the end of that, as if it were still possible that Jonah had inherited some part of his father's temperament.

"God, no!" Jonah burst out. "After seeing the way he disrespected my mom? Are you kidding?"

Lucas nodded. "Some kids don't learn that there's an alternative to what they've grown up with until it's too late."

"I've worked with some of them."

Lucas looked around at the office as if he'd only just walked in. "That's right. I forgot. We should talk about that. I'd be interested in hearing about your research, and your practice."

Jonah came away from the desk as Lucas stood up, and the two men shook hands.

"I'm glad I met you at last," Lucas said, "despite my best efforts."

Jonah laughed, but Lucas was sober.

"I'm sorry about that. I didn't mean for this to become an ambush. I know that you and your father don't get along. I never would have put you in the same room if I'd known."

"I'm a big boy," Jonah said, guiding him out of the office. "I'll get over it."

Would he, though? Now he had even more reason to hate Peter, even as he had less reason to hate Matt. Not that he hated Matt. He just... oh hell, he didn't know. He didn't want to know.

He walked Lucas to his car, and they shook hands again, a warm handshake with a promise to get together again. Then he drove home without remembering a single turn of the journey, and sat in the dark in his apartment, listening to the noises of revelry coming from Sullivan's, and fighting the wash of emotions that battered at his carefully protected heart.

Chapter Fourteen

LAUREL WAS WORKING out the busboys' tips with the waitresses in the kitchen that night, when the back door opened.

"Jonah!"

He never came to her at night. The deal was that she went to him. "Hi," he said.

Oh, my God. He was here, at a time of night that made it obvious they were more than just casual acquaintances. How could she explain away the presence of Jonah Gardiner in her bar at one o'clock in the morning? Nothing came to mind except the obvious, which was annoying because she'd wanted to have more control over the story getting all over town.

Laurel froze for a second, but the waitresses didn't. "Well, hi, Jonah!" one of them began.

Goddammit.

"Hi, Helene," Jonah said, and Laurel's brain made an abrupt about-face. The atmosphere had suddenly gotten as thick as gravy.

Extra double shit and dammit. He'd dated Helene. Laurel had heard that tone of voice before, and the knowing way that Helene said, "Hello, *Jonah*," and then raised her eyebrows at them. Helene had been in Jonah's crowd in high school, going for the goth look and, as far as the rumors went, engaging in a smorgasbord of pharmaceuticals before she, too, cleaned up. She worked hard and was polite to the customers, so until right this second, Laurel had liked her.

"Did you leave your cut for Alejandro?" Laurel asked loudly.

"I was just waiting for him to come out of the bathroom," Helene replied, keeping her eyes on Jonah with absolutely no shame. "How's it going, Joe?"

Laurel was happy to see him grimace a little. "It's going fine, Helene. How are you?"

"Busy. But never too busy to take a phone call from an old friend," she said, and winked.

"Thanks, Helene!" Laurel almost shouted. "You can just leave Alejandro's money there. I'll give it to him when he comes out."

Helene pouted, took her purse out from under the counter and walked past them. She made sure to pass very close to Jonah on her way out of the door, almost close enough for her breasts to touch his shoulder. But Jonah moved away at the last second and, Laurel was pleased to see, didn't follow her out of the door with his eyes.

Pushing Helene out of her mind, Laurel focused on Jonah. He didn't look so hot. His eyes were sunken and his face was thinner than usual, or maybe that was his expression. He looked as though he'd been punched, though she couldn't see a mark on him. "Did you have dinner?" she said.

"What?" He frowned, as though he was trying to remember. "I had something… before…"

"Before what?" she prompted. "Oh, the talk thing. How did it go?" Not well, she'd guess, given his deer-in-headlights look.

"That's what—"

But Alejandro, the busboy, came out of the bathroom at that moment and Laurel was distracted, using her worse-than-it-should-be Spanish to give him his money and send him on his way. Alejandro gave Jonah a searching look, but Jonah just smiled vaguely at him and said, "*¿Qué pasa?*" Alejandro replied in the same casual tone and left them to it.

"Sit," Laurel told Jonah, and he folded onto the stool as though shot. She pulled eggs and fresh spinach out of the refrigerator and began cutting thick slices of bread from the loaf she'd made that morning. The familiar movements and the sounds of metal utensils echoing in the large kitchen soothed her, so that she was able not to interrogate Jonah until he'd eaten.

Jonah only revived when she had a spinach and feta cheese omelet in front of him, with a slab of warm bread and butter beside it. "Lor," he breathed, lifting the plate up so he could take a good sniff. "You get me every time."

"Just eat it," she ordered, though she blushed, and brought him a glass of water.

She allowed him five bites, and then she said, "Okay, now tell me what's so important you couldn't wait for me to come to you."

Jonah took a mouthful of water before he answered. "It's hard to articulate."

"One word in front of the other." She folded her arms. "Come on, buddy. Spill."

"Okay… The guy who was giving the lecture tonight… he's my brother."

Laurel instantly got an image of Matt, aged twenty because that was the last time she remembered seeing him, standing up in front of a crowd, in full battle fatigues. "Matt?" she said, even though she knew it couldn't be him.

Sure enough, Jonah shook his head. "Someone else. Dad had another son. Before me."

That made her uncross her arms, quick. "*What?*" Everyone knew the sad tale of Matt's family versus Jonah's. Had Peter done the same thing to someone else with Jonah's mother?

"I know. That's why I… and you don't even know."

Laurel stayed on her feet while he talked about New York City, and a long time ago, a woman Peter had treated worse than he'd treated Pam, and secrets that had lain undisturbed for years. He was vague about the details. Laurel was afraid to ask, afraid to bring any more hurt to his eyes.

"And he—Dad—wants to meet with me tomorrow, and I just don't know how I can ever look him in the face again," Jonah finished, poking at the remains of his meal.

"I'm not surprised." She tried to imagine if it had been Frank, but that was impossible. Frank could never have been the kind of man Peter was, even though they had shared the same affliction.

"So you think I shouldn't see him?" Jonah asked.

"Oh." Laurel moved her stool next to his, so she could put her arms around him. She'd never seen him look so lost. "No, honey. I'm not going to tell you that. I know that's the easiest way out, but it won't help you in the long run."

One corner of his mouth quirked up, though he kept his head down. "You sound like a therapist."

"I know a really good one, if you're looking." She smiled.

Jonah focused on his fork, which he was twisting on the plate as if picking up spaghetti.

"Speaking of therapists," she went on, when he didn't say anything, "tell me what's going on in your head right now."

He thought about it, then shrugged. "Nothing. I'm a blank."

"You're in shock."

"Yes… but I've told you before… I don't do drama anymore. This is… this was my old life. I'm not going to get sucked into a world I didn't ask to join."

"No one *asks* to join their family. They just get put there."

"But this time I get to choose."

"You're saying you won't even let this... Lucas... into your life?"

He didn't answer again.

Laurel shook him with her arms, which still held him tight. "Jonah. He's blood. You have a *niece*."

"My dad's blood too, and he doesn't exactly enrich my life."

"Maybe he would, if you'd let him in."

But Jonah was already shaking his head. "Not after what I found out tonight."

"At least listen to him once. You *have* to, Jonah. You know all your training would tell you to. And I can't help but remember that for all his mistakes, he brought Matt up just fine. And he's been trying to reconnect with you for years. Maybe he could have—"

Jonah's eyes met hers and her voice died. "My training," he said, "has told me that there are times when you have to cut toxic people out of your life. And he was toxic to me. I'm a better person because he's out of my life, and I'm okay with keeping things that way."

She didn't know when the tears had come into her eyes. But she didn't move away and she didn't hide the tears when she said, "You know that my dad made mistakes. God knows. You witnessed some of them." Jonah winced, but she wasn't stopping now. "He swore blind to me that he would change, so I set up countless opportunities for him to get well, and he didn't take them. If anyone should have cut someone out of their life, I should have done that with him. In a way, I did, by moving to the city and leaving him to—" She closed her eyes, feeling the tears spill onto her cheeks.

"Lor," Jonah said, putting up a hand to wipe them away.

"But I didn't," she went on, the tears choking her voice. "Because he loved us. And right now I have trouble remembering this, but there were hundreds of good moments in our life together, and they have to outweigh the bad. I went back in every time because he *tried*. And you're not giving your father the chance to *try*."

Finally, she saw a crack in Jonah's carefully constructed veneer. His face was stricken as he tracked her tears with his thumb, loosening her arms to do so. "You can forgive in a way I'll never be able to," he said.

"You don't know that," she said, taking in a shaky breath.

She hadn't meant to get upset; after all, this was about Jonah, but her emotions had gotten through to him in a way that logic couldn't.

He cupped her cheek with one big hand. She leaned into it, and he pulled her into his arms, turning the two of them so she could rest her head against his chest, as she had the other night. They stayed motionless for a few moments. Laurel listened to Jonah's heart, that beat so strongly but was too afraid to feel anything, while she felt everything and was afraid she'd never be able to rein it all in.

"Okay," Jonah said at last over her head. "I'll talk to him."

"Great." She pulled away. "You won't regret it, I swear you won't. And if he says or does anything you can't handle, come see me. We can deal with it."

Jonah's hand went to her hair this time, fingering the strands that had escaped her braid, patting them back into place. Laurel leaned back in and kissed him, a closed-mouth kiss this time, with less of the passion of the nights they'd shared, but more promise.

He reached out for the plate but she said, "I got it."

When she stood, he did, and they hugged like that, Laurel reaching up to get her arms around his neck, to press into him all the support she hoped he was feeling from her.

A bang from the kitchen door made them jump and look to it. Helene was standing there, looking smug and pissed at the same time to see them in each other's arms.

"I'm *sorry*," she said insincerely. "I forgot my scarf."

Well, that was that. Laurel looked at Jonah while Helene sauntered past them. He hadn't, she was glad to see, taken his arms away from her. They gave each other a small smile.

"Worth it," he whispered.

Laurel put her head on his chest. Screw Helene and anyone else who talked about them the next day. She had her man, and they didn't.

Helene rummaged around among the coat hooks for a minute and then came back. "Nope. Must have come without it in the first place." Laurel rolled her eyes. Helene had just come back to catch them at something. "So, you two, huh?" Helene added.

They both looked at her, their bodies still entwined.

"Us two," Jonah said.

Laurel couldn't interpret the emotion in his voice.

Helene obviously wanted more but there was a long, awkward pause while they stared her out. "Okay, then!" she said at last. "Cool. I'm happy for you, boss. See you tomorrow!"

"Goodbye, Helene," Laurel said pointedly, and when the other woman had left the room, she closed and locked the kitchen door. "So," she said, turning to Jonah. "It's going to be all over town by tomorrow."

"No reason for it not to be," he reminded her.

"No. Except for the shit my mom'll give me, and your mom'll give you. Come on," she added. "You look exhausted. Let's get you home."

"Is the front door locked?"

She nodded.

"And you just locked that door?"

"Uh-huh."

"Turn off the lights."

His voice was a tempting, dangerous murmur. "Really?" she said, though her body reacted at once to his change in tone. She put a hand to her throat.

Jonah walked over to her as though she were a mouse he

was stalking. Laurel's breath came faster, fluttering her chest under her hand. "On the counter?" she whispered.

"Wherever you say, sweetheart," he answered, reaching her now, stroking her jaw with his hand, moving down to cover her hand and then cupping her breast. Laurel groaned and her head fell back.

"Is this you letting people in?" she breathed as he kissed her neck.

"I don't know," he said. "It's me not giving a fuck right now."

"But the staircase…" She was already hitching herself up onto the counter so he could reach her breasts with his mouth.

"So turn off the lights and quit talking," he mumbled, his breath buzzing her skin beneath her blouse.

"Oh, shit," she gasped, giving up, grabbing his hand and pulling him with her so they could find the switches. In seconds he was back where he'd been, the room almost pitch dark, bar the lights of the exit signs and the hum of the refrigerator and freezer, and their own panting, and a hurried question that was answered with, "It's okay, I'm on the pill," and then muffled laughter, and stifled groans, and a quiet scream into his shoulder and a cry that he hid in her cascading hair.

So the next day, when Laurel came in and saw the thoroughly scrubbed counter and the knowing smiles of the other waitresses and students, the rumor obviously having done its rounds, she was just able to smile like the cat that had got the cream, give them all a sunny, "Good morning!" then send them off to their work.

Chapter Fifteen

WHEN THE FIRE department and EMTs came in for their usual Friday night get-together that night, Laurel swapped ends with Walker so she could hear what they were talking about. She'd paused her search for a new bartender, because she was learning more about her business being a bartender than weeks in front of the spreadsheets had taught her.

They were excited about something that was for sure. More drinks got bought tonight. Laurel noticed that the EMTs who weren't drinking because they were on call also ordered more sodas. So she took a pitcher of cola and one of lemon-lime, and carried them to the tables herself.

"Hi, guys," she began, suddenly awkward.

She'd never had a problem talking to her diners before, but she didn't know these people, and they only remembered her as Frank's young daughter, who'd left and been forced back. They might also know Jonah, who'd been in town for years, and have heard about their relationship by now.

But she lifted her chin and plunged in. "Soda, for you

guys on call." She put it down. They all stared at her. "On the house," she specified. "And for those of you who aren't working, would a pitcher of beer go down okay? Also my treat."

The captain was one of Laurel's few female customers. An olive-skinned woman with long black hair in a ponytail, and a tattoo of thorns wrapped around her bicep, she said, "Thanks. Is this a special occasion?"

Laurel felt her cheeks getting hot. Had she been glaring at their drinks that hard before now? "I just wanted to let you know I appreciate you all coming here every week, especially now. I know there are a lot of other bars who'd love to take your money. I appreciate—and my dad did, too—that you choose us."

One of the men at the table said, with a laugh, "Yeah, well, you're the only place that has room for us!"

But the others shushed him. "Sully was a good guy," another man said. "We miss him."

He probably gave out more free drinks. Well, hell, if anyone deserved it, these guys did.

As if they could read her mind, the firefighters' table yelled from behind her, "Hey, who are we? Chopped liver?"

Laurel turned and gave them a big smile. Hey, they were firefighters, for God's sake. A couple of pretty hot ones in that mix, too. "No, no. I was coming to you next."

They jeered and booed, grinning at her. "No, I swear I was!" she teased back. "These guys just seemed to have something to celebrate."

More hissing and pantomimes of how bad the firefighters were dying of thirst. Laurel got them their pitchers and then hovered between the tables.

"You gonna tell us how much you appreciate *us*?" one of the cuter firefighters said before she could get to her real purpose.

"Nah. The money you made on that calendar last year should have told you that."

The kid frowned, though the others laughed. "We didn't make a calendar," he said, confused.

The man next to him elbowed him. "That's her point, genius! She's flirting with you."

Laurel laughed but put up a hand. "In a purely professional sense, obviously." The cutie pouted. "Does everyone have what they need here?" she asked them.

"No," the cutie said. Laurel ignored him.

Someone nudged him. "Didn't you hear? She's taken."

Laurel blushed, and covered any more comments by saying, "I'll come check on you in a little while." Spinning around so she faced the emergency squad. "So what's the celebration?"

For some reason, the captain looked a little put out. One of the others, a heavyset white man about Laurel's age, answered. "I thought the whole town knew by now. Matt Van Allen is coming home."

The name buzzed around Laurel's head for a second before slotting into place. "Jonah's brother?" She gasped, before she could stop herself.

The captain, whose name Laurel just couldn't remember, gave her a sideways look. "Jonah's *half*-brother," she said, "if it's any of his business."

"Wow, that's—" Jonah's brother?

Her mind was still full of the *other* brother Jonah had met last night. Matt's story had faded way into the background. But they were all looking at her, expecting more of a response than *wow that's*.

Laurel's biggest memory was of how Jonah had talked about Matt when they'd been dating; a period so long ago she should have forgotten it, except Jonah's bitterness had colored so much of his life. Matt had been the golden child, doing everything right where Jonah had done everything wrong. But Matt had had two parents in his life and Jonah's mother had been... who she was. But then something had happened... something Laurel couldn't remember right now. Anyway, the next she'd heard, Matt had joined the army.

He was four years younger than Jonah, give or take, so when she'd dated Jonah he'd still been in high school. And now, looking at the crew who was looking expectantly back at her, she remembered something else. "That's right. He was an EMT before he joined up, right?"

"Right," the man said. "Now you're cooking with gas."

"And he's coming home?"

Did Jonah know this? How did he feel about it? Perhaps

having Matt out of the way had helped Jonah's recovery. Now he would be home and the contrast between them would be made clear.

"Getting discharged in a couple weeks. I hear the town's talking about having a parade for him."

Jesus. Talk about a golden child.

"Banner across the street and everything."

"Wow." In the midst of trying to remember what it was she couldn't remember about Matthias Van Allen, something else clicked in Laurel's brain. Parades meant crowds. Which meant customers. "What'll you do after the parade?"

"Hadn't really thought about it," another medic, a young girl with a short blonde ponytail, said. "Back to Bill's, maybe, right, Bill?"

A third man, a slim African American with glasses, grinned. "I do give the best parties," he said with no small pride. "But I dunno if we could host the whole town."

Laurel thought fast. "What if we had a party for him here? And used it to raise some money for the squad?"

That blew their hair back. The captain said, "I don't know…"

But the first man said, "Oh, c'mon, Raya, it's a great idea. You're gonna turn down the chance to raise some cash? And then everyone can come in."

"It's just an idea," Laurel said, though she was already figuring out logistics and sourcing meat and working out how much of a percentage would be generous enough to give the squad, but would also make room for a few expenses she couldn't afford to give away.

"Maybe we could talk about it tomorrow? Can you come by for lunch?"

Bill and the first man nodded, but they both deferred to Raya. "Up to you, Cap."

Raya threw up her arms. "Fine, then."

Laurel didn't know why she was being so pissy about it, but the tips of her own fingers were tingling at her audacity to make an offer like this without thinking it all the way through. Other people's motives were their business. She wanted to get Sullivan's on a bunch of flyers and on the map and Raya's feelings weren't her problem.

Jonah, though...

As if reading her thoughts, Raya said, "Are you sure your *boyfriend* won't mind?"

Would he mind? Could he possibly still be so pissed at his brother that he'd be upset at her idea to raise money and exposure at the same time? Or would the distraction of getting to know Lucas make him feel more charitable to Matt?

"He'll be fine," she said robustly. "Okay, great. We'll see what we can figure out. Enjoy your evening." She went back to the bar, where Walker had been sending her increasingly desperate glances for the last five minutes.

PETER CANCELLED ON Jonah that night, saying he was sick. In fact, his wife texted that he was sick. She asked if he could come to see Jonah the next day, if he felt better.

Typical Dad, Jonah thought, texting back that he would be home after dinner on Saturday. He had an idea of eating dinner, or at least lunch, at Sullivan's, and getting all the gossip out of the way in one go.

But he walked on eggshells all day, waiting for his father to arrive. He could barely send Laurel off to work with their usual kiss and warm words, and it was only because of her that he didn't cancel on Peter altogether. He didn't eat at Sullivan's.

At eight o'clock, Peter knocked on the front door and Jonah walked without any hurry down the stairs to let him in. As he recalled from the lecture, Peter had shrunk a little since the last time Jonah had gone near him. Realizing that he was the taller of the two embarrassed Jonah somehow.

The expression on Peter's sallow face was painful—a mixture of regret and loss that made Jonah's heart twist. And here he'd thought Peter could never have an effect on his heart again.

"Have a seat," Jonah said when he'd led him upstairs, as though Peter were just another one of his clients. Peter took the corner of the two-seater couch and Jonah sat in his usual low-backed armchair at right angles to him. The sky outside had already darkened, but Jonah had turned on all the lights, as if trying to banish the shadows Lucas's story had thrown over their father. "Are you feeling better?"

Peter sat down and crossed his long, bony legs, automatically arranging his pant crease so it was straight over his knee. Yet his collar still stuck up wrong out of his sweater. "Yes, thank you," he answered formally. "Thank you for seeing me."

"I don't know what good it will do."

Peter's eyes, the same blue as Jonah's, examined him. "I've wanted to see you for so long."

"I know. I didn't want to see you."

"After all this time?" Peter chided gently.

"I think we're way beyond you judging me for my actions," Jonah retorted, getting to the point. "You want to explain what you did to Lucas's mother?"

Peter's head fell, making his shoulders stick up like bare bird wings. "I can't." He covered his face with his hands. "I'm not here to make excuses for that."

"You should be in jail."

"Yes." Peter didn't ask for clemency, at least, which Jonah appreciated.

"Should have been castrated, if you ask me."

Peter shook his head. "In which case, you and Matt would never have been born."

"That would have been fine with me," Jonah said, before he could think.

Peter's head came up, fast. "Is that true?" Now his eyes were piercing. "Do you really feel that way? Did you feel that way when you were young?"

Jonah cursed his choice of words. He knew better than to want to throw away the life he had. As soon as he'd gone into therapy, he'd learned that real oblivion had never been what he sought. Once he knew that, it was easy to leave the temporary kind and make a life less selfish, more giving.

And now, Laurel had come back. He wasn't allowed to count her as one of his blessings, because they could only be... whatever they were now. But, damn, life with her in it was a hell of a lot more interesting than what he'd been surviving on before. "No. It's not true. Knee-jerk reaction. Being around you makes me feel like that teenager again. I get melodramatic."

"I *have* felt that way," Peter said. "For years. After Sarah... Jesus, if I stayed sober for an hour at a time I remembered that night and I hated myself... still hate myself for it."

"Good."

"I'm not asking forgiveness. I've never asked it from Lucas and I'm not asking it from you. Not for that, anyway."

Peter's hands were now clenching and unclenching the baggy material of his pants.

"I never loved your mother the way I should," Peter said.

Jesus. They were really getting into the thick of it.

"I couldn't love anyone then, but she was a giving person and she put up with a lot from me—"

"What do you call a lot?" Jonah asked sharply.

"Not that! No, Jonah, I swear. No, I just neglected her... and you. And then I met Mariah." His face changed, the lines smoothing out, a smile playing on his lips. "It's not an overstatement to say that she saved me. Without her..."

Jonah saw the love that made such a difference to his father's face. Mariah had left him, everyone knew, only a short while after Matt was born. Her actions had woken Peter up to what he was giving up on if he continued to drink. Mariah and Matt, the golden child, had saved him.

Laurel had done the same for Jonah, though he hadn't been crazy enough to bring a child into the mix, thank God. He'd had other girlfriends back then—like Helene, he remembered uncomfortably—but only Laurel had brought him to his senses.

Ugh. Could he be glimpsing a small amount of understanding for his father? If so, that would be a good thing, wouldn't it? Could it bring him closer to forgiving Peter?

Nope. "You hurt people while you were running through the fields with the love of your life," he said, with a tightness to his voice.

"I know." Peter's face tensed again. "I know. Again, there's nothing I can do or say to you or Lucas to make it right." He leaned forward so that their knees were almost touching. "But I want you to know, Jonah, that if there was *anything* I could do, I would do it."

Jonah kept silent. He'd never allowed himself to go down the road of thinking of the words Peter could say that would erase the last thirty years. These weren't bad, he had to admit. But acknowledging them would mean opening a door Jonah had kept locked shut. And he wasn't about to open it in front of Peter.

Laurel, though. Laurel would be there if you did.

Dammit. He wasn't supposed to be thinking of her right now. He had to sort out his own life. He was going to move on in any case, either with Peter in his life or without him. Those were his choices. The one choice was familiar; it didn't hurt. The other was the unknown—it involved emotions, and introspection. Jonah would far rather work with other people on that kind of thing than go into it for himself.

"Have you said this to Lucas?" he said.

"Of course, I—"

"Have you told Mariah?" Jonah interrupted, for it occurred to him that that was more important now. Peter could be as sorry as he liked, but without confessing his full history to his wife, he was just hiding behind the words.

"Yes."

That made Jonah sit back. "What did she say?"

"She was pissed. To say the least. She… she made me go to therapy."

Jonah's eyes widened. "Who are you seeing?" he asked at once, feeling a professional curiosity. Then his personal side kicked in. "Never mind." He put up a hand. "None of my business. Is it helping?"

Peter shrugged. "I still feel like a total shit."

"Then it's working."

They sat for a few seconds in silence. Then Jonah said, "Will you tell Mom?"

Peter rubbed his hand over his mouth, choosing his words. "She'll have to know about Lucas. I think she hates me enough not to need to know about… the other thing, don't you?"

Jonah didn't know how to answer that. "Why did you call her the other night?"

Peter looked, for some reason, shifty. "To tell her to tell you Matt was coming home," he said. "You never answer your phone."

"Why would I need to know Matt was coming home? What's going on?"

For the first time, Peter went on the defensive. "Why does something have to be going on? I want my sons to get to know each other." That brought him up short. He took a deep breath. "All my sons."

And there they were, back in the past again. Jonah didn't think he'd learned anything that would change his opinion of his father. But perhaps he could make room in his life for Lucas, who, after all, had never done anything to him.

Matt? Talking to Matt would highlight that Jonah had no good reason *not* to talk to him, and he wasn't ready to deal with that yet.

"I'll tell Mom," Jonah said. "I won't make any promises

as to how much I tell her."

"All right. Thank you."

"When does Matt get back?"

"The third. They're having a big party for him over at Sullivan's."

"What?" Jonah's tentative feelers toward his brother shriveled. "No, they're not."

Peter's eyebrows rose. "Apparently they are. Picking him up from the airport and then the whole town's invited to the bar. They're giving some of the day's earnings to the squad."

Jonah's issues with his father faded into the background. Laurel was doing this? For the brother she knew he…

Okay, he had no business messing with *her* business, just because he didn't like Matt a whole lot. Opening the bar up to the town when their homegrown hero returned was a great idea. Jonah's jealousy—sure, yeah, he could call it that, not that he wanted to be a hometown hero, but everyone just kept going *on* about it—was irrelevant.

"Will you go?" he asked. Peter felt the same way about bars as he did, and with more reason.

"No," Peter said at once, rubbing his hand through his bird's nest of hair. "I'm sure his mother will. I'd rather see him later, alone, anyway."

"You're going to lay all this on him his first night home?"

Peter winced. "Perhaps. Probably not."

"Thinking of someone else for once?" Jonah said. Yeah, it was nasty. That was how he was feeling. "I'm impressed,

Dad."

"That's a first."

The snort of laughter was forced out of Jonah, and it made Peter smile too. For a brief moment they looked at each other, man to man, or even father to son, and Jonah felt the tiny shift that could be the more frightening choice.

For the first time in ten years, he thought he might need a drink.

Peter left pretty quickly after that, probably feeling, as Jonah did, that any more conversation would ruin the small connection they'd made. When he'd gone, Jonah sat on in his leather armchair by the window, looking at Sullivan's lights and the new awning Laurel had had installed, and thinking of Peter, and himself, and Frank, and Brett.

Chapter Sixteen

When Laurel got home late that night, he was asleep in his chair, his neck at an angle that made him wince when she kissed him awake.

"How did it go?" she asked, lifting the top off a to-go container of a pulled-pork sandwich. Another container was in a plastic bag hanging off her wrist.

"Thanks," he said, rubbing his neck.

"Lemme just put this one in the freezer," she said, walking into his kitchen. "There's ice cream in it. Eat your sandwich."

She came back and stood behind him, massaging his neck like a pro, her hands warm and soothing after his roller coaster of emotions.

"God, that feels good," he said after a while. "I'm sorry I didn't come over for dinner."

"I didn't expect you, though it was a nice idea. Eat."

Fried apple slices, which gave an autumnal flavor to the spicy-sweet pulled pork, raised their sweet aroma to him. "Sweetheart," he said. "Don't be so good to me."

"Why not?"

"Because I'm going to fuck this up. I know I will."

"You won't."

"I already am. Dad told me you're planning a party for Matt?"

"Oh. Yes. I meant to tell you last night. Are you mad?"

"Not at you. But my reaction when he told me was all wrong. And that's what I mean."

"Well, hell, Jonah. You've got a ways to go. No one said you haven't. And anyway, it was my impetuousness that got me into the mess of planning a whole party for two weeks from now. I could use some of your cold logic myself."

He let his head fall back, too tired to argue. Her hands were still rubbing his neck and shoulders, gently pulling his head to one side, then the other, and pressing on each shoulder until he felt so relaxed, his head could have rolled off altogether. "I don't feel cold right now."

"Nope," she said, moving in front of him and taking the fork she'd put with the food to scoop up some of the pork. "Not cold at all." She fed him the pork, and Jonah forgot about everything else.

LAUREL COULD HAVE begun to worry, after that night, about Jonah's commitment to making their relationship work, but she just didn't have the time. Matt's party was going to be a massive undertaking. Her to-do list stretched over three pages, and much of it would involve people she wasn't sure would help.

There was one task, however, she decided to do first. She'd enjoy it, and it would take her mind off all her other tasks—finding some new decorations for the bar.

She had no money to spare, so she began at the town's consignment shop, which was only two blocks away from Sullivan's. The store's sign was cracked and aged, but the window was clean and there was a display of clothes and accessories in the window that wouldn't have been out of place in a mall. In the window were several signs advertising other charity events, including, she noticed, a Dress for Success fundraiser in a few weeks. That wasn't the charity the consignment store raised money for. Laurel thought it was damn decent of them to help out a competitor. Then she noticed that the fashion show Dress for Success was running would be featuring "model and local businesswoman, Pamela Gardiner."

Huh. She hadn't known Pam was a model.

She opened the glass door and a bell tinkled. Inside, the store looked much as she'd expected—racks and racks of clothes blocking her view of the cashier in the back, and beneath them, shoes and boots that looked cleaned and polished. She smelled the slightly musty smell that always came with secondhand clothes, but the lights were bright, and hanging from metal grids on the walls were more outfits, complete with accessories. Eighties music was playing in the background.

She pushed past the clothes and shoes and into the back of the store, which was bigger than she expected and carried household linens and knickknacks. This was more like it. Laurel thought of the moldering netting, dusty picture frames and cracked ashtrays Frank had seemed to think were appropriate decorations for an Irish bar, knickknacks which he had nailed to the walls with little regard to whether or not the nail could be seen.

She needed to brighten it up, and after a long night on Pinterest and gazing at pictures of the top one hundred restaurants in America, she knew what she was looking for. She couldn't do anything about the boring brown, heavy chairs and tables, though a coat of paint might give them new life. Everything else, however, would be beaten metal and old leather. If the surface was mirrored, so much the better. No more squinting at the barman in the corner, unable to see him because the light was so dim.

She homed in on a set of large mason jars at once. They were perfect to use as lights over the bar. An old set of carpenter's tools in beaten wood and pitted steel also went into her arms. Silver and black picture frames which she planned to use to reframe the photos of Irish celebrities Frank had so lovingly collected. A large mirror with a rusty metal frame tempted her, but was too big, and too expensive, for her to think of now. Still, since she no longer had her own apartment, redecorating the bar was the closest thing to a labor of love, apart from cooking, that she'd had since Frank had died.

"Can I give you a—oh!"

A woman holding a polishing cloth had appeared from behind another row of knickknacks and jumped when she saw Laurel's face. This made Laurel jump so hard, she dropped one of the mason jars. Somehow the woman caught it and then stood in front of her, her eyes running over Laurel's face.

"You're Laurel, right? Gail's girl?"

"That's right."

Belatedly, Laurel made the connection between the poster outside and the woman who ran this store. *Way to walk into the lion's den, Laurel.*

Laurel had forgotten how beautiful she was. With her long, straight, black hair streaked with gray, and her heavy-lidded eyes, Pam Gardiner looked like Cher. Nothing like Jonah, certainly. But as Laurel scrutinized Pam, she saw something of Jonah in her jawline, and her expression, which right now was surprised and calculating.

Laurel felt a blush steal across her cheeks. "Um, how are you?" she said.

"Good. I'm good." Pam broke eye contact and began to polish the mason jar with the cloth in her hand. "I wanted to say, I'm so sorry about your father."

"Oh. Thank you." Laurel hadn't expected her to begin

with that. The knowing look in Pam's eye told Laurel she'd heard about her relationship with Jonah. The town had had a whole thirty-six hours to spread it around.

"How's your mother? Here, let me take some of that." Pam relieved her of some of her purchases and began walking back to the counter.

Another topic Laurel wasn't expecting. "She's not great," she said. This woman was Gail's friend, right? The one who hadn't come to see her?

Pam paused and her head half-turned to Laurel, before she continued on her way to the counter. Placing Laurel's things on the surface, she began to arrange them in a fussy way, wiping the cloth over them all, even the ones that didn't need it. It was as if she wanted Laurel to look at them instead of listening to her. "I'm sorry to hear that," she said. "So sorry."

Since the spotlight seemed to be off Laurel for the moment, she decided to stir the pot. "Mom'd love to see you."

"Oh!" Pam's eyes flew to hers. "Would she? I thought she—well, I thought that we—"

"No one has come," Laurel stated flatly. "I think none of them know what to say, because Dad was…" She allowed the silence to finish her sentence.

Pam was blushing. "I didn't want her to… to be reminded…" She arranged the mason jars just so in front of her. "I never made a secret of what I thought of your father. I'm sorry."

"That's all right. He was difficult." Laurel thought about what Jonah had told her about Peter. "Their history was very different to yours, though. Mom knows that. She won't hold what you said against you, if that's what you're worried about."

Pam smoothed her beautiful hair down one shoulder. Really, it was a shame she'd never remarried. Maybe Gail wasn't the only one holding onto a man who'd never existed. Then again, Jonah had always made it clear that Pam's bitterness outshone any good qualities she might have had.

But she'd run this store for decades and as far as Laurel knew, no one had ever said a word against her customer service skills. And here she was, being nice as pie to Laurel, whose mother hated her son… whose son Laurel was sleeping with…

When Pam met Laurel's gaze this time, her eyes were damp. "I've been meaning to call. Honest. I just…"

"Don't know what to say?" Laurel repeated, pressing her advantage. She'd received the same radio silence from her friends in New York. Death was so damned awkward. She'd attributed it to her friends' youth, but apparently the bug could hit at any age. "I think your son would tell you to just sit with her and let her talk. Drink coffee and eat a Danish. Be normal."

"Yes." Pam sniffed and touched her fingertips under her eyes, the cloth still firmly in one hand. "Yes, that sounds like a good idea." She sniffed again and gave Laurel a more direct look. "Are all these lovely things to cheer her up? Brightening up your apartment?"

"No." Maybe Laurel should have thought of that. "They're for the bar. I'm redecorating a little. We're having a big party there in a couple of weeks and I want to change things up."

"Sounds like fun." Pam had gone back to store manager mode. "What's the occasion?"

Too late, Laurel remembered Pam's relationship, or lack thereof, with Matt. "Um… the emergency squad is hosting it. A fund-raiser for them and the fire department."

"That sounds great," Pam said. "And from what I remember of your bar, these will really brighten up the place." She finally put down the cloth and began to wrap the mirrored frames. "Did you see that mirror in the back?"

Danger over. That one, at least. "I saw it," Laurel said, "but it's not in the budget right now."

"I see." Pam must have heard that a lot, because she didn't push.

"And I'm going to open up the garden in the back," Laurel went on.

Back in her dim and distant past, she remembered running in and out of metal tables and chairs in the small area in the back of the bar, seeing bright flowers hugging the fence and the smell of grilling wafting over the diners. But with the clientele dropping off and Frank consolidating what energy he had into the bar, the area had become seriously neglected, and Gail had been too depressed to keep the flowers going.

"My God!" Pam exclaimed, pausing in her work. "I'd forgotten all about that! Gail worked on it... what, must be years ago now?"

Laurel nodded. "Dad closed it down for the winter and then just never opened it again."

"That's such a shame. Gail made that area so pretty, with the raised beds against the walls and all the flowers she planted there." Pam moved on to the mason jars. "She's the one who got me into gardening, you know. Speaking of budgets, she knew where to go and what to buy out of season."

"Yes, she did love it." Laurel felt a pang of nostalgia for Gail's long-forgotten smiles and contented humming when she worked on the garden. "I'd forgotten."

"If you're opening it up again, it might be just the project she needs." Pam suddenly put out a hand to cover Laurel's. "He's only been gone a couple of months or so, right?"

"Right."

"So don't ask her for miracles, hon." Pam's face held so much sympathy that Laurel's heart began to hurt. "But a positive project like cleaning up the garden might help jolt her out of her... wherever she is now."

"She's sad now." A lump formed in Laurel's throat. "That's all. Sad and not seeing any way to get out of being sad."

Pam nodded and squeezed her hand again. "I can imagine."

There was an awkward silence.

"You've taken on a lot," Pam said, changing tack. "I know Sullivan's is in trouble. I know that you had other plans. But you've come here to try and help it, and you haven't complained once."

"Not out loud," Laurel confessed. How did Pam know?

The answer came to her way too fast.

"Still," Pam went on, "you're here for your mother, and that's a wonderful thing in this day and age."

"Did Jonah tell you this?"

Pam took her hand away and now her hooded eyes pinned Laurel in her place. "So, you and Jonah are... together?"

"Yes," she said warily.

"You know his history." Pam laughed but without humor. "Everyone knows his history."

"Yes," Laurel said again, but added, "emphasis on *history*. He's different now."

"That's very nice of you to say," Pam said. "I don't think your mother sees it the same way, for all we're friends."

"Like I said, he's different now." And much, much more irresistible.

"Still," Pam went on. "I wouldn't like you to get too mixed up with him, Laurel."

Laurel's mouth fell open.

"You're a good girl, and a sweet one. Jonah will chew you up and spit you out, and I'm saying that as his mother. Oh, he won't do it on purpose," she added, preempting Laurel's splutters, "he'll just… suck you in and then… drift away. You know the phrase, 'Physician, heal thyself?'"

Dumbly, Laurel nodded. Her mouth was still open.

"Well, he can't. And I wouldn't want you to exhaust yourself trying to do it for him."

Too many words, too many emotions, pressed into Laurel's throat to express any one of them now. All she could manage was, "We're just—" She couldn't even finish the lie. He'd been more than "just" to her from the moment he'd saved her from that bus.

Perhaps the worst of the reasons that kept her silent was that on some level, she knew Pam was right.

Chapter Seventeen

Phase two of Laurel's plan went into effect the next morning, a Sunday. She stayed at home the night before so she wouldn't be tempted to spend an extra hour in Jonah's bed, baked oatmeal raisin cookies, and made sure the coffee was good and strong before she went into Brett's room with a tray.

She hadn't entered his room in years, but she'd seen him come in last night and it had been reassuringly early. She reckoned she had an even chance of getting him in a helpful mood.

She put the tray down on top of a pile of books on his childhood desk and crept over to the lump in his bed. Then, putting her hands on the highest lump—his butt or his shoulder, she wasn't sure which—she began pushing him up and down, while yelling at the top of her voice, "Bork! Bork! Bork! Bork!"

Now bounced half out of bed, Brett's fair head appeared from under the blankets, cursing and groaning. It was a ritual they'd each done to the other many times in their teens. "Wharrrrr?" he said.

"I bring sustenance," Laurel said, stopping the borking long enough to hand him the tray. The smell of fresh coffee opened his eyes and Brett sat up in the bed, his bare chest heavy and pale in the dark room.

"Mm," he said, grabbing a cookie. "I almost forgive you."

She waited until the coffee and sugar had hit his bloodstream before she told him why she was there. "So I told the emergency squad we'd host a party for Matt Van Allen when he comes back."

"Uh-huh." Brett obviously didn't see how this was relevant.

"And he's coming back in a couple of weeks."

"This involves me doing some unpaid labor, doesn't it?" Brett grumbled.

"It's paid, if you count the fact that you're living off Mom right now and her income comes from the bar. But if you work front of house—sober—on the day, I'll pay you a going rate."

The word *sober* made him roll his eyes. Laurel didn't like this—had he even talked to Jonah these past couple of weeks? If he had, he wouldn't be so flippant about it, but then again he had "been good" all week—but she had to focus on what she needed now. "And the yard in the back is a dump and I thought we could open it up to the customers on the day, maybe launch a new garden seating area."

Brett collapsed back against his pillows, almost spilling his mug of coffee. "Jesus, Lor. It's a freaking dump out there."

"Yes. That's what I said. Nothing a strapping young man with time on his hands can't handle. And I'll help you."

"You already do everything else around here."

At least he'd noticed that. "I'm going to ask Mom to do some plantings in the beds she used to have against the fences."

"It's October," Brett pointed out. "What's going to grow?"

"We'll plant mums for now. And get some lights. And check on the music. There used to be speakers out there."

Brett didn't say anything for a moment but started on his second cookie, chewing thoughtfully at her. He might be marshaling a reason not to help her.

So, she said into the silence, "We need to do something different, bug. We need more customers. Different customers."

He made a movement as if he had to flick off a fly. "What's wrong with the customers we've got?"

Echoes of Jonah. Why couldn't anyone see the writing on the wall? "Nothing. But there aren't enough of them, and they don't spend enough. You know the debt Dad left this place in. I can't pay it back unless we do something grand. Something different. With a garden area, and a few updates to the décor, and the menu, we could market ourselves more as a family restaurant, and get the new residents in. But the old customers will have somewhere new to sit and will still feel welcome."

Brett frowned up at her. "You just said we're in a ton of debt. How are you going to pay for upgrades?"

The idea flooded her with fear, but she'd made up her mind. Her credit cards were going to have to groan for a few months—or years, if this didn't work. "I don't plan on spending more than I have to, and I have some... funds." She put her hand on his covered leg. "That's why I need you, okay? The more we can do for free, the less we'll go in the hole. And if we can get a whole crowd in here on that day, it could make all the difference going into the winter."

He stretched his arms above his head. The sheet fell down to his stomach, revealing a pale pot belly that did him no favors. "Ugh," he said, and Laurel knew she'd won. "I guess you'll want to be starting on this indentured servitude today?"

"Right now, if possible," she agreed, patting his leg. "Don't bother showering; you're going to get dirty. I'll see you outside in ten minutes." She jumped off the bed, avoiding the poke in the side he tried to give her. With the tray in her hand, she paused at his door. "Thanks, bug," she said. "I really can't do this without you. Any of it."

A strange expression came across his face—she would have said it was half shame, half fear, and half pride. With no time to figure out the equation, however, she left him and went to talk to her mother.

Gail was drinking coffee and eating an English muffin at the kitchen table. Laurel's continued attempts to distract her had so far been gently and lovingly ignored. But this was different. This wasn't busywork; this was the future of their business. Of their family.

"Hey, Mom," she began, and got the usual querulous "Hello, Laurel," in return.

"Mom," Laurel went on, dropping into the chair opposite. "I need you to do something for me."

Gail's expression of pain and hopelessness was familiar, but Laurel didn't give her a chance to say no. "I'm opening up the back seating area, and I need your gardening expertise."

"Oh, I don't know, honey…" Gail said at once.

"No, listen, Mom, please." Laurel grabbed Gail's hands around her mug in her intensity. "I've told the emergency squad that we'll have a party for Matt Van Allen when he comes home from the military in a couple of weeks—"

That put a different expression on Gail's face. Surprise was a very welcome change. "What? Matt Van Allen? Pam's ex's son?"

"Yes. And I thought we could—"

"Why on earth did you say you'd do that?"

The question made Laurel pause. "Why on earth not?"

"Because she's a friend of mine! And that's the son of the woman who screwed up her life!"

Laurel was glad to hear some passion in Gail's voice, though she could have done without being its target. She'd heard this tone only once before—when Gail had gone off on Jonah. "It's not Matt's fault his father cheated on Jonah's mom."

Some pink had crept into Gail's cheeks. She pulled her hands out of Laurel's. "His father turned Jonah Gardiner into what he is, and forced Pam into that job at the consignment store!"

Really? This is the thing that's going to bring you back to me? A decades-old feud I'm having enough trouble getting Jonah to rethink? "First of all, Mom, Jonah *was* like that. He's not anymore. Saying differently is being really unfair. And again, what does any of that have to do with Matt? The emergency squad loves him. Looks like everyone else does too. Whatever Jonah's dad did, he brought up Matt okay."

The logic didn't sit well with Gail, as it hadn't with Jonah. Only he'd finally allowed it. Laurel wasn't so lucky with Gail, who sat mutinously across the table, her jaw set. "How am I going to tell Pam that my own daughter is celebrating the boy she was pushed aside for?"

This was a disaster. Laurel was going to have to figure out the flowers herself. "I don't think it's like that, Mom. Will you please think about it? This could bring us in a whole new clientele and we can finally start paying off the debt on this place."

Also the wrong thing to say. "What do you mean, a

whole new clientele?" Gail's voice went up a few notes. "What's wrong with the community your father built up? You're not going to turn us into one of those fancy *gastropubs*, are you? Jack up the prices and leave all the regular folk with nowhere to eat?"

It was Laurel's turn to blush. Gastropub wasn't a dirty word in her circles, at least not the way she'd planned it. "Not raise the prices, no. But I don't see why I keep getting slammed for trying to increase our turnover and introduce a little actual *food* into this place!"

Gail's face drained of color. She put her hand to her chest. Laurel could see her bosom heaving as though her corsets were too tight. "How could you say that about what your father worked on for thirty years?" She stood up, began reaching behind her as if she wanted to get to the door but had forgotten where it was. "I don't think I know you anymore, Laurel. I knew that cooking degree was what you wanted, and I was sorry that it meant you spent so long in the city, away from us, but I didn't think you'd come back and look down on all of us like this!"

"I'm *not* looking down on you!" Laurel retorted hotly. "I don't want to lose our regular customers, either! I swear to God, Mom, I'm trying to do what's right for *everyone*! We can't live on what we take in now. That's the cold, hard truth! What do you want me to do? Sell the business for pennies on the dollar because of all the debt? Move you to some tiny apartment?"

Gail didn't seem to be listening. She'd worked herself up into a first-class tantrum. "You'll stop all the regulars from coming in and the bar will die, and that'll work out great for you, won't it, because you'll be able to go back to New York and tell them all about when you slummed it with your working-class parents—"

"Mom!"

The voice made both of them jump. Brett was standing in the doorway to the kitchen. He'd thrown on a wrinkled T-shirt and jeans, and was holding his coffee mug.

"Did you hear what she said!" Gail said to him at once.

"I didn't say anything!" Laurel disputed.

"Jesus, ladies, calm down," Brett said. "You're giving me a headache."

His calmer voice, and his general lack of energy, took some of the tension out of the room. Gail's shoulders slumped and Laurel noticed that her own hand was about to crush her coffee mug.

Crap. She hadn't fought often with her mother and had forgotten where she got her passion from. When Gail was in full flow, she was hard to stop. That was why no one could ever tell her that she had enabled Frank's addiction. Suggesting such a thing would have set off a full-blown shouting match, and who needed that with a room full of customers downstairs?

Gail collapsed back into her chair and Laurel wasn't surprised to see tears falling down her cheeks. She herself could feel the tightness in her chest that presaged tears and took a couple of deep breaths to hold them back. There was a time and a place for passion, and it wasn't when she had a garden full of crap to move.

"Mom," Brett went on. "Don't accuse Laurel of things she hasn't done."

"Thanks—" Laurel began, but he interrupted her.

"Lor, don't forget why the people who *do* come to this bar come here, while you're dreaming your big dreams."

Her cheeks burned. She didn't think she *had* forgotten anyone, especially after listening to Jonah, but since Brett had stopped her mother yelling at her, she wasn't about to contradict him. She restrained herself. "I haven't," she said. "Are you coming downstairs now?"

"Yeah, yeah. Tyrant," he said with a grin, and turned back to his room. "Hell of a day when I'm the one in this family being rational," he said to himself as he went.

"Hell of a day," another voice said from the front door. Laurel whirled around and Gail looked up from her pity party at the table.

Pam was standing in the door, which none of them had heard her open. Framed in the doorway, she was impressive, dressed for work in a dark pair of jeans and a long, floaty, lavender tunic that emphasized her height and brought out violet tones in her eyes. Her hair was braided, like Laurel's was today, down one shoulder. She couldn't have been more of a contrast to Gail, whose hair stood out in a gray-blonde frizz around her head, and who had been wearing the same pajamas for three days.

The tableau was still for a few seconds. Then Gail said, "Oh, *Pam*!"

Pam was there at once, sitting at the table and taking her friend into her arms. Laurel got out of there, fast.

Chapter Eighteen

Downstairs, the kitchen was empty, so Laurel didn't have to worry about her own tearful face for a while. She went through the bar doors and past the bathrooms to the door that had remained closed for years, opening it up to unseal the garden.

Brett followed a couple of minutes later. "What's happening up there?" Laurel said at once, nodding up to the apartment window.

"Mom's crying," Brett said with no emotion. "Ms. Gardiner's hugging her. I think there's some coffee brewing."

About the best that Laurel could wish for, for now at least. She wished she'd had an extra second to ask Pam not to tell Gail about her and Jonah. She nodded and pointed to Brett's first task.

She and Brett spent the morning pulling broken pallets and boxes out of the small space, through the gate in the back wall, and into the dumpster in the alley. Then they were able to assess what was left. The list was not impressive. Several tables that had buckled from being blown over in gales and ignored, chairs with rust showing through the old black paint, and shredded umbrellas, one of which had an old wasp's nest in it that sent Laurel back into the kitchen until Brett swore it was empty.

The Sunday bar and kitchen staff took a moment to peer into the back and marvel that they'd never noticed the door before. A few of the customers also looked outside and reminisced over hot summer nights and celebrations after softball games. Their conversation made Laurel remember the longevity of Sullivan's. No one who worked for her today had been here twenty years ago—not even Reg and Brian had been there that long—but plenty of their patrons had. As Jonah and Gail had said, if she forgot that, she would kill Sullivan's just as fast as if she did nothing.

WHEN MIGUEL, JUNIOR, and the students arrived on Monday, Laurel and Brett were already in the garden. There was still so much to do. The flowerbeds were rotted out and would need new wood and new potting soil if they were going to do anything but kill whatever she put in them. The fence needed painting and repairing. And the old bluestone patio floor needed to be in-filled with sand, if not completely replaced.

The crew came out in ones and twos to look at what they were doing. "I wondered where that door went," one student said.

"It's a mess," Junior said, then blushed.

"I know," Laurel agreed, following him back into the kitchen for a second, and keeping her dirty hands away from the food. "Anyone know any strong, young studs and studettes with a little extra time on their hands? I need new flowerbeds built into the borders out there, and I need the fence painted."

The students looked regretful. "We're booked," they said. "Between this and classes…"

That was a disappointment, but then Miguel said, with diffidence, "I might know some guys."

"My cousin's been out of work for six months," Junior added. "He could really use the work, if you're paying."

"I'll pay an expert," Laurel said, "and minimum wage for anyone else who can help," she added to Miguel. "Have your cousin call me."

Junior nodded. "I'll text him right now."

"Right," she said. "Thanks. The rest of you? You might have heard by now that we're hosting a party here on the third for an EMT who's coming back from the army. I could use all hands on deck that day. It's a Saturday, so if you can come, let me know." She made sure they were all looking at her. "We're going to put Sullivan's on the map, with new food, new décor, and the space outside for parties and families and… whatever else it's needed for."

"What kind of new food?" asked one of the students.

With the new staff, Laurel had already been able to upgrade the cooking methods, using the microwave and the fryer less and the griddle and sauté pan more.

"Stuff like the lamb chops. More local produce, more flavors. Twists on the traditional, that kind of thing. I've had an idea for a truffle burger that's going to knock the pants off anything we serve now. I'll put it on tomorrow's menu and you'll see how quick it goes out that door." To make her point, she pointed at the swing door to the bar. "Any questions? Cool. Let me know about working on the third."

She went out to check the bar. The music was loud in there, the bar bustling, but she still almost knocked the servers over like bowling pins, because they'd been huddled around the swinging door.

Laurel decided to find it funny, rather than seeing the uncertainty in some of their eyes. "Did you catch that?" she said with a laugh, and told them the plan all over again.

One or two didn't seem convinced, but seemed to decide now wasn't the time to question her. Laurel got while the going was good, washing her hands and leaving Brett to the yard while she closed the door to Frank's office.

As the afternoon wore on, she had to come out again, to check the turnover from morning to night staff, visit the farmer's market for the night's special, welcome the new bartender she'd finally found, and perform a hundred other tasks that required her personal and immediate attention. But as the daylight waned and the neon lights in the bar's windows began to reflect on the patrons and the street outside, she found herself thinking about Jonah.

He'd told her about the conversation he'd had with his father. She'd sensed that his feelings were changing, and that he didn't know how to deal with them. He couldn't reconcile understanding Peter with condemning him for what he'd done to Lucas's mother. Maybe there was no way to reconcile it. Maybe that was just life, like Laurel's love for her father even as he made her life harder and harder each year until she left.

On the plus side of Peter's scale, there was Matt. He was a good guy, or so everyone said. There had to be something in Jonah's father that had made that happen.

She'd held Jonah to her, comforted him the best way she knew how, and didn't talk about Matt. One step at a time.

The evening customers arrived and Monday night was soon in full swing. Laurel ran around as usual, happily in her comfortable chef's whites rather than her bartending outfit. Bill and the rest of the emergency squad who were free came to hash out the details of the party. The bar would give 10 percent of the day's take to the two departments, and in return, they would advertise the event as far as their networks and social media accounts would take them. When she mentioned the outside area, they got all kinds of excited. She had five volunteers for building and painting and a donation of fine-grain sand for the patio before she could draw breath.

"You're real sweet. I'll take all the help I can get."

THE NEXT DAY, Laurel was halfway to dancing on her tiptoes in anticipation and anxiety of the reception of her new burger. She coached the servers to mention the special recipe and hoped the patrons would need their fix of red meat enough to trust her. Some small instinct of logic told her not to mention that the recipe included a mushroom-like fungus that pigs had dug out of the ground under filbert trees. And she didn't add anything to the price, despite the cost of that small pot of seasoning and the shaved truffles she'd found—with a guilty flush—at the Wegman's on 32.

She'd spent last night at home, not wanting to have to hide this from Jonah. Because of course she wasn't going to tell him. She'd tell him when the burger was a huge hit and she could watch him eat crow… or burger, or something. She'd texted him and he'd replied that that was fine, and she almost immediately wanted to change her mind, afraid he was going to go too far into his own head again while she was absent. But she shook herself and stuck to her resolve. She couldn't fix all Jonah's problems with sex. Most of them, she thought with a self-satisfied wriggle, but not all.

She recognized many of the lunchtime regulars now and was relying on their goodwill to make her experiment work. She made the patties herself and in a burst of joie de vivre, added a pinch of the seasoning to the ketchup dish she'd also introduced instead of dumping a plastic bottle on the table.

Jennie and Bethany looked at the plates, looked at her as she hovered over them, shrugged, and took the plates out.

Laurel held the swing door ajar and spied on the results, her heart pounding through her chest. This wasn't a little dish of salad that the customer could ignore, or a lamb chop they could choose not to choose. This was a Sullivan's staple, a good ol' American burger. With cheese. Which she'd also switched out for swiss, although she'd at least given them the option of sticking to that disgusting yellow processed stuff most of the country was so inexplicably hooked on.

Two guys sitting in the front of the restaurant were the first to try the meal, two Realtors who worked across the street, under Jonah's apartment.

The men flipped their ties over their shoulders, tucked a few paper napkins in their shirts, and dug in. Laurel clutched the edge of the door. The first man took a giant bite of roll, cheese, shaved truffle and seasoned burger—and made a face.

"What's wrong?" she imagined the other man asking. Could she learn lip reading in one second? She really wished she didn't have to guess what they said.

"It tastes... funny," she thought she heard. The other guy had eaten a couple of fries first and so hadn't gotten to his burger. Now he looked at it as if it were about to bite him.

"Funny?"

"Yeah... kind of..."

Musty. Laurel sighed, her hopes sinking. She knew what

some people said about truffles. That they tasted how they looked—like muddy balls of dirt and mold. They were so much more than that, once they got to know them, but…

Too soon. She held her stomach against a twist of disappointment and remorse. *And too much.*

It was that damn jar of seasoning. It had smelled so good. It had reminded her of all that she'd learned and experienced at the restaurants where she'd worked in the city, where difference was celebrated, where the same old same old would get you fired.

She hadn't tested it on the staff, like she'd promised. She hadn't even tested it on Jonah. Or Sadie. Or anyone. She'd just plowed ahead, so damned sure that she was right and everyone else was wrong.

"Behind you," Bethany said, and Laurel melted back into the kitchen. She couldn't face the crew in there, so she sat on the stairs leading to the family apartment and hid her face in her hands.

Within about a minute, Bethany was back. "Is Laurel around?" she asked the room in general.

Laurel took her hands away. She hadn't been crying, just hiding from her own stubbornness. She came down the stairs. "I'm right here."

"Table two didn't like this," Bethany said, holding out the offending plates. Each burger had only one bite taken out of it. Even the fries had hardly been touched.

Laurel gave a big sigh and mentally kicked herself again.

"That's fine. Miguel, can you make them up a patty the usual way?" Miguel went straight to the refrigerator and pulled out the freshly-ground chuck. At least the quality of the meat was good in the first place.

"Apologize to them, please," she said to Bethany, "and offer them a free dessert."

"Man," Bethany said. "You must really feel bad."

"Just this once," Laurel swore, thinking of the half-dozen patties she had ready to go and figuring she was going to be getting a lot of iron in the next few days. Not to mention the crow *she* was going to have to eat if Jonah or her mom found out about this.

Chapter Nineteen

Laurel had said she was so pooped from cleaning up the yard and her full day in the bar that she hadn't slept at Jonah's in four days. Jonah had tried to convince himself that she was telling the truth, and that she wasn't running as far and as fast from him as possible, after what he'd told her about his so-called family.

Still, after fighting with himself for four days, he got up early on Wednesday morning and brought two mugs of coffee across the street. If the kitchen door was locked, he wouldn't ask her to stay anymore. He needed to figure out his own shit like a grown man, not rely on the kind of emotional backup she'd provided the night he'd met Lucas.

The door was unlocked. But when he pushed it with his forearm, making sure he didn't spill her coffee, the kitchen was empty. The door to the bar was open, and there was the unmistakable scent of baking coming from one of the ovens. Cookies, he guessed. She had to be nearby, then. Maybe in the bar. The door he'd sworn never to walk through again.

He moved across the room, past the stools where she'd

hugged him, around the counter where they'd made such delicious, and dangerous, love the other night, and past the griddle where she'd made his omelet. Laurel was everything about this room. If she hadn't been his favorite chef before now, her care of him over the last few weeks would confirm it.

The door to the bar was held open with a wedge, and he could feel a breeze as he approached it. He heard a strange hissing noise coming from his left, on the other side of the wall, followed by a curse, and the sound of a spray can being shaken.

Jonah reached back to his memory of the bar. Where would the patio be? He didn't remember ever seeing it open.

He walked through the swing door and around the corner, and saw a door that opened up beyond the restrooms. The chilly October day was sweeping past him, and the spraying noise had resumed. He followed it and stepped out into the courtyard.

It was about twenty feet square and tucked into a corner of the building, with the restrooms along one side and the kitchen on the other. A stockade fence in need of serious TLC closed in the other two sides. The lower portions of the fence were darker than the tops, as though something had been growing up them and had recently been pulled down. Café tables and chairs were standing or leaning in various stages of disrepair all over the crooked flagstone floor.

The sun was hardly up and dark shadows sliced the area,

hiding Laurel from him at first. Then he spotted her, in one corner, standing on old cardboard, spray-painting a metal chair black. The wind was whipping around the yard, and as Jonah walked closer, he saw Laurel's cursing coincided with specks of black paint she now sported on her white long-sleeved shirt and skinny jeans. Skinny jeans which, he couldn't help notice, hugged her curvy butt beautifully as she bent over to spray a chair.

"Hey," he said.

"Argh!"

She screamed, jumped a foot and dropped the can. He had misjudged how much the shadows would hide him from her.

But it was still funny. Jonah laughed and raised the coffee mugs. "Don't kill me. I bring coffee."

Laurel looked slightly mollified. She stretched her arms over her head—making her breasts jostle most appealingly beneath her shirt—and groaned. "The damn wind keeps blowing the paint in my face."

He handed her a mug and noted the black flecks which had, indeed, added to her freckles. "They suit you."

"Shut up." She pushed him, and Jonah pretended to fall backward.

But Laurel got the last laugh, because his clowning made him spill hot coffee on his hand. "Shit!" he exclaimed, switching hands and sucking the burned area.

"Oh, I'm sorry." She didn't look particularly sorry, especially when she took his hand and sucked the spot herself.

The light pressure of her lips on his skin stole his breath. Jonah stayed very still, feeling every brush of hers with every nerve ending he had. Then her tongue flicked out, tasting the coffee, and she gently laughed as her eyes darted up to take in his expression.

He could throw the mugs against the fence, pull her into his arms, and take her right here on the uneven floor. Or he could stay exactly where he was, loving the feel of her, vibrating with his longing, knowing she knew what she did to him and loved it in her turn. When she finally let go, he wanted to whimper in pain, but to thank her for such a simple pleasure.

Laurel straightened up and took a sip of her coffee as if nothing had happened. Jonah's hand was still buzzing. "So?" she said.

"What?" He almost shook out his hand.

"What are you doing here?"

Jonah couldn't remember. "Let's just… drink our coffee a while," he said.

"Okay." Laurel gave him an impudent smile, glanced at his jeans and back up again. "I'll wait until you can walk again."

Jonah shifted position. Of course he was turned on. Jesus, the woman had licked him! What red-blooded male could stay cool after that? It didn't matter that she smelled of spray paint. And had he mentioned how her breasts jostled against each other when she moved? He swallowed hard. "Next time, warn me before you lick me."

Laurel laughed. "No."

"I knew you'd say that. How's it going out here?" he added, to distract himself.

"Worse than I expected. Dad closed it up for the winter years ago, and never got around to opening it again. It was around the time the leather factory shut, so we lost a bunch of customers."

His blood cooling now, Jonah leaned against one of the tables. "Is this part of your rebranding?"

She brought herself to her full height. "Are you going to give me more shit about trying to get new customers in?"

He held up his hands, pacifying her. "No! I was just asking. I think it's a great idea. Square footage like this is rare in the middle of town." He gauged her ability to take a suggestion. "It might rain on the day."

She sighed. "I know it might. And we might get the fire department and the emergency squad and no one else, and I'll have made hundreds of hors d'oeuvres for nothing. And I'll pay the evening and the morning shift to come in to help out, and they'll be sitting here twiddling their thumbs." Her shoulders slumped. "I don't know what I was thinking."

Jonah looked around at the space with new eyes. "So this is all for Matt?"

"No. Well, yes, because I'm sorry, Jonah, but he *is* a hero and just because you're mad at him for something that's not his—"

"I know, I know." He stopped her, but circled his hand in front of him. "Move on—like I'm trying to."

"Okay. Then I'm doing it for me. For the bar. I need customers, and Matt is a draw. If I open up the front windows—"

"The front windows open?"

"They're supposed to. There's a picture on the wall in the bar of the whole front of the bar opened up to the street. Must have been back in the sixties, when the factories were still open. St. Paddy's Day, I reckon." Her eyes widened. "Oh, my God! St. Paddy's Day! We have to push all the boats out for that one." He watched her brain whiz through the possibilities. "Super Bowl. July fourth. Halloween—no, that's too soon before Matt's thing, but if we could make it a party kind of place for the town, make ourselves a destination…"

"It sounds great," he said. "I can see… it could really open up the bar for you. And keep the community involved. You need the fire department and the EMT guys."

"I know I do. And besides." She finished her coffee and plunked it down on the table. "I *want* them there. I like them. Admire them, and all that."

"Then you are going to love Matt." Had a small sigh escaped him? *That was pretty pathetic, Jonah.* "He's got that cute Latino thing going on, on top of the army medals. Plus, he's *happy*."

"You sound jealous."

She was smirking at him. Jonah grunted. Hell, yeah, he was jealous. Laurel and Matt could easily take a fancy to each other, and then where would Jonah be?

Before he could talk himself out of this train of thought, her hand slid over his forearm and up to rest on his shoulder. Laurel had gotten a lot closer to him. Her chest and stomach brushed against his, and she looked into his face with that teasing smile still on hers. "Don't worry, Dr. Jung. I don't look at a man unless he's got a PhD after his name."

She was so close now. He smelled coffee and cookie dough. He could kiss her, but he had to be fair. "Matt's smart. Just not book smart."

"Would you shut up about your brother for one freaking second, you idiot? I'm angling for a kiss, here."

That was all the invitation he needed. Lowering his face the last inch, he took her lips, cool from the fall air and warm from the coffee, and tasted every inch of them. Then, when she gave a little groan and a gasp that released him, he moved on to her jaw and her cheeks, kissing wherever there wasn't a black freckle of paint.

"You'll get a mouthful of Krylon," she murmured. The table she was leaning on shifted backward with a loud scrape as he moved down to her neck.

"Don't care." He buzzed against her skin. With her head to one side, he could access that sweet, warm spot where her neck became her chest and he gave it his full attention, his tongue darting out to sear the place she revealed to him. The table scratched against the patio again.

"*Laurel!*"

The high, horrified word echoed around the yard. Laurel pushed on his chest, hard, and Jonah backed off. They both looked up to the source of the voice.

To his considerable discomfort, her mother was glaring at them from an open window. Dammit. Where was an umbrella when he needed one?

"What are you doing with *Jonah Gardiner* in *my yard* at *seven o'clock in the morning?*" Gail spluttered from the second-floor apartment.

Jonah dropped his hands from around Laurel's waist, but she stopped him, holding one of his firmly in hers and shouting back up to the window, "I'm kissing him, Mother!"

Her honesty and bravado apparently flummoxed Gail out of all proportion. Mouth gaping, she took a couple of ragged breaths, her hand at her neck, before she gasped out, "I could see that, Laurel! What is he doing here?"

Okay, if Laurel could be brave and not feel like an eighteen-year-old caught necking, he could too. To Laurel, he said in a low voice, "I guess no one told her about us yet."

"I thought your mom would. She came over the other day."

"Did she? Good." He looked up at the window. "Good morning, Mrs. Moore," he called up.

"Don't talk to me!" Gail snapped at him. "I told you not

to go anywhere near her! You see, Laurel! They're all the same!"

"I asked him to kiss me, Mother," Laurel went on. "And then some, if you must know."

Jonah's cheeks burned. Was this how it was going to be? Anyone he'd met while running errands around town had given him a knowing look over the weekend, proving that Helene had done her job of telling everyone in a ten-mile radius. But the reality of Gail knowing, as well as the whole town, made him not know where to look.

"And stop calling me 'Mother' like I'm the one being unreasonable!" Gail's gray-blonde hair was falling around her face. She looked… terrified.

Jonah couldn't let Laurel do all the explaining. "Things are very different now, Mrs. Moore—"

"I told you to stop talking!" she shouted, in much the same way Laurel might do if she were pissed at him. "And what's that burning smell coming up the stairs?"

That changed Laurel's calm rebellion. "Oh, shit, the cookies!"

She let go of Jonah and ran through the open door to the kitchen. Jonah looked one more time at the mess in the yard, then up at her mother who was giving him the gimlet eye and seemed to be winding up for another pitch. Handling a tray of burning cookies sounded safer.

The kitchen wasn't full of smoke, as he expected, but in its closed atmosphere he could definitely smell burned cookies. Laurel had pulled out two trays of singed... somethings, and was grabbing at another one, cursing all the way.

Chocolate chip. Hell of a shame. "Can any be saved?"

"No! Look at them!" She slammed the last tray down on the stainless-steel counter, and Jonah saw defeat in the set of her shoulders. "Now there's no fresh dessert for this afternoon."

He didn't know how to make it better for her. What he wanted to say was that she was doing too much, working on the yard and still baking, and taking on the catering for a whole party by herself. He didn't need his doctorate, however, to know telling her this right now would get him a swift kick out of the door, and he'd have earned it.

Instead, he said, "I have an hour or so before I have to leave for work. I can go change and come back and help with the spray-painting. It's a good, dry day today. We should work on it while the weather holds."

It worked. Her face brightened and she gripped his arm again, though this time in relief, not passion. "Really? You have time? I didn't ask because I know you have clients all day, but there's so much to work on. And each one of those damn tables takes so much paint..."

He squeezed the hand that held him, said, "Be right back." He almost ran across the street.

GAIL CAME DOWN just as he was disappearing out of the door. "Has he gone? Good."

"He's coming back. He's going to *help* me. Which is more than I can say for some people," Laurel retorted, still sore over the cookies and that Gail had given her such a hard time for resurrecting the yard in the first place.

"I can't believe you'd let that man into your life, knowing his history—and his father's history!"

That brought Laurel's head up fast. What could Gail know already, when Jonah had only just found out? But she just meant Pam's experience with Peter. Laurel relaxed again. She poked disconsolately at a burnt cookie. "What did Pam tell you about Peter?"

"That he was all charming until they were married. That was when she realized how much he drank—they didn't live together before they got married, so she had no idea. And he ignored her and Jonah most of the time and when he did come home he was either silent or verbally abusive." Gail paused so the words echoed around the kitchen. "And then he came home less and less, until he finally confessed that he'd been seeing that Mariah."

Laurel wished she hadn't asked. It had been an intrusive question and her nosy side had asked it before remembering that if anyone should tell her about his childhood, it should be Jonah.

Gail took her silence for capitulation. "Is that the kind of man you want in your life, Laurel? Is that what you want for your children?"

"Mom!" The spell was broken. "No one has said anything about children! And Jonah, I'll say it again, is not his father! I thought Pam was your friend! How could you think that about her son?"

Gail sniffed. "Pam agrees with me."

Then Laurel remembered Pam's words at the consignment store. *Jonah will chew you up and spit you out, and I'm saying that as his mother.*

Pam's dismissiveness of her own son robbed Laurel of breath and with her body still zinging from Jonah's kiss, and her appreciation that he'd promised to come back and help, Laurel said, "Mother. I am seeing Jonah Gardiner. I am sleeping with him." Gail winced and opened her mouth, but Laurel talked over her. "He's a better man now than he's ever been, despite being abandoned by his father and, I'm sorry to say it since she's your friend, by a mother who's done nothing but make him feel bad about himself his whole life. I'm not going to stop seeing him for you or anyone. All right?"

Gail's cheeks flushed red, and Laurel steeled herself for a full-blown tantrum.

But it didn't come. "I suppose you *are* thirty years old. I can't tell you what to do anymore," Gail said with a sigh. "I can warn you he's going to break your heart, for all the reasons you just told me, but I suppose you won't hear it if I do."

"No, I won't," Laurel said stoutly, though a tiny voice in her head repeated the warning. "Now I have to go back and finish those chairs before the staff arrives."

Gail twisted to look at the open kitchen door to the bar, and the hallway to the garden. "What are you trying to do out there, anyway?"

"You want to come see?"

Laurel held her breath.

Gail stared at the blank wall beside the door for a second, then said, "All right."

JONAH CAME BACK to an empty kitchen, but he could hear voices through the open door. He slipped around the corner and into the dark hallway that led to the garden. But he stopped before stepping into the morning sun.

Laurel and her mother were standing at the fence, looking down at the ruined flowerbeds. Gail was talking and Laurel, one hand holding her up at the fence, her head bent to hear her mother better, was listening and nodding. Gail crouched down and picked up a handful of the dirt that spilled over the narrow raised bed. "What do you do with the food scraps?" she said. "The vegetable peelings?"

He watched Laurel wince. "Throw them away."

Gail tutted and brushed her hand against the other. "Let's get a composter and make some use of them. Doesn't have to be a big one, and we could keep it in the alley behind

Chapter Twenty

LAUREL PUSHED OPEN the screen door that led into the farmer's market's barn. Warm air from a heater welcomed her—Upstate New York was firmly in October and the temperature had trouble making it out of the forties.

A little behind her, and blinking as though she were just waking up, stepped her mother. This was the first trip Laurel had been able to convince her to take since Frank's death. Laurel suspected Gail had come because it would mean Jonah was definitely *not* with Laurel for a few hours.

"Hey!" Sadie called from the register. "How's it going?"

"Good." Eschewing the chance to browse the displays between the door and the cash register, Laurel went over to say hi. "This is my mother, Gail. Mom, Sadie runs the market."

Sadie shook hands with Gail, then turned back to Laurel. "Haven't seen you for a few days."

"I know. I had to hunker down a little with the menu. We've got a big party coming up and I've been concentrating on sprucing up the bar."

the garbage."

"Compost takes years to make, doesn't it?"

"So?" Gail straightened; at her full height she matched Laurel. "You going anywhere?"

Laurel regarded her for a long moment. "No, Mom," she said. "I'm not going anywhere."

Gail put her soil-covered hands around Laurel's middle, and they hugged.

Jonah gave them a few moments, then stepped into the yard. Without saying anything, he went to the area where Laurel had been working before and picked up a can of spray paint. Out of the corner of his eye, he saw Gail break the hug and look at him, so he smiled at her but didn't speak, and got to his job. Laurel stayed with her mother and they worked separately but in a delicate truce for the hour he had before work.

Laurel kissed him goodbye, keeping the kiss chaste but obviously determined not to hide from her mother anymore. Leaving her in the yard, Jonah found Gail walking with him through the hallway.

She scowled at him. Feeling he couldn't keep quiet anymore, he said, "Believe me, Mrs. Moore. I'm aware of how lucky I am to have Laurel even look at me."

Gail's face softened and her shoulders stopped poking at him like weapons. "As long as you remember that, I guess we'll be okay."

"I will," he promised, and left them to their day.

She didn't look at Gail while she said this. Gail had not been happy with some of the editing of the decorations Laurel had made.

"Ooh!" Sadie fluttered her eyelashes. "Big party? Am I invited?"

"Of course." Laurel laughed. "I could use a friendly face." She told Sadie about Matt coming home.

"Don't know him," Sadie said. "We only came here about five years ago."

"Well, you're still welcome. In fact, I'd be happy to put a sign in the bar, if you can help me out with some local ingredients for the menu."

"What are you planning on serving to all the town? And do you want some apple cider?" She already had her hand on the Crock-Pot that had been sending a sweet, delicious smell over to Laurel the whole time.

"Sure, thanks."

"Gail?"

"Oh." Gail looked as though she really couldn't decide.

"I'll just put it here. You can have it if you want it," Sadie said with an empathetic warmth to her tone.

Laurel propped an elbow on the counter and they started talking turkey—and corn, butternut squash, sausage, pies, and cookies. After a few moments, Gail picked up the paper cup of hot cider, and drifted off to the house plants. The next thing Laurel knew, she was through the back doors and in the small greenhouse.

Taking advantage of her absence, Laurel confessed to Sadie, "I think I bit off way more than I can chew, and the way the fire department and emergency squad have been advertising all over Facebook, the whole town's going to be there. And Mom's not happy with any changes to the bar."

"Yeah. I can see that would be hard." Sadie's face reflected her sympathy. "But the changes will keep the bar going, right? She knows it's in trouble?"

"Knowing and accepting are two different things." They both looked in the direction Gail had gone.

Sadie sighed and went back at the list they'd been making. "You'll have to cap the dining to however many tables you have."

"What would you think of making the whole menu a sharing, finger-food kind of thing? Charge a cover for the party—not including drinks—and give everyone a taste of what I'm trying to do? Then each order gets the same thing, we don't have to restrict it to tables, and I can close for dinner that night."

"You'll have to make sure you keep a balance between the familiar and the new," Sadie warned.

"Don't I know it." Laurel winced, remembering the burgers. She'd hidden the jar of truffle spice in the back of one of her mother's kitchen cupboards, unable to face it again. "Some of the town is looking for me to fail. For the bar to go back to the way it was when my father ran it. Which will kill it." Her eyes slid to the greenhouse again.

Sadie reached her hand across the counter to squeeze Laurel's shoulder. "One crisis at a time. You studied for this kind of thing. You know how much is too much. And if you run out of food, you run out of food. They can still drink, can't they?"

"Yeah. That we'll have plenty of. Oh, and I forgot—we're giving a portion back to the first aid and fire departments."

Sadie threw up her hands. "Then don't worry about it! That's a bunch of good will, right there. Hey, I have a little whisky in the back. You want me to spruce up your cider?"

Laurel laughed and shook her head. "No, thanks. I have more errands to run. Which is the other thing I want to ask you about." She waved at the front of the store. "Decorations. Specifically, mums, and whatever goes with mums."

"Sure!"

"I need a lot of them. We have sixty linear feet of flowerbed to fill. That's why I brought my mom. She was always the gardener in the family."

"Oh, I'm awesome with mothers!" Sadie slapped the counter. "We can get you whatever you want, and I'll tell you what, you can have it wholesale. Since you'll be advertising us and all."

Laurel let out a breath she hadn't realized she'd been holding. "Oh, that'd be great. I was really kind of hoping you'd say that! This is all going on my credit card and…"

"Say no more." Sadie unclipped the walkie-talkie at her

belt and talked into it. "Paul! Come cover the front, 'kay?" A man came through the front door and Sadie came out from behind the counter. Taking Laurel's arm, she propelled her out of the door and in seconds she'd found Gail, who was gazing at a shelf of thick ferns.

"We used to have these in the bar," Gail said unexpectedly as they approached. "I'd make baskets and put them out front in the summer, and in the winter, we'd hang them from the ceiling to help the air."

Laurel hardly dared breathe. Gail hadn't volunteered that kind of information in weeks.

"Not that it helped the air much, back then, with everyone smoking, but they did look pretty."

"That's what the hooks in the ceiling were for!" Laurel said. "I wondered why they were all out of the way."

"People's morale is improved by house plants," Sadie nodded. "It's a scientific fact."

"We couldn't afford the luxury," Gail said, "in the end."

Sadie drooped a little, but rallied. "Well, it sounds like you're focusing on the patio for the fall, and that's a great idea. Not so much commitment and everyone'll be bundled up against the cold. Oh! You wanna hire a couple of those outdoor heaters?"

"Yes!" That had been another thing on Laurel's list. "You know where I can find some?"

"The farm that we get our pumpkins from has them for their haunted hayride. I'm sure they'll lend you a couple for one afternoon. Now, Gail, these celosias, they give a great contrast to the mums, don't you think? And you might want some greenery, too. Check out this croton…" She held up a large houseplant with bright yellow and green leaves so Gail could caress the foliage.

Laurel's head reeled as she tried to remember everything. But there was no denying that this was Gail's happy place, and despite the small amount of stock on hand, Gail had an eye for variety. Ten minutes later, the Expedition's axles were groaning with as many chrysanthemums and croton as it could carry, and Gail had a small—very small—smile on her face.

PAM CAME TO the point so fast when she opened the door to Jonah that Friday night, he took a step back.

"The party at Sullivan's is for Matthias," she said, advancing on him with a finger pointed at his chest.

Jonah wished he could take another step back, right off the porch and back to the safety of his apartment. But he could only tell the truth. "Yes. Laurel heard the squad talking about him and offered them the space."

"Why didn't you tell me this before?"

"Because…" He looked at the floor, where he'd instinctively removed his shoes, despite his mother's verbal assault. "Because I didn't want you to have another reason not to visit Gail."

Pam shook her head, her long, sleek hair showing more of its gray hairs in the bright light of the hallway. "Since when did you care so much whether I visit Gail?" Then he saw the unwelcome penny drop. "You care about Laurel. That's why."

He rolled his eyes, hoping he was conveying an indifference he didn't feel. Time to change the subject. "How did you know about the party being for Matt?"

Distraction achieved. Her eyes slid away from his. "I went to see Gail. Yes," she snapped, before he could say anything, "like you told me to!"

"I'm glad, Mom. How did it go?"

"Fine." Her voice was still caustic, but less so. "It went fine. She's my friend." Pam drew her hair down one shoulder again, in the sign Jonah knew she was uneasy. "We talked for a long time. I should have gone sooner."

"Don't beat yourself up, Mom. It wasn't easy for you to go back there, either."

"I knew you'd say that." She squinted up at him. "Once a psychologist…"

"Better than a criminal."

"Anyway," she said, not really listening. "Gail perked up when we talked about gardening. I'll have her over here one evening to look at the last of my Lenten roses. I've been putting potash on them and they're the best I've seen anywhere. Honestly, if I had the time to call them, I'm sure I could get on the cover of *Country Garden*."

Jonah made a noncommittal noise. She never *had* called any of the many places she was sure would love to hear her story.

"Come on in for dinner," she said.

She led him into the kitchen, but her interrogation wasn't done. "I wish you'd told me about the party being for Matt, though. It really blindsided me when Gail mentioned it, and now she thinks she's betraying me by letting Laurel have it."

"You told her she isn't, right?" he said, sitting down at a plate of baked lemon chicken that was drying out in the warm kitchen air.

"Of course." But she chewed her lip. "I think I did. It'll be hard to see everyone making a fuss over him, when they still look at you like you're about to rob a bank."

That's how you look at me, Mom.

Could he say those words out loud? It turned out he couldn't. Not tonight. He had bigger chicken to bake. Looking at the unappetizing food on his plate, he steeled himself to say what he'd come here to say. "Speaking of brothers, let's go in the living room a second."

Pam's face fell. "Oh, God, what?"

"Just… let's sit down."

He gently drew her napkin from her hand and led her into the tiny living room, onto the French blue couch with the faded corners. So much of this house had been a reason for him to hate his life, but now he was almost nostalgic for those days, when it seemed that what he hated and what he loved were so cut and dried.

Where to begin? Keeping both Pam's hands in his, he said, "Dad had another son before me."

Pam's hands froze. "What? No, he didn't. He wasn't married before we met."

"No. But he had another son anyway. He and the mother were never… he…" He wasn't sure if he didn't tell her all of it as a concession to Peter, or because he simply couldn't say the words. "He left her before Lucas was born."

Pam's hands slipped out of his altogether, to hover in front of her open mouth. "He had another… you mean he did this to someone else?"

"Years before he met you. Lucas is forty."

"Lucas…" She tried out the name. "Oh, my God…" She still spoke from behind her hands. Her voice was strangled. "How do you know?"

"I met him the other night. He was giving a lecture. He's a psychologist too. He recognized me. Dad and he have reconciled… to a degree, and Dad told him about us."

"Your father was *there*?"

This was indeed out of character for Peter, who had never come to Jonah's life events. But then again, what did Jonah know about Peter's character? About anything to do with him anymore? "A lot of things have changed."

"You're telling me," she said from behind her hands,

which made Jonah laugh a little. "So you're saying he was a shit *long* before he met me... and that means... that means that it wasn't just me."

Jonah looked harder at her. Big tears swam in her eyes and spilled down her cheeks. "Mom," he said, in anguish. He'd known the news would upset her, but he wasn't prepared for the reality of it.

Now her voice was full of the tears that streamed down her face. "I always wondered... what was wrong with me," she sobbed. "She wasn't as pretty as me, and yet she saved him when I couldn't... But it wasn't just me."

Jonah went to hug her, but Pam, even though she was crying, pushed him away. "No," she said. "Go home, Jonah."

"Mom. I don't want to leave you like this." He hadn't seen her cry since the early days of Peter's desertion.

"I don't want—you to—I have to think," she said between gulps of air. "Please, Joe. Go home."

Did she really need to think, or was she so vain that she didn't even want her son to see her cry? "If you're sure..."

"Go!" She pushed him half off the couch and covered her face, her black hair falling down, around and on her hands, blocking her from him.

Jonah had no choice. He stepped into his shoes in the hallway and looked back through the archway into the living room. Pam hadn't moved.

Chapter Twenty-One

Laurel left Jonah's bed as usual the following Saturday and got to work in the kitchen. At least she didn't have to sneak back upstairs anymore to turn on the coffee machine, pretending she'd just gotten out of her own bed. But this morning was different, because at seven o'clock, Jonah came through the kitchen door.

"What's up?" she asked, kissing him. He'd brought more coffee, which was reason enough in her book for him to be there, but still. His mornings off were precious.

"I came for the key to the front windows," he said. She loved looking up at him like this, his beard at her eye-height, his light blue eyes looking down at her with appreciation and, always, what she might have called confusion. *Yeah, baby. I am the best thing that ever happened to you, and if you can just get out of your own head long enough to realize it, we'll be fine.*

"What for?" she asked, pulling away reluctantly to get the key from the keychain in her purse. "They still don't open. I put it on Junior's cousin's list but he hasn't gotten to it yet."

"It shouldn't be hard," Jonah said. "Just scraping away some of the old paint and debris. You shouldn't have to pay someone else to do it." He took a sip of his coffee and didn't look at her. "Thought I'd give it a try."

Giving up his Saturday morning to help her? That wasn't the action of a man who wanted to keep their relationship physical. Laurel gave in to a swell of hope that made her take in a deep breath. "Well, thanks, Jonah. That'd be awesome, if you can get those suckers to move. Let me show you how they're supposed to work."

"Keep pointing that chest at me like that and we won't get anywhere," he said, smiling now. Of course Laurel "wasted" a couple of minutes pressing against him, running her hands through his hair and kissing the crap out of him, Jonah laughing and kissing her back.

An hour later she went to check on him and he had the first window unstuck and open to the chilly October morning. A toolbox stood next to him as well as a broom, a wire brush, and a dustpan. He was covered in flecks of black paint and held a utility knife, which he used to scrape down the cracks between the window frames.

"Muffin?" she said.

Jonah turned and wiped his face with his shirt, which deposited more flakes of paint on him than removed them. She giggled and held out a plate. "I can't believe it's working."

"Just elbow grease and a bit of time," he said, stepping

through the freed window into the bar, where he'd left his sweater. Laurel followed him to get out of the wind, which didn't seem to bother Jonah. He was sweating lightly, she assumed from pushing and shoving the window open. When he wiped his hands on his sweater before taking a muffin, she watched the play of muscles in his arms and withheld a sigh.

Again, by brute strength and the willingness to take the time, Jonah had saved her time and money, and shown he cared. Laurel's chest swelled again, this time with a little fear. The last time she'd loved him this much, he'd let her down and she'd had to push him away. There was no way history would repeat itself, was there?

WHEN THEY OPENED for lunch service, Laurel went to the front with a roast beef sandwich and a glass of ice water. But Jonah wasn't there. In fact, it looked as though he'd never been there. The windows were closed up tight again, the debris removed, the sidewalk in front of the bar cleaner than even her staff could make it. But when she looked closely at the cracks between the panels, she could tell that he had, indeed, broken through all the old black paint and the windows now worked.

But where was he? She walked through the bar, plate and glass in hand, but didn't see him talking to the staff there or taking a load off at one of the tables. Out back, on the patio, she heard voices and laughter, so she followed them.

Jonah was in the back, his shirt removed, his chest glistening with sweat, tattoos on full display, wearing a thick pair of gloves she didn't know he'd had, helping the workers out there lift the bluestone pavers so others could pour gravel under them. The flowerbeds were lined with the pavers and a gate in the back of the fence was open, revealing a truck parked in the street behind Sullivan's and some industrial pieces of equipment Laurel couldn't name.

Those pavers were at least an inch thick, and judging by Jonah's sweat and the way two men had to lift them and carefully place them on their edges around the patio, heavy as hell. But he kept going, laughing and joking with other workers, friends of Miguel supervised by Junior's uncle, in Spanish and English. She vaguely noticed that Brett was there, too, but she only had eyes for Jonah, his wiry biceps and shoulder muscles popping every time he lifted a stone.

Laurel had to stand in the shadow of the doorway for a moment, his lunch threatening to fall from her numb hands. She'd planned on bringing a whole platter of sandwiches out to the others, and now here she was, stuck with one plate and a melting in her loins and a hyper-focus on one man in ten in the yard. She leaned on the doorframe and stared. Jesus, he was hot. No one had ever said he wasn't, but now he was hot *and* helping her. How else was a girl supposed to react?

He saw her first, happening to look in her direction and

seeing her white chef's jacket in the shadows. "Laurel!" he called.

She waved with the glass holding the water and he loped over to her. *Oh, Jesus, don't come over here.* She wanted to lick him.

"Is that for me?" he asked.

Oh yeah, baby. All of it. "Um, yeah," she said, looking up at him. "I have a round of sandwiches for everyone else."

He took the plate from her. "I'll help you bring it out. Let me just clean up a little."

From this close, she could see he was covered in fine dust. It was caught in his beard and whitened his cheeks and tattoos. His T-shirt was stuck in the back of his belt. *Okay, maybe I don't want to lick him so much anymore. But giving him a long shower sounds pretty good.*

Jonah turned left into the men's room, giving her a small smile that said, "See you in a minute," but Laurel wasn't about to let the chance to see him wash go that easy. She followed him in.

"Hey!" he laughed. "This is the men's room!"

"It's my men's room, and it's empty," she pointed out.

"Don't touch me!" he said, holding out his hands. "You'll get dirty."

"You have no idea," she replied, unbuttoning her chef's jacket. When she got it off she laid it on the sink counter and wrapped her arms around his sweaty, dusty, hot torso.

Jonah got with the program fast. He put his arms around

her waist and squeezed, almost lifting her off her feet.

"Oof," she said. "You're strong."

"You're soft," he answered. Then she could have sworn, through the dust, he blushed.

"You're something else, Lor," he said. "I don't even want to kiss you. That gravel dust gets everywhere." He smacked his lips to demonstrate.

Laurel put out a hand to turn on the tap and wet her fingers before running them over his mouth. Jonah moaned but kept his mouth shut. With more water she cleaned off the worst of the dust on his beard. She always had loved the way it looked with water dripping off it. And now she got to watch it drip down onto his chest. She washed each tattoo, the tangle of vines on his arms and shoulders with their thorns and roses, showing a contradiction she wasn't sure even he understood, before turning him around to those on his back—logos of My Chemical Romance and Linkin Park that didn't seem to go with the artistry of the ones on his arms. Well, the bands had certainly shown emotion, so maybe their tattoos were a good thing.

She turned him back around and got one more scoop to caress his neck and collarbone before Jonah groaned more loudly, said, "Fuck it," and kissed her.

Her T-shirt was instantly soaked, and a customer could come in any minute, but who cared? The man she loved was powerless before her. What more could any woman want?

After some really hot kissing and grabbing of asses, abs

and breasts, however, Jonah pushed her gently away. "Come on," he pleaded. "We've caused enough of a stir as it is. You have a room full of customers, and I have to finish up and go check on my mom."

Laurel sighed and backed up. "Way to ruin the mood, Jonah. Mention your mom, why don't you?"

"She took the news of Lucas hard. She hasn't replied to any of my calls, and I'm worried about her."

"Isn't she working today?"

"I called there. They said she's been off sick."

Laurel sighed again. "Okay, then. I guess you'd better go."

"I'll eat my sandwich first. And help you with the others' lunch. They got the luckiest gig in town, being fed by you."

"Thank you, but you're only partly forgiven." She rearranged her T-shirt, brushed off some of the dust he'd transferred to her, and put her chef's jacket back on. "You'd better make this up to me tonight."

"Promise," he said, kissing her one last time and opening the door.

K<small>NOWING</small> J<small>ONAH HAD</small> gone to his mother's helped Laurel get back to business. She had prepared a menu for the party that would capture the season and the variety of local farms surrounding Tanner and Boon, but give the customers familiar flavors that would make them come back another day. Every finger food or hors d'oeuvre she created was a direction she wanted to take the menu in, with a fresh take on spices or a quirky mix of savory and sweet that she loved. If she never saw another frozen breaded chicken breast, she would be quite content, but she had listened to Jonah and the others, and knew she wouldn't be able to just start over.

One or two things still rankled with her, however, and those things walked into the bar for a late lunch that afternoon.

Laurel was a good chef. She knew this as surely as she knew she loved Zumba and her body might not be what society accepted, but was strong and capable and womanly. So knowing even one person had come into her restaurant and eaten something they didn't love had bothered the crap out of her all week.

The two Realtors worked strange hours like she did, so she wasn't surprised when they came in at two o'clock, talking about the showings they'd done that morning. They sat in their usual spot by the front windows and Daniel, their server, took their drink order. Laurel watched it all from the swing door and waylaid Daniel before he could take their beers over. "Let me," she said. Daniel raised his eyebrows in surprise, but handed her the tray.

Having run the bar for almost two months now, Laurel was pretty sure all the regular customers knew her, but she was still glad to be wearing her chef's whites as she approached their table. "Hi," she said, smiling at their wide eyes as she put down their drinks. "Who had the Oktoberfest?"

The blond one recovered first. "Me."

"Great. That makes you the pale ale." The men nodded their thanks but didn't make a move toward their drinks.

"Can I talk to you for a moment?" she went on. They nodded again, their eyes still wary. They'd remembered the burgers and the fact that she'd probably cooked them. They might be thinking she was here to give them a hard time for sending them back.

Laurel pulled a chair over from another table and sat down, not too close to their table but enough to make the conversation easier. "This week you guys were kind enough to be my guinea pigs for a new recipe."

Now both men were avoiding her eyes. Laurel went on quickly, "A bad recipe, it turned out—okay, not *bad*, but not what you were expecting and perhaps not what we should be serving here. Am I somewhere near the truth?"

Her honesty made both men stare at her. The blond one said, "Not what we were expecting, no."

"Well, I'd like to make up for it."

"You did," the dark-haired one said. "The burgers we got the second time were great. And we got dessert."

"Yes, but I don't want you to leave here thinking that everything's changing and our best customers aren't being consulted. Could I bring you over a small taster plate of what we'd like to serve at the party next week? On the house."

The men glanced at each other and then back at her. Laurel held her breath. She was counting on their natural arrogance to make them believe she needed their, and only their, opinion.

She got it. "Sure," the dark-haired one said.

"Great! Go ahead and figure out what you'd like for lunch, and I'll get you the plate in just a second."

She hurried into the back and put together a tray of two different soup shots, the lamb chops she'd made for Jonah, a square of sausage and sweet potato bake, a mushroom and Gruyere tart, and a twist on green bean casserole made with puff pastry and caramelized onions.

"Here you go," she said, putting the tray in the middle of their table with a flourish. "Enjoy. I'll send Daniel over to get your lunch order."

Much as she was dying to hover over them to gauge their reaction, Laurel forced herself back into the kitchen, where she stood at the door and once again tried to lip read.

"Do we get to eat those, too?" Annie, the weekend lunch chef, asked behind her.

"Yes, please." Laurel had left all the prepared food out on purpose. "Everyone, please try something as you go past it." But her eyes hadn't left the sliver of gap in the door, watching the two professionals—part of the future of the bar—she most wanted to impress.

She saw appreciative looks on their faces, and they certainly ate everything, except the mushroom tart. What was it with these men and fungi? Daniel brought the tray back with an encouraging smile and took three of the menu items she'd left on the counter before going back outside. "Mmmf," he said, his mouth full. "Sausage 'n' sweet 'tato. Killer."

"Good," Laurel said firmly, though what she wanted to say was, "Oh, thank God. Thank you. I love you." But she was still the boss, and showing a lack of faith in her cooking wouldn't exactly rally the troops before the big party.

When the Realtors had finished their main course, Laurel went back out. "So?" she said.

"Excellent," the blond said. "That's what the menu's going to be from now on? Count us in."

"I'm so glad." She smiled, though inside she fist-pumped the air. "We'll still have your burgers, don't worry, and many of the other things that made people love Sullivan's in the first place"—*though no more goddamn mozzarella sticks*—"but it'll all be local, New York State-grown food and I promise you, it'll put Tanner on the map."

"We'll be sure to add you to our list of town restaurants," the brunette said. "And if you ever want to expand…" He whipped out his business card.

"Hey!" the blond laughed. "No fair!"

"Snooze, you lose, buddy," the first man said.

"It's okay," Laurel assured the blond. "The Moores have been Sullivan's, and Sullivan's has been on this corner, for decades. We're not going anywhere."

THAT NIGHT, LAUREL kept an eye out for a few of the old-time regulars and gave them the same dish she'd given the young men. But this time, she added more to the sample plate, and also gave them their main course on the house. Later on, they'd ask their server to pack the main course up so that they could have a free meal the next day.

She hovered more closely and listened to them talk about the area, gave them details of where the food had come from, and listened to the stories about how the town had changed through the decades. These stories inevitably led to reminiscences about Frank's life. No one mentioned his habit. Everyone talked about his good heart, his compassion for his regulars, and his lack of bitterness when they began to leave Sullivan's.

Each telling eased Laurel's heart a little. She could begin to move away from all the pains of bad memory, and begin to let in the good memories of Frank that were reflected in the good things she needed to keep at the restaurant.

"Sully'd be so proud of you," Terry said. He was wearing an old auto parts baseball hat and a jacket with ground-in mud on the elbows. His dirty pale skin made her believe he was in the habit of rubbing car oil into it.

"Always was," added Bruno, a black man with a grizzled beard, his checked collar frayed under his padded vest.

"Thank you," Laurel said, not hiding the tears their stories had brought to her eyes. "It means a lot for you to tell me that." But she still had work to do, and the tears didn't fall. "What kind of food would *you* like us to serve?" she asked the old-timers.

"The chicken and fries basket is good," Terry said.

It would be, if the chicken were freshly breaded. "How about if we used panko breading?" she suggested. "And a little Asian slaw and a soy sauce dip on the side?"

"Is Asian slaw like regular slaw?" Terry asked, looking skeptical.

"Basically. How about if I make it one day, and you guys can be my taste testers again?"

They nodded. Laurel beamed.

That night she found her copy of *Nobody's Fool* and re-read the ending. She'd forgotten something about it. Sully had indeed had no job, no money, and a bum knee, but he'd had a family. A community. Slightly beaten and not very pretty from the outside, perhaps, but a community nonetheless. Something Laurel could be a part of, if she worked hard enough.

Seeing the big picture for the first time, she felt more optimistic than she had since Frank had died.

Chapter Twenty-Two

JONAH DROVE TO his mother's house. He hadn't called first, afraid she'd keep him off with some excuse if he gave her a chance. He knocked on the faded front door and waited for her to see him through the high window panes in it.

There was a pause while her shadow hovered behind the door. "Mom," he pleaded.

"All right," she said, unlocking and opening the door. "I suppose you'll just keep coming back if I don't let you hassle me now."

"*Worry* about you," he corrected, following her into the kitchen. "It was a lot to take in, the other day. I wanted to see if you'd processed it all yet."

"Jesus, Jonah," Pam snapped, taking a bag of coffee out of the freezer. "Could you not talk like what you are for once?"

Jonah laughed and sank into a kitchen chair. "When you figure out what I am, you be sure to let me know."

"I meant, a psychologist. But you're your father in so

many ways it makes me crazy," she answered, measuring out the coffee and taking the pot to the sink.

Jonah let the comment pass. It was par for the course.

The next thing Pam said, however, was not.

"You know how many times in my life I wished Peter would die?"

Jonah stared at her, mesmerized by her honesty. She'd never spoken about her feelings like this.

She was still at the sink, her back to him. Her shoulders slumped. "I could have killed Peter myself for the life he introduced you to. No, don't talk now." She held up a hand, stopping Jonah's response without even looking at him.

"Then in the end," she said in a quieter voice, "it wasn't Peter, but Frank, my best friend's husband, who had actually loved her, who died. And Gail has suffered more than I ever did. That was why I didn't want to visit with her. I never made any secret of how little I thought Frank deserved her. But I never wanted him to *die*." The pink spots in her cheeks grew to a full blush.

"You weren't the only one, for a while, who wished Dad dead."

She began picking at the hem of her T-shirt. "Your father is a lying, cheating piece of shit."

"You're not wrong there."

"I kept you from him, and him from you, because I was just waiting for him to turn on Mariah and Matt the way he turned on us, and I didn't want you exposed to that again."

This might have been the first time that Pam had talked about Peter in terms of what he'd done to Jonah, rather than to her.

"But that's not what happened." She opened a cupboard door to take out mugs. "Mariah cleaned him up. He got sober. He's done well with Matthias, apart from the reading thing."

Jonah wanted to correct her, but Pam seemed to have stolen all the words from the room.

A little of the old Pam resurfaced as she said, "Don't look at me like that." But she sank back into her chair, her body wilting with defeat. The two mugs clattered onto the scarred wooden table while the coffee machine bubbled in the background. "You get into a habit of hating someone, you know?" she said quietly. "Then one day you wake up and that energy is gone, and all you're left with are the consequences of that hate."

Jonah didn't think he wanted to go further with this conversation. His mother was pushing, hard, on doors he'd left well closed. *He* was left with the consequences of that hate, just as badly as she was.

Her head came up. "I always understood why she stayed with him, because there was a while there when I would have done anything to keep Peter with me."

God, what was it about his father that made these women line up to be with him?

"He was so smart," Pam went on, as if she'd heard him.

"He opened my life up like no one else ever had. He can talk about anything, did you know that? Like you." She gave him a small smile which he tried to return. "He never stops reading and learning, and he never, once, talked down to me. When he was sober."

The moment of connection made him reach out to take her hand. "But he wasn't sober, Mom."

"No, not once we got married and he could relax." But Pam seemed sad rather than angry about it now.

Jonah added his other hand, and she enveloped his in both of hers. "So he lied to you," he said. "Then he lied to you again. It's okay for that not to be okay. It's not surprising you hated him."

"But I didn't. I just told you, I loved him." Her face tightened. "And hated him." She sighed. "And loved him."

Then her eyes got snappy again. "And he *did* ignore you at first, and I don't know if you can ever forgive him for that. But he tried to rectify that *before* you cleaned yourself up, and I never gave him credit for it. And Matt is a good kid. That doesn't come from nowhere.

"The bottom line is," she went on, and now Jonah was alarmed to see a glint of tears that made her eyes huge, "I loved him long after he left us, and it's taken me thirty years to accept that he loved Mariah more. I think… I think I wish Mariah a long and happy life with him."

Jonah dropped her hands in shock. "Holy crap, Mom."

She looked at him across the table. "All right, all right."

She sniffled and wiped her eyes with quick movements. "Don't look at me like I've never had a thought in my head. That's the problem with you intellectuals."

Jonah sipped his coffee, but the burn that went down his chest was from more than the hot drink.

"You hungry?" Pam said.

He shook his head. He'd make himself something when he got home, where he'd be going the second he'd drunk an acceptable amount of this weak coffee.

While he was looking disconsolately at the clock on the stove, Pam spoke again. "Speaking of Gail. What are you doing with Laurel Moore, of all people?"

"What do you mean, of all people?"

"You're getting involved with the nicest girl in Tanner."

"And?"

"And, Jonah, you shouldn't be. Have you even thought about a future with her? With her owning a *bar*? How do you plan on being part of a life with alcohol all around you? You think you're that strong?"

Yes, he did, as it happened, though obviously she didn't. But arguing with her would prolong this painful conversation. "We're just… seeing how it plays out, Ma."

Her lips tightened. "For her sake, Jonah, don't 'play it out' at all."

That brought his eyes to hers again. His mother was giving him girl advice. About Laurel. He was actually in hell.

And she wasn't done. "She's a good girl with a lot of love

in her, and she likes hopeless cases. Like her father, and her brother. She'll die, beating herself against that caged heart of yours."

Jonah opened his mouth as the jab morphed into a cascade of hurt that rushed through him. "So you think that Dad can change, but I can't?" He stood up. "Jesus, Mom. I thought you'd actually gained some insight. That maybe you were seeing things through new eyes. But apparently not."

"What are you talking about?" Her surprise could have been comical, except that Jonah was shaking with horror. Just the other night he'd offered her all the compassion of which he was capable, but she didn't have any to give back. At least, not to her own son.

"You literally just said I'm incapable of love."

"And I told you who's to blame for that. What?" she said, as he turned to head out of the kitchen and to the front door.

Shit. Could any relationship with his father, or with Matt, be as toxic as this one? "I'll see you, Ma," he said, putting his boots on at the door.

"Aren't you going to stay to eat?" She still didn't know what she'd done. And how could he explain?

"No." He pulled open the front door. "I'll be back to plow when the snow comes," he said.

"But that could be weeks from now!"

"Right." And he walked away from his mother, for the first time in his life.

As he drove away, the tension in his chest pushed into his head, almost blinding him. He pressed his finger and thumb to his forehead, trying to erase the headache and her words.

They'd hurt so much not because she was wrong, but because she was only saying the truth he'd been pushing away for weeks. He *was* broken, and getting in touch with someone as giving as Laurel had been a huge mistake. He'd done it once when he was young and stupid. He didn't have that excuse now.

WHEN THE NIGHT staff came in later that day, Laurel had several plates of tarts, puff pastry, wraps, delicate lines of meat and vegetables on skewers, and stuffed mushrooms for them to taste. They loved them, as she'd known they would—or should, if they had any kind of taste buds at all— but there was someone else whose opinion she wanted more. Or maybe she just wanted to watch him eat.

She let herself into the apartment as usual, but Jonah wasn't home. Laurel was surprised. He'd gone to Pam's hours ago and it was past dinner. Had he really eaten Pam's food, which he'd told Laurel about, rather than come back to the promise Laurel had left him with?

She left the platter of food on the kitchen counter and walked into his bedroom. She loved this room as much as she loved the man who lived in it. This space meant safety in a way her house never had. She whispered, "Thank you for that," into the room, before heading for the shower.

Her idea grew as she was washing herself down, her body starting to buzz with anticipation of whenever Jonah finally did get home. She remembered him in the yard that day, busting a gut to make her party for his brother—who he didn't like—the best it could be. The brother he still couldn't talk to, a small voice reminded her, making her happiness wobble a little. She wasn't Matt, she reasoned with a toss of her long, wet hair. She'd brought him nothing but joy in the last couple of weeks, and he would remember that, and they would be fine.

To make sure, she slipped into the sheets, naked, her hair still wet, her skin glowing in the one lamp she left on.

When she woke up, it was because the bed had been jostled. Jonah was sitting on his side of the bed. He wasn't touching her, but looking at her as if someone had died.

"What's wrong?" she said at once, blinking sleep out of her eyes. "What time is it?"

"I don't know." He looked at the alarm clock. "Ten o'clock."

"Shit! I slept through dinner service!" She began to get out of bed, but Jonah's mood laid over her like a thick blanket, slowing her down. "What is it? Is it your mother?"

"In a way," he said, the heaviness in his voice like the dread that was stealing into her limbs. He was still barely looking at her.

"Come on, Jonah," she said in a louder voice, hoping to break the mood. "Spill."

He shook his head, with such finality that Laurel wanted to cover her breasts with the sheet. But that wouldn't help her case, so she stayed sitting up in the bed.

"Lor," he began.

"You're overthinking this, aren't you?" she interrupted. A cool prickle ran over her skin.

"I'm doing the right amount of thinking, as far as we're concerned," he said.

"What the hell does that mean?"

"It means that we should never have gotten involved. That I shouldn't have given in, that I've opened you up to a world of hurt. That I can't give you what you deserve in a man."

"Why don't you let—"

"And I'm not going to let you settle for second-best—or even third-best, which is about where I am these days when it comes to personal relationships."

"What the hell happened at your mom's house? What did she say?"

He shook his head again. "Yes, I agree. She is toxic, and I'm going to limit my visits to her now. But she was also right. I have no idea what love is."

The distance between them on the bed opened into a gulf. Now Laurel did try to cover herself with a sheet, but it was too far underneath her. "Why didn't you argue with her?"

"Because she's the closest thing to love I've ever known." Laurel felt her cheeks turn scarlet. "And it was a terrible kind of love, a love that's made me unable to accept anyone else's. Even yours."

The dread turned into anger. She stopped fighting the sheet. "You coward," she said.

He didn't contradict her.

"You're not incapable of love. You're scared of it. Hiding behind your 'rules,'" she went on, sarcastically. "You've done it for years—first, the rules about rebelling against your father because it was easier than accepting him as a flawed human being, and now the rules about letting me, or anyone else, into your heart because you're afraid you'll actually feel something back and you won't know what to do with it."

She clenched the sheet to her stomach, which was as far up as it would go. It was still warm, and damp in places, and it made her even angrier. "Let me ask you one question," she went on, when he didn't speak. "Ten years ago, were you in love with me?"

His mouth opened. He didn't say anything for a long moment, long enough that Laurel got her hopes up. Then he said, "No. I didn't know how then either. I could blame my mom, but it was me being too wrapped up in myself to be that generous with anyone else. I'm sorry."

She'd expected the answer, but it still hurt. She lifted her chin. "And are you in love with me now?"

He looked at her steadily. She searched his eyes for any weakness, any crack in the wall.

"No," he said.

That sure the hell put a crack in *her* wall, but she was damned if she'd let him see it. "Like I said," she said, standing up, pulling the sheet with her so it slid off the bed and he had to stand up to let it. "You're a fucking coward, Jonah Gardiner, because you've never *been* in love with anyone the way you love me, and you just won't admit it. Well, I'm not waiting around for you to figure it out."

She locked herself in the bathroom, where she tried to control her rioting emotions, put on her dirty clothes, retied her half-wet, half-dry hair into a braid, and hoped she could reduce the pink flush in her cheeks. She walked into the kitchen without looking back into the bedroom.

On the way to the stairs, she noticed the platter of food. With one hard, final shove, she sent it over the edge of the counter where it, and its collection of delicious morsels, smashed to pieces on the floor.

Chapter Twenty-Three

JONAH COLLAPSED BACK onto the bed and, more alone than he'd ever been in his life, used his comforter to cover himself. A pillow fell to the floor, sending her wonderful, unique scent up to him. He scrubbed his hand through his hair, then just held his head, which might burst with the size of the lie he'd just told.

He could hurt her now in one crushing blow, or he could hurt her in tiny, endless cuts as he failed again and again at the kind of emotional intimacy she deserved. He'd gone for the grand gesture—not the one the romantic movies preferred, but the one that would save the heroine in the end anyway. Sure, he loved her, but his love wasn't worth much, especially when it came with the kind of baggage he had.

His head was pounding. He hadn't anticipated how badly this would hurt *him*. The pressure was building up behind his eyes, so he made his hands into fists and held them there.

Coward. Coward. Coward. She was right, but so was his mother. So was he, if he was following his own logic. The problem was, his body didn't want to hear it, but forced him onto his back on the bed, his limbs leaden, his chest constricted. He hid the sight of his room, and the memory, by covering his eyes with his forearm, this time, but the pain didn't lessen.

Finally, physically and mentally exhausted even though he hadn't moved, he admitted it all to himself. *She was right. It's all been bullshit. I love her so hard I can't stand it. I can't stand it.* And then he couldn't keep the tears back at all.

MUCH LATER, HE was awakened by the buzz of his phone somewhere in the apartment. He stumbled up and through the dark hallway into the kitchen, where he stepped into a kind of soft sludge, and something sharp embedded in it transferred itself through his sock to his foot.

Swearing and hopping around, he ripped off the sock, grabbed a dish towel and held it to his foot. His phone stopped ringing. All the lights were out and the front room was lit only by the streetlights outside. He leaned back against the counter to examine his foot, but quickly jumped off it again when he remembered the first time they'd made love there. If he'd only stopped things then… if he hadn't been so much of a coward that he'd allowed himself to fall into her arms, to take all the luscious gifts she was giving him. His eyes hurt. His face hurt. Everything hurt. Including his foot.

He found the phone next to the armchair by the window and folded into the chair, holding his foot up high. He didn't recognize the number, so he put the phone down and went to turn on the lamp. The shard of pottery, or whatever it was, didn't seem to be causing a massive hemorrhage, but he was still a mess.

His voice mail beeped. He had nothing else to do with the rest of his life, so he listened to it.

"Yeah, hi, Jonah," a deep voice said. "It's Lucas." The voice paused. Jonah sat forward, forgetting about his foot. "So... I thought we should talk again... You let me go on about myself the whole time last week, and never told me anything about you." Lucas laughed. "I guess that makes you a good therapist."

A great therapist—as long as I'm not trying to help myself.

"I—we—wondered if you'd come to dinner one night next week. You can meet my family. My immediate family, I mean—not Peter." Most people would count their father as immediate family, but this was something that Lucas had in common with him.

"I know Matthias is coming home next Saturday," Lucas went on. "I don't know if Peter's told him about... me... yet."

Jonah remembered Peter's reticence when he'd asked him if he'd tell Matt about Lucas his first night home. *He won't tell him. He'll be waiting for you to do it yourself, like you had to with me. Matt's the one person whose opinion Peter really cares about. He's the only son who's ever said he loves him. He's going to hold off telling the truth as long as possible.*

"I heard there's going to be a big party for him. Peter's wife invited me, but she was being nice. I'm obviously not going."

Another thing they had in common, though Mariah hadn't spoken to Jonah in years.

"If you want to come over for dinner, let me know." Lucas gave out his number, then said, "If not, don't worry about it. I get that this is real weird. Just don't respond and I'll get it. I just... my wife is close to her siblings, and she says... it'd be worth a try." He laughed again. "I'm not a serial killer, or a cult member, or anything like that. There's more of Peter in me that I like, but I'm guessing, from looking at you, that you feel the same way. Still, I think—I *think*—he's really trying to do what he can to make amends."

There was another, longer pause. "Anyway," Lucas said. "Talk to you later. Or not." And the message ended.

Coward, she'd said. Jonah sat in the dark, watching the neon reflection from Sullivan's signs, tapping the phone against his lip.

Then he called Lucas back.

LAUREL WOKE UP the next morning feeling as though she had a hangover. Her anger had seen her home from Jonah's, into and out of another shower, through closing up the bar, and making her way upstairs in the dark. But her family was in bed, the apartment was quiet, and in the end she couldn't find anything to do but think about what Jonah had said, and the memory sent her into her bedroom, where she had to hold her aching middle, relive that one word, *no*, and swear at him, and cry for him, and for herself.

"Oh, he won't do it on purpose," Pam had said. "He'll just... suck you in and then... drift away."

Jesus, she should have realized then. Pam wasn't damaging *her* by saying that, she was damaging Jonah. Laurel just got caught in the fallout.

Then again, he sure had told her he didn't love her on purpose. That wasn't drifting away. Laurel had done what she'd told herself not to do ten years ago—she'd fallen in love with him, and he'd known it, and had pushed her away because of it.

She slept badly and for the first time since she'd moved home, it was Gail who awakened her. Gail, and the smell of coffee. "I brought you coffee," Gail whispered. "Don't get up."

"Mm," Laurel said, trying to open her crusted eyes. Gail sat on the edge of her bed. "I heard you last night."

She *couldn't* cry about Jonah in front of the mother who hated him. But the damn tears weren't done coming.

"Oh, honey," Gail said. And Laurel didn't have to say anything, didn't have to do anything but collapse into her mother's waiting arms and sob, while Gail stroked her hair and told her she loved her, and put little pieces of Laurel's heart back together.

"Thanks for the coffee," Laurel said eventually.

"What were your plans for today?" Gail said.

Laurel let her head fall into her hands, her hair covering her face and shoulders. She could hardly think beyond the next ten minutes, let alone the rest of the day. Apart from maybe taking a baseball bat to a certain person's nuts, she had no plans.

"I can look in on the bar, if you'd rather spend the day in bed. And the kitchen."

"Oh, Mom." Well, shut the front door. Her mom had offered to help. "That's nice of you, but I think I'm better off in the kitchen. I'm going to the farmer's market first. I think we could use some donuts up here. You want to come?"

"Okay, honey, if you want me to." Gail stroked her hair again, smoothing it onto her shoulder.

Laurel hadn't received that kind of touch in months. Not since Frank's death, certainly. "I appreciate your help," she said. "Really."

"You're welcome." Gail smiled, something that seemed easier to do, now that she had a project to give her talents to. "The patio's coming out real nice. They'll reinstall the pavers tomorrow, and then we can get the tables and chairs back and we'll be pretty much good to go!"

"Thanks," Laurel said again. She might be able to focus on that coffee now, so she sat up.

Gail hugged her again. "Don't rush. We'll be fine downstairs."

When Laurel got into the kitchen fifteen minutes later, the lunch service was in full swing, and Gail was supervising it. Laurel choked up again and had to run back up the stairs for a second to get a handle on herself.

Once she got back into work mode, however, her emotions were soothed. She put on her coat and drove to the market. Having to talk to Sadie in a normal voice helped her to create some distance from the memory, and coming back to the kitchen, working on lunch and dinner and then staring at a spreadsheet all afternoon, reminded her of her priorities. So that by the end of the day she could tell herself she'd moved on from last night and the jackass who'd taken her heart and stomped it into the ground and then acted like he was doing her a favor and—

Yeah, she'd moved right along.

WHAT ELSE COULD Jonah do but go to work the next week, as if he hadn't just blown his world apart? Give his clients advice, help them understand and work through their emotions, as if he were a mature, balanced counselor without a care of his own?

The worst of it was, he now knew exactly where his emotions were, and who they concerned. He couldn't go through the rest of his life without contacting Matt, even trying to have a relationship with him, because Matt was as much a part of his life as his mother was. His guilt over the trouble he'd caused his mother as a teenager had made him overlook her more poisonous diatribes and their effect on him. She'd kept him away from his father as well as if she'd moved him to another state.

And he had met the love of his life ten years ago, had waited to find her again, and then had failed her again. He could blame the bar where she worked, that people would judge him for entering. He could blame his professional relationship with her brother and the fact Brett needed many more sessions with him before Jonah would be comfortable sending him off on his own. He could blame Laurel's mother's dislike of him, and his own mother's insightful words about his own abilities, for staying away from her. But, as he ate his lunch, bought from the college cafeteria for the thousandth time, without tasting it, Jonah knew the only reason he wasn't with Laurel right now was because he was too much of a coward to try.

Jonah had arranged to go to Lucas's house that Wednesday night. Lucas and his family lived over the border with Massachusetts, a drive that took over an hour and gave Jonah way too much time to think.

Whenever he got done regretting much of his time with

Laurel, he thought of Matt instead. In three days, Matt would be home. The party would be over. Laurel's business would be back on the map. Matt might know about Lucas.

The only person whose life wouldn't have changed perceptibly by then was Brett. He hadn't heard from the kid since they'd worked on the patio together last Saturday. Jonah called him again now, but only got his voice mail. He asked him if they could meet before the party, because that would be hard for the kid, being around all those drinkers. Brett hadn't replied to his last couple of texts, and Jonah was getting worried. Adult children of alcoholics needed a lot of time to work through the layers of suspicion and distrust that they were forced to assume when around an unreliable parent. Brett had let him in, but only for a week or two.

And what if Laurel had told Brett even a tiny part of what had happened yesterday? And what if she hadn't? Could he really continue to counsel her brother while keeping himself away from her? If he were Laurel, he'd tell Brett to tell Jonah to go jump in Thompsons Lake.

Still. It might not be professional, but he was going to keep trying to contact Brett. He had a bad feeling if he didn't reach the kid, the party would be his undoing.

Lucas's house was a low-slung farmhouse on several acres of land outside a neat little tourist town. A truck with a snowplow on it stood in an open barn, along with a ride-on mower and other machines. As soon as he drove his Wrangler up the winding driveway, he heard dogs barking, and two pit bulls raced out of the garage, their butts wriggling ecstatically, until a high voice shouted from the house, calling them off.

Jonah stopped his truck and got out to a welcoming slobber from both dogs up and down his pants. They had apparently decided not to listen to the voice. He laughed and held out his hands, and they sniffed him and made little jumping motions, as if they wanted to crawl all over him but knew better than to test the voice too far.

The owner of the voice came out of the shadows of the long, deep front porch. "Little devils!" she called out, her tone not indicating anger at all. "Look what you did to his pants!" She came down the steps and held her hand out to Jonah. "I'm so sorry. We're still training them." Then her cute face twisted. "Still."

She was smaller than Laurel in every way, with platinum-blonde hair in curls and a curvy body enhanced by a baby bump. In her arms, she carried a child Jonah guessed to be about six months old, though he hadn't been around many babies. This one had latte-colored skin, silky black curly hair, and dark brown eyes like those of her father. She was dressed in a thick onesie and a blanket that almost trailed on the ground, and had one hand firmly attached to Piper's ear, threatening to pull out her earring.

"Mrs. Richardson, I assume?" Jonah said with a smile.

"Mr.—what is your last name? Do you use Van Allen or your mom's name? Oh, the hell with it. Jonah. I'm Piper."

With one hand she managed to envelope him in a hug. "We're so happy you came," she said into his ear. "Lucas needs this so badly."

Jonah pulled back in surprise. Piper's blue eyes were suspiciously bright.

"Well," he said, feeling like his feet and hands were too big. "Maybe he's not the only one."

Piper grinned. "I had a feeling. I know Peter's better now, but I also know what you've both been through. Come on in. Lucas is out back with the grill."

Inside the house, everything smacked of comfort and ease. A low L-shaped couch stood at one end of the open-plan room, a stone fireplace reaching to the ceiling in front of it. On the other end, a dining table and chairs of old chestnut and a chandelier made of beaten iron made Jonah feel that he'd stepped back in time. The kitchen was in the back, framed by windows that faced the yard and a French door through which Lucas now entered.

"Hey, Jonah," he said, coming in for a bro-hug, which Jonah appreciated even as it surprised him. Even more surprising was how glad he was to see his half brother. With all the craziness going on in his other relationships, at least he hadn't screwed this one up yet.

They sat down to a pork tenderloin and began to talk about mundane things—their work, as Lucas had promised, and the baby's progress, and Piper's decision on how many hours she could bear to leave her each day. After the main meal, which was excellent—though of course, nothing on what Laurel could have provided—Piper took Sally to bed, depositing her in Jonah's arms first for a few minutes so he could give her her final bottle.

She smelled and felt soft, delicate, and perfect, though when he said this, Piper and Lucas laughed.

"Yeah, just wait till she's teething. She's got lungs on her," Piper said.

"I dread making her give up that bottle," Lucas agreed.

"Does she sleep through the night, now?" Jonah asked.

"Yes." They nodded.

"Until she doesn't," Piper added. "And now we've got five months until this one starts it all up again."

She couldn't even sustain the fantasy that she wasn't thrilled to be pregnant again. She rubbed her belly and Lucas gazed at her as though she were the Messiah come again, and Jonah felt what he'd lost even more keenly.

When Piper had gone, Lucas offered Jonah coffee and they went into the kitchen, to the high-end machine that stood there. For some reason, it was the coffee machine, not the big house or the acres of land, or the new farm equipment, that made Jonah realize Lucas and Piper were seriously rich.

"What made you move out of the city?" he asked.

"The job. A change of career, and of lifestyle. Neither of us wanted to bring up kids in the city, or any city. Piper's from Boston but her family lives not far from here. It's a good compromise." The machine ground up fresh beans. "Have to do that now," Lucas said over the noise, "rather than later when Sally's asleep. Keeps us from the caffeine too." Lucas pulled two glass mugs from the rustic wood shelves.

Together, they stood at the counter, watching the machine drip their espresso into the mugs. Jonah almost missed what Lucas said next. "It's peaceful here."

"It's a good life," Jonah said, a hint of a question in his tone.

"It's my best life," Lucas said, then smiled. "That sounds like a poster. But honest. I could never have imagined myself here. Not in a billion years. Without Piper... who knows where I'd be now?" He looked out into the backyard, which was dark now, the lights from the kitchen falling only on a large deck with covered furniture and a shining stainless-steel grill.

"This is all because of Piper?"

"The means to buy this place? No. That was money I inherited from my neighbor." Lucas's eyes softened. "Stubborn old woman wouldn't even let me replace her stove, and meanwhile she was saving her nest egg for me." He shook his head. "No, Piper was the one who got me here. I... got to a bad place. Piper made sure I didn't stay there."

As Laurel had been trying to do for Jonah. "How did you know you were in a bad place?" he said, his voice hoarse.

"I didn't." Lucas laughed. "I had every intention of staying there. Blocking myself off from everyone and everything after Mrs. K. died—she was my neighbor. My tenant, really, but… it's a long story. Anyway, Piper was angry enough and smart enough to break me down and remind me that I could have the things I really wanted. Like her. And peace."

His eyes down, Lucas busied himself with the coffee and getting milk out of the industrial-sized refrigerator. Jonah didn't say anything, though the parallels between Piper and Laurel were obvious.

Not until they were sitting back at the dining table and Lucas had brought over a New York cheesecake with a strawberry coulis did Jonah find his voice. This was his brother. He'd known what Lucas was feeling, at least a little bit. "I had someone like that," he said.

"Had?" Lucas stopped before taking a forkful of his own cheesecake.

"I lost her."

"That's what Peter said about you, the first time he told me about you."

Was Jonah acting like Peter by closing off his heart to Laurel?

"I was trying not to be selfish. I know my flaws. I know what Peter did to me—and my mom didn't help. In fact, she was the icing on the cake. She basically said I was incapable of love."

Lucas's gaze was steady.

"Laurel deserves better," Jonah finished.

"That's what I thought about Piper," Lucas said. "But I

reckon that's just another way of saying you're too scared to open up and let her in."

"Fuck, yeah," Jonah laughed ruefully, rubbing at his beard. "Scared to death. She knew that, too. Called me a coward." The words still stung.

"So," Lucas said, finishing a mouthful of cheesecake. "What are you going to do with the rest of your life?"

Jonah sat back, toying with his fork. "How do you think that far ahead when…" He shifted position. "You don't know how much fucking up I've done in the last few days. Few decades, really."

"I can guess." Lucas grinned, a white slash in his amber-toned face. "The way I figure it, if Peter can find someone to love him for the last thirty years, we should be able to, right?"

Jonah didn't smile. "But how do you walk it back?"

"Groveling," Piper said, coming into the room unexpectedly. Jonah hadn't realized that their voices had carried. "Lots and lots of groveling." She sat on Lucas's lap and stole his fork, scooping up a big portion of his cheesecake. "And probably keeping her in bed until she can't walk," she added, her mouth full.

Jonah gasped, then choked, then laughed. Lucas shrugged as if to say, *This is who my wife is. Take us or leave us.*

"Advice noted," Jonah said with mock seriousness. But inside he quailed. He had a feeling he'd need more than groveling before Laurel would believe he'd changed.

Chapter Twenty-Four

SATURDAY ARRIVED AND it seemed even the weather loved Matt Van Allen. The air coming through Laurel's bedroom window that morning was fresh and cool, the sky was the kind of blue that highlighted the colors of the turning leaves, and a clear day was forecast through the evening.

With everyone's help, and every minute Laurel could spend when she wasn't cooking or doing paperwork, the bar and garden had come back to life. Gail had overseen the purchase of new dirt and wood for the flowerbeds. Armfuls of chrysanthemums, celosia and black-eyed Susans now lined the newly painted fence and served as a backdrop for the shiny black tables and chairs. The heaters were in place, the new decorations were brightening the bar, the jukebox was piping music through the new speakers, and the folding wall at the front of the bar had been repainted and tested so it would open everything up when the time came.

Laurel, Miguel, and Junior prepped all morning. Laurel was confident that with the help of the students who were coming in, they wouldn't need her for the cooking part of the afternoon. Miguel had found a young cousin who was happy to earn a few bucks washing dishes and being put to whatever use Laurel needed her for.

Pam had come by almost every day in the run-up to the party, keeping Gail's spirits up and making her tea when she was too sad to move. Laurel tried to avoid her, too angry with her for what her words had done to Jonah and, through him, to her. But she heard Gail talk to Pam as usual, rather than railing on her for the mess her feckless son had left Gail's daughter in, and for her part, Pam didn't bring up Jonah at all. This made Laurel even angrier. Days had gone by since Jonah had said he wasn't going to talk to Pam any more. Wouldn't she bring that up to her best friend?

There was one other dark cloud on Laurel's horizon. The closer they got to the weekend, the more she realized she hadn't seen Brett. He'd been so helpful in the back patio, but since then he seemed to have disappeared. She'd been hoping he could help her give out the tickets at the front of the bar on the day. That way he'd be occupied with something that didn't involve drinking; he might even be able to stay out of the bar altogether.

Unlikely, but Laurel was too busy to think of a better idea.

She went upstairs an hour before the bar opened, changed into a pretty faux-wrap blouse and knee-length skirt instead of her usual chef's whites, and left her hair down.

Thanks to the town's contacts, a photographer would be in the crowd, and that warranted a flash of leg and a little cleavage. Also, she couldn't help but think, if Jonah Gardiner happened to look down from his high horse in his apartment and saw her greeting customers, he could eat his cowardly heart out.

The fact he'd told her she was beautiful in beat-up T-shirts and jeans squeezed at her bruised spirit. She ignored the pain and put on enough makeup so she wouldn't look bleached out in the photographs.

Gail was up there, watching TV. "You look beautiful, honey," she said when Laurel went in to check on her.

"Thanks, Mom. Will you come down in a little while?"

"Oh… I don't know."

"Please?" Laurel had hoped for more than this, with Pam's encouragement. "You haven't seen the finished garden yet."

"I've seen it." Gail waved to the windows, the ones she'd seen Laurel kiss Jonah from. Damn him.

"Yes, but—" Laurel didn't want to tell her she'd tucked a surprise into the corner of the garden that Gail couldn't see from the window. "Please come down anyway. People have asked after you."

"I might," Gail said vaguely.

Laurel figured that was all she was going to get right now, and turned to go. Then, as nonchalantly as she could, she said, "Seen Brett?"

"He caught a cold," Gail said, looking back to the TV. "Spent a couple of days in bed."

Wow. Laurel really had been busy. "I had no idea. How's he feeling now?"

"Better."

Gail obviously wasn't worried about him, so Laurel would try not to be either. She tried to roll the pinch out of her shoulders that appeared whenever she thought of him and went down the stairs in her gold high-heeled pumps.

The front wall, when opened, showed off pillars dividing the space into three. Laurel arranged tables between two of the spaces so that the customers who wanted to eat would pay their cover charge to her, and get a ticket, at the third. She'd found a podium in the basement and so, long before Matt and his entourage arrived, she began greeting customers, and the party started.

The dynamic in the bar changed as the clientele filled it. Space was made for the strollers containing the offspring of the fire department and emergency squad and their friends. Coffee was ordered almost as often as beer, at least at first. And when the taster menus came out, arranged so tables could share, the talk and laughter rose as everyone tried to steal from everyone else.

Sadie's signs were on every table, and a larger poster stood on the bar. Laurel greeted her with a hug and a free ticket, which Sadie refused, paying for herself, her husband and two of her staff who she'd brought with her. Laurel could have talked about the food with her all day, but she was too busy with newcomers and had to allow Sadie and her group to be swallowed up in the crowd.

Her students came. So many had offered to work that day that she'd had to draw names, so she appreciated the rest had shown up in support anyway. Andrew Largo from the college also came with his family. He was full of praise for the improvement the students had made in just a few weeks.

The auto mechanics, Terry and Bruno, came, as did the real estate agents from across the street. The agents who couldn't come to the party, because they had clients, popped over anyway to introduce her to the newcomers and sing the praises of the restaurant. Laurel hoped to hell she'd live up to their exaggerations.

The cute firefighter made as if he was about to faint when he saw her in her girly clothes, and tried to engage her in conversation while she was taking money and giving out tickets. Laurel's increasingly short responses to his come-ons finally got through to him, and she lost him in the crowd.

After about an hour, Gail crept around the corner from the alley. "Mom!" Laurel cried, coming out from her podium to hug her.

Gail's mouth was open as she gazed at the opened-up space. "I forgot they did that," she said, her voice thin. "We used to have tables on the street, but we had some vandals come through one night and…"

"It's okay," Laurel interrupted. She didn't want to lose

her mother in sad memories again. "Did you see the garden?" Gail had probably gone through the kitchens so she wouldn't have to face the crowd inside the bar.

"It looked pretty good from my window."

"You should go in there, Mom." Laurel chewed her lip. "I left something for you."

Gail's eyes met hers. "Oh, that's nice of you, honey." Then her gaze slid over to the crowd inside the bar. "Maybe in a little while."

"You can slip back through the kitchen and around the corner," Laurel pressed.

"Yes, I could." But her tone told Laurel that Gail wouldn't. Well, she'd hardly expected to see her at all. This would have to do for now. Gail kissed her cheek and went back the way she'd come. None of the crowd noticed she was there.

After about an hour, the cry went up that Matt was arriving. Laurel stepped out from her spot to look down Bridge Street. Pretty soon she heard car horns and blipping police sirens, along with human yells and whoops. Approaching her, stopping all traffic, was a small cavalcade of cars, trucks, and an old red fire truck with flags waving. Men and women hung out of every open car window and waved to the people on the street, who were turning to gaze in wonder at the excitement.

The people inside Sullivan's heard the ruckus and swarmed out of the bar. Laurel flattened herself to one of the pillars and allowed them to take over the road. They were hooting and hollering as if a war had just been won. The old-fashioned fire truck stopped right in front of her and, with the help of nine or ten friends, a good-looking man with olive skin and black hair got out and encompassed everyone in his huge grin.

"Hi, guys," he said.

The cheers got bigger. Laurel had to laugh at the out-of-proportion reaction to simple words.

An older woman got out behind him, seeming unable to allow him a few feet from her side. Judging by her skin tone and black hair, and the adoring way she gazed at Matt, this was the famous—infamous—Mariah. Laurel saw a proud, relieved mother, unable to believe she had her beloved son back in one piece. Not the scarlet woman any friend of Pam's had heard about. Laurel wondered if Pam was secretly as proud of Jonah as Mariah was of Matt. As Frank had always said he was of Laurel. She sure the hell should have been.

Laurel watched the rest of the crowd get out of the fire trucks and cars, but didn't see Peter.

Mariah didn't get too long to cling to her son. Laurel watched the rest of the squad all but carry Matt the few steps to the entrance.

"Here's the girl who made it all happen!" one of his friends said. "Matt, this is Laurel Moore."

"Hey!" Matt gave her his grin. "The guys said you put all

this together. Thank you."

His smile was infectious. His black hair was cut military-short on the sides but long on top, almost flopping over his dark eyes. His dimples were the only possible sign that he was related to Jonah. "Not just me," she said. "Your friends are the ones who wanted to welcome you home in style," she went on.

"Well, I really appreciate it. In fact, I could hug you."

"Go right ahead," she said recklessly, well aware whose windows they were standing in front of. Could Jonah see from up there? Or was the fire truck in the way?

Matt laughed and swept her up in a huge, brotherly hug that made the others grin and Laurel squeal. When he let go, she smiled up at him. "Welcome home," she said again.

"Home," Matt said. "I like the sound of that."

He looked at the crowd surrounding him. They all grinned back, repeating, "Welcome home!" and adding, "You're buying!"

The squad captain ducked into the crowd, looking like she'd drunk sour mix neat. Not surprising. The few occasions Laurel had met the squad to talk about the party, the captain had hardly ever smiled. She probably wanted to make sure everything went according to plan and, like Laurel, didn't trust someone else to make it happen.

"Come on in!" Laurel said to Matt. "Take your ticket; that'll get you food. Everyone else line up if you want to eat!"

Mariah took his arm again and they began to make their

way through the bar. Everyone else paid their cover and the bar was soon full of people eating, drinking, and enjoying the mood. Laurel stayed at her post for a while longer, but now that Matt had arrived there were few other new guests who wanted to stay and eat. Most just wanted to buy Matt a drink—Laurel didn't notice any change in his manner, so she had to assume he'd refused the majority of them—and catch him up on the gossip from his seven years away. Eventually she asked one of the servers to stick around the front of the bar, and went to see how the garden was faring.

The sun had dropped behind the trees by that time, though it was still light out, and shadows crossed the packed patio. When she switched on the fairy lights strung around the fence, it turned into a magical autumn grotto. The red and yellow plants glowed in the lights and the heaters made the small space cozy enough for the guests to stay out there as night fell.

The tables had been grouped into twos and threes or pushed to the side altogether, used only as places to put down drinks. That was fine with Laurel. She liked the casual attitude out here and wanted to reflect that inside. She wanted the food to improve, but that didn't mean she wanted white-glove service at Sullivan's. *So there.* She still felt delicate about the subject.

Laurel began to circulate among the crowd, asking which of the tasters they had liked more, making mental notes. The pulled pork and apple sloppy joes had been a big hit; the porcini and Gruyere tarts less so. Too much Gruyere. Or too much porcini. So maybe it wasn't just the Realtors.

She'd had Walker, and Brittany, the new bartender, create two cocktails and checked in with them on how they were selling. Very well, was the answer, like everything else Sullivan's offered to drink. Walker, Brittany, and the weekend bartenders were circling each other like boxing opponents—ready to fight, but with a certain grudging respect. The space was a little crowded, but so far everything was going just as Laurel had hoped it would.

The photographer was also circulating, even, Laurel was happy to see, asking permission to go into the kitchen and take shots of the platters of food before they went out and got devoured.

Best of all, Gail came down again, accompanied, this time, by Pam, who had a good grip on her arm. Well, toxic or not, she'd gotten Gail into the party and Laurel had to say thank you.

She hovered while Pam propelled Gail down the hallway to the garden, saying, "Come on, Gail, it's your garden." She brushed off the photographer and anyone who tried to say something sympathetic to Gail.

In the corner Gail couldn't see from her window, and lit up by the fairy lights, was an Adirondack chair painted a dark green, lined with cushions of red and gold. Above it was a hand-painted wooden sign that said, "Gail's Garden." Laurel had cordoned off the chair with a white chain and another sign saying, "Reserved," and she was relieved to see that everyone had respected it.

Aware something momentous was happening, the crowd shushed and watched as Gail's hand flew to her mouth. Laurel snuck up to her side and put her arm around the smaller woman's waist.

"Laurel," Gail breathed. "Why did you do this?"

"Because," Laurel said, in a voice low enough not to carry, "all we ever did was talk about how this bar was Dad's, and what it meant to him to keep it going. But he couldn't have done any of it without you."

Gail let out a sob.

"This was always your space, and it got taken from you by the recession and the factories closing and all that, and I wanted to give it back to you."

"Laurel," Gail choked out. She turned into Laurel's arms and began crying. The crowd murmured in respectful sympathy and went back to their conversations. Pam patted Gail's back and Laurel saw her eyes shining with tears in the lighting. So she did have feelings for someone other than herself, after all.

After a few moments, Laurel said, "Do you want to sit?" Gail nodded, still hiding her face in Laurel's shoulder. Pam produced a tissue and they took down the chain and gave Gail her chair. Laurel whisked a chair from underneath another patron, who wasn't about to complain, and put it next to Gail so Pam could be with her. Wiping her face, looking around the garden, and laughing, Gail relaxed into the pillows.

"I'll get you a drink, shall I?" Laurel smiled at her. "Walker made up this twist on an Irish coffee that's really warming and buzzy."

Gail laughed again. Laurel had never heard a better sound. "Whatever you say," Gail agreed, and Laurel left her to rule over her small domain.

"That went well," a voice said as Laurel bustled through the hallway to the bar.

Laurel jumped and peered into the shadows. Brett.

"There you are!" she said. "Where have you been all day? I could have used your help out front." Then she heard what he'd said. "Wait. You saw that just now? Why didn't you come over?"

Brett shrugged.

"Come on, Brett. This is for the whole family. You helped out. You should get some of the credit too."

"I didn't know about the 'Gail's Corner' thing," he said, and she detected a bite to his voice.

Deciding to ignore it, she kept on walking. As Brett fell in step behind her, she said, "I'm glad it went so well. I thought she might hate it, or want it to have Dad's name on it."

"And that would never do."

Laurel stopped before she reached the bar itself and spun around to face her brother. "What does that mean?" And then she focused on him for the first time. *Shit.* Of course, he was drunk.

Brett gave her a smirk so unlike the happy smile Gail had just had that it hit Laurel like a punch in the stomach. "Isn't that what this is all about?" he said. "To get people to forget Dad was ever here?"

"That's totally unfair and you know it." She hissed, trying to modulate her voice as someone passed them on their way to the bathroom. "And I'm not going to talk to you when you're this hammered."

"Hey, it's a party," he said, throwing his arms out. "Whaddya expect?"

"I expect some self-control!" she said, her voice rising, even though she'd already lost the argument, as she'd lost every argument of the kind that she'd ever had with her father. Worse… she'd created an event that had set Brett up for failure.

But she'd been so proud of herself—she'd even forgotten about Jonah for a moment in her success at making Gail happy—and Brett had been doing so well. But now here he was, reminding her. The things she cared the most about were the ones she was least able to fix.

"Oh, cool your jets. I haven't had that much to drink." Brett sneered. But his eyes were unfocused and he kept one hand on the wood paneling beside him.

"How much is not much?" Asking him these questions was futile, but she didn't seem to be able to stop herself.

"Three beers. Swear." He crossed his heart and pointed to heaven. "I still have this cold."

Laurel could only shake her head. "Well, go on in the kitchen and get something to eat. Tell them I sent you. And no more alcohol, all right?"

"Sure thing, boss," he said, the smirk firmly on his face, and he turned away from her, around the corner into the kitchen, while she continued to the bar to get her mother's drink.

But she was stopped, again, by a sight so bizarre she almost tapped on someone else's shoulder to confirm what she was seeing.

Jonah was standing in the entrance.

Chapter Twenty-Five

JONAH HAD WATCHED. Not obsessively, not all afternoon. But still, and shamefully, he'd hopped up from his desk and taken quick glances through the window, until Laurel had left the front entrance.

Laurel looked radiant. Her bright strawberry-blonde hair was so luxurious, and she wore it down so seldom. It, and she, easily drew his eye. She wore an emerald-green floral blouse with a short black cardigan, and a black pencil skirt that showed off her magnificent hips and calves.

Then again, she'd looked perfect to him when she had tomato sauce in her shoes, but it was a treat to see her dressed to kill.

It sure the hell killed him.

When Matt arrived Jonah had to move, to hide himself behind a curtain and watch his little brother welcomed in like a four-star general after a victory. His view was blocked for a while by the old-fashioned fire truck that Matt rolled up in, but when it moved forward a few feet he got a good shot of Matt hugging Laurel close and her smile when he pulled away.

Jealousy like he'd never known pierced Jonah, a pain sharp enough to make him gasp in the quiet room. "Goddammit," he swore, scrubbing at his beard. What a waste of an emotion. Matt was that way with every woman—if the woman wanted him to be, of course. After not laying his eyes on his brother for seven years, and after that brother had been in life-threatening situations, was Jonah's first thought really that Matt should take his damn hands off Laurel? He shook his head in wonder. His brilliant logic about not giving in to his emotions was dying in flames.

By the time he'd pulled his head out of his ass and noticed that Mariah was standing right next to Matt and could hardly let go of him for a second, Matt and his crew had disappeared inside, and Laurel had resumed her place at the entrance to the bar. Jonah made himself walk into his bedroom and change, putting on a pair of black jeans and a shirt the color of Japanese maple leaves, before smoothing down his hair and beard and forcing himself down the stairs.

This is the only way. No more thinking his logic was the best way not to get hurt, or to hurt others. The bottom line had moved. It was no longer about keeping his life safe and unemotional. It was about winning Laurel back, and to do that, he'd have to talk to Matt. And to Peter. And step one of that was walking across the street, into that crowd, and hoping to hell his brother would shake his hand.

He didn't recognize the kid at the front door who took

his money and gave him a ticket—not that he could have eaten right now, not even Laurel's food, with his heart in his throat—and used the advantage of his height to look over the crowd to see one particular dark head. But then he remembered that Matt hadn't inherited Peter's height, and there was nothing for it but to plunge through and hope he found his brother before Laurel found him and kicked him out.

It didn't take long. Matt was in a knot of admirers, sitting on a bench facing out, a large round table in front of him. A server was taking a huge tray of empties away from the table while another added a new round. Briefly, Jonah wondered if Matt was going to inherit the family disease, but his brother looked relaxed and happy, not buzzed and sloppy, and he was listening with clear attention to the person next to him. One of the other EMTs, if Jonah remembered correctly.

Then Matt turned his head slightly, and saw Jonah. Jonah watched a panoply of emotions cross his face—surprise, of course; uncertainty; perhaps a little apprehension? However, Matt being Matt, his expression settled into a broad smile that echoed Jonah's dimples. "Jonah!" Matt said across the table.

And before Jonah knew it, Matt had stood up, looked to left and right, decided there were too many people penning him in, and walked across the table itself before dropping down right in front of him.

"Laurel'll have your hide for those footprints," Jonah said. Not the first thing he'd planned on saying to his brother after seven years.

Matt wasn't listening. "You came. Mom said you wouldn't."

"Yeah, well." Jonah rubbed at his beard. "Someone had to come and make sure the big hero remembered he's still someone's dweeby little brother."

Matt grinned. He was wider than Jonah and could probably flip him with one hand tied behind his back.

"Hey, Matt," Jonah said, and held out his hand.

Matt took it in a firm grip with both of his, his big grin getting bigger. "Good to see you, Bro. What's going on?"

"Um…" Jonah thought about Peter and Lucas. "Quite a lot, to be honest." But now that Matt was actually here, back in Tanner, back with his family and friends, Jonah felt a small piece of his life that he hadn't realized was missing click into place. "It's good to see you home safe, little bro."

Matt looked surprised. That was probably the nicest thing Jonah had said to him in his entire life. The strange thing was it was true. Jonah might have spent years being pissed at Matt, but he couldn't imagine his life without him.

"Thanks," Matt said. "It's good to be back."

They stood for a moment, taking each other in. "Nice beard," Matt said. "Hippy."

"Jarhead."

"That's the marines, doofus. The term you're looking for

is 'dogface.'"

"Dogface." Jonah looked at his brother's handsome face, seemingly untouched by all he'd seen in the war. "Perfect."

They grinned at each other again. "Well, I'll let you get back," Jonah said, nodding at Matt's friends, who were watching them closely.

"Okay. Don't go away though, 'kay?" Matt said, shaking his hand again in emphasis.

"I'll stick around for a while." Now he had to find Laurel, the thought of whom brought his heart—or his stomach—into his throat again.

"Cool. I'll come find you before we leave. Hey," he said, as Jonah turned to go back into the crowd. "Thanks for coming."

"I'm glad I did," Jonah said sincerely.

Okay, that was enough of that. Everyone was really staring at them now, and he could swear one or two of Matt's friends had tears in their eyes. He pushed through the crowd, aiming for the fresh air of the patio and to see the results of his handiwork.

But he didn't get there. Because Laurel was in his way.

"What are you doing here?" she said, but Jonah was still recovering from seeing her close to. Her outfit hugged her curves to perfection, and her hands on her hips, and the heels, made her look like a pinup girl. The scowl on her face wasn't exactly pinup-girly, but Jonah deserved worse than that. She wore perfume tonight, and because she hadn't been near her own food, she smelled of that instead of pulled pork and chicken satay and apple tarts. In other words, she smelled as unapproachable as she looked.

"You look stunning," he had to say.

She shook her head, which only drew his attention to her hair cascading down over her shoulders to her breasts. "That's what you came to say?"

They were feet apart, enough that people began to walk between them, until a server noticed who they were and stopped dead, drawing the crowd's attention to them. Whatever rumors they'd heard about a passionate affair going on, the look on Laurel's face seemed to suggest something else, something they wanted to listen to.

"No, of course it isn't," he said, trying to keep his voice low, though with the buzz of the party he could hardly whisper and expect her to hear. "Can we talk somewhere?"

Laurel let out an exasperated sound. "I'm a little busy, Jonah. Can you come back? Like, never?"

Behind her words he knew she was hiding a world of hurt. "I can't leave," he said. "I came to welcome Matt home. He wants me to hang around so we can talk later."

Laurel's mouth dropped open. "You came for Matt?"

"Partly. Seriously, Laurel, can we go somewhere and talk? Just for one minute?"

The stares of the crowd were pressing in on him. Laurel's eyes narrowed. Between her and the crowd, though, he'd take her. "Fine," she said, turning around and walking back the way she'd come, through the garden.

Jonah followed, but was again stopped before he'd gone more than a few feet into the garden by a familiar voice. "Jonah!"

He turned to see his mother, rising from her place next to a kind of throne that Laurel had set up for Gail. He'd known about the special chair; Laurel had talked to him about it, back when she'd liked him.

But Laurel didn't stop when Pam called. She parted the crowd, walking toward the gate in the back of the fence and going through it. "Yeah, Mom," Jonah said, not taking his eyes off Laurel. "In a minute." And he continued in Laurel's steps.

Outside the fence, with the gate shut and the early evening closing in around them, the sound of the party seemed muted. Laurel crossed her arms under her chest and glared at him. This did not make her any less beautiful, or any less intimidating.

"Yes, I came for Matt," he began. "I had dinner with Lucas the other night." This made her eyes widen. "I met his wife, and his daughter. My niece."

Laurel's stance softened. She unfolded her arms. "You really did? How did it go?"

"Great. We have a lot in common." He fixed her with his gaze. "We both fucked up royally when it came to women."

That made her straighten to her full height. "You got

that right."

"I know, Lor. I'm trying to say—"

"Where's Laurel?" a voice said on the other side of the fence. "Have you seen her?"

"She was just here."

"Laurel!"

Goddammit. He knew she couldn't resist a call like that. Not if something might be going wrong with her party.

Sure enough, she pushed past him and opened the gate. "I'm here. What is it?"

And she bustled through the crowd, listening and talking to Miguel, who was recognizable in chef's whites and his dark, curling hair.

Jonah had lost his chance. He stayed in the alley for a moment, scraping his hand through his hair. He didn't want to go back into that crowd. He'd wanted to say what he wanted to say and then leave. But Matt had asked him to stay, and Laurel had been interrupted.

"Shit," he said aloud. He'd just remembered his mother was on the other side of that fence too. This party was getting more and more fun.

THE REST OF the afternoon went by in a blur of spying on Gail without looking as though she was, avoiding Jonah, shutting down one more attempt to ask her out from the cute firefighter, keeping an eye out for Brett at the bar, avoiding Jonah some more, asking everyone she could find what they thought of the food, and continuing to avoid Jonah. Once she realized he was staying close to Matt, he was easier to track, and Laurel could try and concentrate on her party.

Before she knew it, seven o'clock had rolled around, and the squad member who'd first talked to Laurel about the party, Ellie, found her in the garden.

"It's time for us to drag our main man outta here," she said. "Thanks for everything, Lor. The food was amazing, and so were those cocktails. Those of us on call appreciated the virgin ones, too."

"You're welcome," Laurel replied, hugging her. "I'm so glad it all worked out. When I get the receipts added up for the day, I'll get you and your buddies over there at the firehouse your check."

"You couldn't just 'forget' to split it, could ya?" Ellie said, her grin turning devilish. She nudged Laurel with her shoulder as she backed away. "Just kidding. Will you come meet with Matt? He wants to say thank you in person."

"Sure!" She took one last look at Gail, who seemed quite content, and followed Ellie's swinging blonde ponytail into the bar.

Since the meal ticket had only covered lunch, many of the partygoers had gone home to their dinners, or a nap before the Sunday night game, so she could now see straight through the room and out of the open windows in the front. The street outside was shining in the streetlights and the light spilling from Sullivan's. The windows of the retail store opposite reflected everything back to her. The bar was vibrant, alive. Working. Laurel breathed a huge sigh that made Ellie, who was in front of her, put a hand to the back of her neck.

The squad was near the door, talking and laughing as they had done all day. They'd taken up most of the tables for the last few hours, so now that they were standing, the floor was almost bare.

Ellie led her to Matt, who beamed at her, as he had to everyone, and hugged her again, the way he had before. "Laurel," he said. "You're my hero."

Jonah wasn't there. Laurel let out a breath and had to laugh. "You're the one they practically strung a banner across the street for. I just did my job."

"Ah." He shrugged. "So did I." And his smile was so big and uncomplicated, he wasn't humble-bragging. He really was a nice guy.

"Well, Tanner's lucky to have you back. You're going back to the squad?"

"If they'll have me," he said, winking and inclining his head toward the crowd.

"You think they would have done all this if they didn't want you back?" she replied, incredulous.

"Most of them," he said, tapping his finger on the side of

his nose.

Laurel thought back to the squad captain's scowl when Matt had first arrived. Was that who he was talking about?

Anyway, not her business. She shook her head and smiled. "I'm sure you'll bring them round."

"Thanks."

"Don't be a stranger. I'll expect you here with the rest of the squad next Friday night."

"It's a date," he said, and winked before turning away.

See how easy that was? Just a little flirting, a little banter. No deep dark conversations to be had. Why couldn't her relationship with Jonah have been this easy?

Because Jonah was a hell of lot more important to her than his brother, and the only reason Laurel wanted to be nice to Matt was because she wanted Jonah to connect with him again. Jonah, who'd rejected her, who she'd called a coward because he was afraid of his own feelings. Who'd tried to say something earlier but hadn't been able to get it out.

"Buddy?" Matt's voice cut into her thoughts. "Dude? You okay?"

She refocused on him. He wasn't near her, however, but at one of the open spaces at the front. There were three or four people between them, so she couldn't see what—or whom—he was looking at.

One of the other EMTs said, "Not waking up. Hey. Hey!" Two of them were leaning over one of the tables that blocked the open space, their voices getting increasingly loud and professional.

"He's ice-cold," Matt said. "Better call it in. Who was on the soda today?"

A couple of voices answered him, but it was still Matt whom Laurel heard say, "Okay, buddy, we'll get you warmed up." Laurel saw coats coming off and being handed forward.

All this happened in slow motion, one voice after another, as if they were each a jigsaw piece that Laurel had to solve before she could be told what she wanted to know. What she already knew.

"It's Brett," one of the EMTs said. "Somebody get Laurel."

Chapter Twenty-Six

JONAH HAD MOVED away from Matt when his friends had begun looking at their watches. He had to talk to Pam, too, since she was here, but staying near Matt had meant she wouldn't come anywhere near them. Matt's mother had seen him, and had given him a neutral look that didn't scream friendliness, but didn't exclude him either. With a soda in his hand and a position in a dark corner of the garden, he'd been able to stay mostly invisible, thinking about what his mother might say if she found him. Once the party began to thin out, that became a distinct possibility, so he moved back toward the bar.

A scream broke into his thoughts. Although he'd never heard her do it before, he knew at once it was Laurel. The people in front of him were knocked aside like nine-pins as he ran the last few feet into the bar.

Laurel was crying Brett's name, her voice tear-soaked, sobbing, "Help him! God, Brett! *Brett!*" The EMTs laid a figure out on the ground in front of the bar.

As Jonah got closer, he heard a cacophony of calm, reassuring voices under Laurel's cries, saying, "Shallow breathing... but it's there... It's okay, Lor." Laurel couldn't hear them, and anyway Jonah's long stride had reached her by then and he did the first thing he could think of, which was muscle his way through the crowd that wasn't helping Brett and gather her into his arms.

Laurel gasped in surprise, but then her body shuddered and she seemed to lose all the tension that was holding her upright. Jonah maneuvered her so she could sit on the table behind her and he could sit with her, his arms still tight around her, his face close to hers. Her hair was across her face, wet with her tears, but he couldn't move it yet while he held her to him.

"He'll be okay, sweetheart," he said, while she cried. "He'll be okay."

"He swore he only had three beers," she sobbed. "He swore! God!" She felt boneless in his arms. "What was the point? What was any of it for?"

"It's okay," he said again. "You're in the right place. We're all here. We'll help. He'll be okay."

He wasn't sure if this was true, was hardly aware of what he was saying, but her need far outstripped any logic he might have told himself.

A siren blipped and one of the town's ambulances pulled up behind the old fire truck. At the same time, Jonah saw that Gail and Pam had come through from the back garden.

"Mom," Jonah said.

Pam jumped, echoing his surprise. "Jonah! What are you still doing here? And I thought you said you wouldn't come?"

"I wasn't going to," he said. "But I was just being a coward."

Laurel shivered again, as if she'd heard him. But her focus was all on Brett.

"Mrs. Moore?"

Matt had reappeared at Gail's side and now drew her forward to where Brett lay. "Do you know what he drank today?"

"Three beers!" Laurel cried. "He swore! Three beers!"

"He had a cold all week," Gail said. "I gave him the non-drowsy stuff today because he wanted to be here to help."

Matt and the other EMTs exchanged glances, and no one who saw them could miss the concern in their expressions.

"All right," an EMT with a blonde ponytail said. "Do you have the packaging from the medication he took?"

"I'll find it," Pam said, and dashed up the stairs. Jonah kept a tight hold of Laurel, who had descended into a silence broken only by hopeless weeping.

"Liver," the blonde EMT said to the man who jumped out of the ambulance. He nodded and they got Brett on the stretcher.

Pam came back with three different packages. Gail nodded. *All three?* Jonah thought. Jesus. Brett would have been high as a kite if the alcohol hadn't acted as a suppressant.

Matt came into their view again. "Laurel? He'll be okay. We've got him hooked up to everything now and he'll be fine. Just gotta get him to the hospital. Okay?"

Laurel turned her wet face to Matt. Even puffy and red as it was, she was the most beautiful woman Jonah had ever seen. How could he have believed he could close himself off from her?

"Thanks," she said, her voice thick, but Matt's words did seem to stop the hopeless flow of tears. Jonah kept his arms around her, and she seemed not to want to go anywhere else.

"Room for one more in the ambulance," one of the other EMTs called over to them.

Unlike Laurel's loud weeping, Gail had remained stony-faced, staring at Brett on the floor, now on a stretcher and cocooned in a blanket. Brett looked pasty-white in the harsh flashlight that someone was using to help out the team. He didn't stir or speak as they lifted him.

"I can do it, Mom," Laurel said, as Jonah had known she would.

"No, Laurel." Gail set her jaw. "He's my son. I'm going with him."

Laurel nodded and shrank back a little. Jonah held her so tight he could feel the flutter of her heart against her ribs.

Gail took a step forward, and then seemed to see Laurel and Jonah for the first time. She narrowed her eyes at them.

Jonah felt Laurel take a breath. This time he got in before she could. "I love her, Mrs. Moore. I'll take care of her."

Laurel seemed to have stopped breathing. Gail glowered at him. "Will you?" she pressed.

"If she lets me."

Laurel let out a squeak that might have been a laugh. Gail flicked a glance at her, but turned away and followed the EMT to the ambulance. Pam's eyes were wide with meaning, but she seemed to decide that her time was better spent following her friend to the hospital, and left the bar.

Laurel now looked at Jonah. Her eyes were wet and the deepest blue. "What did you say?" she said.

Logic dictated that with a decade of study behind him, Jonah would be able to say what he meant. Still, it was amazing how those three words scared the crap out of him, when he had to say them to their object. But the time to be afraid of his emotions was over. "I love you. I'm so sorry I let you down. I'm sorry I lied to you the other day. I should have agreed to come here from the start. It was important to you, and I didn't want to come because of my stupid, selfish logic. You've been right about me since the beginning. But I don't want you to forget about us. 'Us' was the best thing that ever happened to me. Then and now. And whether or not I've earned a place in your life, I love you."

Laurel closed her eyes and let out a long sigh that blew across the damp patches on his shirt, where he'd held her while she cried. Now he noticed the open doors and the cool evening were starting to chill him. Only where he held

Laurel did he feel warm.

"Let's go to the hospital," he said.

"Yes."

But before he could even set her feet on the floor, Matt came up to them. "Didn't you go with the ambulance?" Jonah asked.

"Nah. I was drinking," his brother said. "They'll take care of him." Then he grinned. "Glad you've got someone to take care of you."

They shook hands again. "When you've settled in," Jonah said, "you wanna grab a coffee? I have some... news."

"Is it Dad?" Matt said at once, his smile fading. "He's sick, isn't he?"

Jonah was the one whose eyes widened this time. "Is he?"

"Haven't you seen him? He wrote to me, asking me not to re-up." Matt frowned, the first worried expression Jonah had seen on him tonight.

"That's why you came home."

"Yes. That and I've been... hiding from something I need to deal with." Matt glanced at the street, for some reason.

"I've been there," Jonah said, leaning his head against Laurel's. Matt gave him a brief smile, but a frown still marred his usual cheerful expression.

When Jonah had last seen Peter, had he looked sick? The evening had been kinda full of revelations; he only remembered remarking on how stooped Peter had seemed. "He canceled a meeting with me last week because he was sick. But he saw me the next day."

"He did?" Matt's voice carried hope. "What did you talk about?"

"I'll tell you later," Jonah promised.

Laurel's arms squeezed him a little more tightly. If the reward was the respect of the woman he loved, of course he'd talk to his brother again.

"Okay, yeah. Let's catch up." He and Matt clasped hands again, and Matt turned to follow his friends onto the street.

JONAH DROVE TO the hospital with Laurel scooched as close to him as she could. Logic told him to tell her not to duck out from under her seat belt. But logic couldn't feel her soft body against his, or smell the sweet, delicious scent of her hair. And the hospital was only ten minutes away.

"Tell me again what a jerk you were."

Jonah laughed, and pulled her tighter, driving one-handed while he dropped a kiss on her hair. "A big, fat, dumb jerk, who didn't grab for what he wanted even when he knew what it was."

Laurel sighed again. "Will he be okay?"

Yes. Tonight was about more than Jonah's declarations. "I'm sure they're taking good care of him."

There was still tension in her body, worry about Brett.

She'd also fussed about leaving the bar, until Walker and Miguel had both shoved her out of the door. So many worries for one person to shoulder.

"Laurel, I swear I'll never leave you to face life's problems alone again."

"And I shouldn't have called you a coward. The way you've been dealing with your mother is the action of a saint."

Jonah laughed. "I rejected what she said, then followed it anyway. That was the action of an idiot, plain and simple."

They drove on a few blocks. "The bar looked amazing, by the way," he said, remembering what he'd seen when he'd been able to look away from her. He'd seen the new touches that she'd added—a wider variety of texture and shine than Frank would have been capable of, and more modern lights over the tables. The place was still welcoming to the old-timers, but with enough modernization that she'd also get the new customers she'd been hoping for. "You fixed it all." He looked down at her fondly. "Me and everything else."

"I almost didn't. When I didn't listen to you, I nearly derailed the whole thing."

"How do you mean?"

"Never mind. Just keep telling me when I get carried away, okay? I need a little of your logic now and again."

"Any time, sweetheart," he promised.

"Jonah!" she said suddenly, taking her head off his shoulder.

The urgency in her voice made his hand slip on the steering wheel. "What?"

"The bar!"

"Yes?"

"What about you and me and the bar? Was Mom right at the beginning, when she said we could never make it work?"

He ran his hand over her hair and tried to put all his newly admitted feelings into one quick glance at her. "Ten years is a long time. Where you go, I go," he said.

Laurel put her head back on his shoulder and played with the fingers of his right hand until he'd parked the car.

"I want to kiss you," she said, turning as soon as the growl of the engine stopped. "But… Brett."

"Of course." He opened his door.

"Come on," she complained. "Don't give up that easy."

He buried his hands in her hair and took her lips in a gentle, brief kiss, murmuring his love, as the door lights dimmed around them, the cold air swirling in from his open door.

IN THE EARLY hours of the next morning, when Brett was out of danger and sleeping in the hospital, Laurel and Jonah made themselves as comfortable as they could in the waiting room. Across from them, Gail and Pam slept, leaning against each other, their mouths partly open.

"Your mom's snoring," Laurel said, nodding to them.

"That's *your* mom," Jonah protested.

Pam answered by taking in a deep, guttural breath that roused Gail for a moment before she helplessly fell back to sleep against her friend.

Laurel laughed, covering her mouth so she wouldn't make more noise than Pam. Jonah was thrilled to see her regain her sense of humor. He took her hand away and kissed her palm.

"I love you," he said again, in case she hadn't gotten it the first three dozen times.

She gave him a cheeky smile. "I love you too, even though you make me nuts."

"I'll learn."

She grabbed the front of his shirt and pulled him to her. Jonah moved closer, wrapping his arms around her middle as tight as he could.

"Don't learn too soon," she said against his lips. Her breasts pressed up against the *V* of her blouse. "I kinda like teaching you."

The End

Recipes

Miguel's Cucumber and Apple Slaw Salad

1 granny smith apple

1 red apple like fuji or pink lady

1 seedless cucumber

3 chives

Dressing:

1 TBSP apple cider vinegar

3 TBSP olive oil

1 tsp honey mustard

1 tsp mayo or egg yolk

Shave the apples and cucumber on a mandolin, or slice very very finely, and fold to arrange in a ramekin (cut if you have to, but folding is better so they don't stick together). Chop the chives into one inch pieces and toss with the apples and cucumber.

Whisk all the dressing ingredients together and add a teaspoon to the salad. Serve with buffalo wings, chicken fingers, burgers and faithful old customers!

Laurel's Brownies

4 oz butter

6 oz (half a bag) semi-sweet chocolate chips

½ cup made coffee (½ tsp instant coffee with ½ cup hot water, or leftover coffee is fine!)

1 egg

1 cup sugar

½ cup all-purpose flour

1 tsp baking powder

½ tsp salt

Pre-heat the oven to 350 degrees.

Melt the butter and chocolate chips in a double-boiler or a glass bowl over a saucepan half-filled with simmering water. Don't let the water touch the bowl. Meanwhile, beat the egg and add the other ingredients to it.

When the butter and chocolate have melted, take them off the heat and stir in the half-cup of coffee. Add this mixture to the flour mixture and beat until well blended (it will be runny!).

Pour into a square pan lined with parchment paper that goes all the way up the sides of the pan. Bake at 350 for 50-55 minutes, until a toothpick comes out clean. Cool in the pan and cut into 16 squares. Find a hot psychologist to share with and enjoy!

If you enjoyed this book, please leave a review at your favorite online retailer! Even if it's just a sentence or two it makes all the difference.

Thanks for reading *Forget Me* by Kimberley Ash!

Discover your next romance at TulePublishing.com.

If you enjoyed *Forget Me*, you'll love the next book in….

The Van Allen Brothers series

Book 1: *Forgive Me*

Book 2: *Forget Me*

Book 3: *Free Me*

Available now at your favorite online retailer!

About the Author

As a teen, award-winning author Kimberley Ash would sit in her English boarding school dormitory and read Silhouette Romances with her friends. They would have passionate arguments about the kind of American hero they really wanted to see in the books, so to settle things, Kimberley wrote one. While she took great pleasure in deconstructing alpha males and exposing their chiseled but vulnerable underbellies, life and inner demons made her put away her dreams for twenty-five years. She was forty before she realized that what she wanted to be when she grew up was what she'd always wanted: a romance writer. So she joined Romance Writers of America, took all the classes she could find, and has never looked back.

Meanwhile, to her great surprise, Kimberley was swept off her feet by her own all-American hero. Now making her home in rural New Jersey (yes, there is a rural New Jersey) with him, two hybrid children and two big furry dogs, she can be found staring into a computer screen, wrestling with plotlines and ignoring the giant dustbunnies.

Kimberley holds a bachelor's degree in French from the University of London (spectacularly useful at PTA meetings) and a master's in English Literature from Drew University. She writes contemporary romances about fish-out-of-water characters who find home where they least expect it.

Kimberley writes about real life and therefore celebrates and supports diversity in all its forms. You can find her obsessing about tea at www.kimberleyash.com, and on Facebook, Twitter, Instagram and Goodreads.

Thank you for reading

Forget Me

If you enjoyed this book, you can find more from all our great authors at TulePublishing.com, or from your favorite online retailer.

CPSIA information can be obtained
at www.ICGtesting.com
Printed in the USA
FFHW020626240519
52634859-58134FF